"**A**re we agr___ Her Ladyship are despicable people?" Angela asked.

"We are."

"But yet Lord Francis is a cocksman of the first degree, is he not?"

"Most assuredly."

"Then use the very passion, which unfortunately and through no fault of your own caused you to become his prisoner, to your advantage. Apply it well, please and pleasure him, and he will not dare part with you, for such ardor is rare. Once you are secure in your position, then we can go about the business of finding a way to escape."

"And are you confident in your position?"

"I am, but much depends on you. That is why I beseech you with all my heart to use the talents nature has seen fit to bless you with. Now do you understand?"

"Yes, I do."

"That is good. Now you rest, for Her Ladyship has requested your presence in her private chamber in an hour's time."

Danielle:
Diary of a Slave Girl

Anonymous

Danielle: Diary of a Slave Girl
Copyright © 1998 by Anonymous
All Rights Reserved

First Masquerade Edition 1998
First Printing February 1998
ISBN 1-56333-591-3

First Top Shelf Edition 1998
ISBN: 1-56333-915-3

Manufactured in the United States of America
Published by Masquerade Books, Inc.
801 Second Avenue
New York, N.Y. 10017

Introduction by the Publisher

We are indeed fortunate and consider ourselves very lucky to be able to present *Danielle: Diary of a Slave Girl* to the discerning reading public. The production of this sociologically important document was a joint effort on behalf of ourselves and our British and French colleagues, and to them we owe an enormous debt. Their unflagging enthusiasm was an inspiration to us all.

Preface by the Editor

Danielle Appleton was the only child of Henry and Sophie Appleton, née Charon. She was born in Orléans on October 24, 1846. When she was three, her parents moved north, taking up residence in Paris.

Henry Appleton was English. Upon completing his formal studies at Cambridge, he took a holiday to the Continent where, as youth was wont to do, he met and promptly fell in love with the beautiful Sophie. Much to the consternation of his parents, he remained in France, became fluent in the language, and listened to his heart, marrying Sophie after a brief courtship.

Henry became an attorney of no particular distinction, a fate similar to the one he would have had had he returned to England. Records from the French Bar Association and also the Fraternity of Attorneys at Law reveal that he specialized in import/export law, a mundane but nevertheless fairly lucrative sphere that, simply put, consisted of a tangled mass of intricately woven laws and covenants supervised by a huge bureaucracy. Apparently, Henry had the kind of personality that enabled him to maneuver his way successfully through this veritable jungle of rules and regulations, effectively navigating treacherous legal reefs and shoals with skills that quickly brought him an excellent income. A modest, self-effacing man, Henry sought fortune rather than fame and in this endeavor, he prevailed.

At the time the *Diary* begins, he was forty-five years old. Descriptions of him indicate that he was a rather plain, ordinary-looking man of medium height, neither ugly nor handsome.

Danielle's mother, Sophie, was much more creative and is credited with establishing one of the first *haute couture* salons in Paris. Although her talents were more of an administrative nature, she nevertheless had excellent instincts when it came to women's style.

As a result, she carved out a small niche for herself in French fashion history. She was not a designer in the true sense of the word. Rather she was an adapter. Sophie made frequent trips to England, where she meticulously observed what women were wearing. Upon her return to Paris, she modified costumes to suit the particular tastes of Frenchwomen. Sophie catered to an upper-class clientele and her successes and failures were well documented in the Paris newspapers.

Records from the Ministry of Health reveal that Sophie had two miscarriages. She was forty-four at the time the *Diary* begins.

Of Danielle we know even less. For all intents and purposes, she vanished from the face of the earth on or about September 1, 1867. One of the remarkable aspects of the *Diary* lies in the fact that it is a literal chronicle of her life. In all good conscience we must warn the prospective reader that there are aspects of her life that are not suited for the faint of heart.

Fortunately, we know more concerning the details of her disappearance and these will be revealed during the course of the *Diary*. We can, in all good faith, believe that her father and mother used all their influence in order to find their missing daughter. All attempts failed.

Henry Appleton never forgave himself. He shouldered all the blame unnecessarily and died of a stroke, guilt ridden, fifteen years later. Sophie, also obviously heart-broken, survived her husband by some eleven years, apparently taking solace in her work. She continued her business until two years before her death.

Herewith *Danielle—Diary of a Slave Girl.*

Entry № 1

Although I am writing this from memory, there is no doubt that my accountings of the events will be accurate in every detail, for they have been branded into my brain as if by a hot poker.

And why am I doing this? To keep my sanity, I suppose, for I have been thrust into a world of madness, where sexual excess reigns in the extreme. I am not here of my own free will; and although I know that no one will ever see my pitiable scribblings, I nevertheless feel that in some small way, I must document what has happened to me.

I shall begin on that fateful evening when, unbeknownst to me, I embarked upon a series of actions that

11

would change the course of my life. Tears come readily to my eyes, but that is of no concern to you.

Spring had finally come, and Paris never looked prettier. Everyone was gay and happy after enduring a long, cold winter. I was a nineteen-year-old student, and my honey-colored hair rested gently on my shoulders.

Maman's fashionable shop was very busy. I remember the lines of carriages, some drawn by matching pairs of horses, that waited by the curb while wealthy women made their selections from among her creations. The fitters fluttered over the matrons while Maman offered advice: careful only to suggest, never to offend.

The shop was located in the Eighth Arrondissement, one of the richest neighborhoods of Paris. Maman was already quite well known, and her business flourished. It was my intention to follow her when I finished my studies. It was apparent that I had inherited some of her talents, and I eagerly looked forward to the day when I finally would join her.

I did what I could to help, although I admit that at times I was overwhelmed by all the beehive activity as the fitters and seamstresses flew back and forth between all the customers, trying to treat each one equally. I also admit that at times I was more of a hindrance than a help, for my mind was filled with thoughts whose nature was of something quite different than the world of *haute couture.*

For the past year, François Lechine, a darkly handsome, thirty-year-old assistant professor at the Sorbonne, had been courting me. He came from a respectable family and it was assumed that he and I would marry. My father's law practice had also flourished, making more demands on his time. I scarcely saw him. Oh, how I regret not spending more time with him! It weighs so heavily on me that I fear it will crush me. But I must go on, for it is my only salvation from the hell on earth that has become my existence. One balmy night after dinner, when my parents were busy discussing some financial affairs, I quietly slipped out of the eight-room apartment we occupied on the fashionable rue de la Rochefort. I wore an ankle-length dark blue linen skirt and a high-necked white cotton blouse. Around my shoulders I draped a beautiful black lace shawl to protect me from the breeze which still could turn chilly at times.

François met me on a street corner three blocks from where I lived, kissing me gently on the lips. Then he took me by my arm and we walked down the gaslit street, the air sweet smelling and warm, caressing my shoulders.

How proud I was to take his hand, knowing that soon I would be called "Madame" and not "Mademoiselle." How handsome he looked!

Was it then that my fate was sealed? At that very moment, when in all innocence I strolled with my love? How many other couples had done the same thing over the centuries? Millions, no doubt. But why was I singled out? Alas, I have no answers. After a short time, we found ourselves entering the Bois de Boulogne. The closeness of his body elicited feelings in me that were strange, yet welcome. Was this the beginning of the hell on earth that I am forced to endure? Again, there are no answers, and even if there were, they would do me no good. Escape is impossible, save for death.

After ten minutes, he led me down into a hidden depression in the sprawling, grassy grounds of the park. When we reached the bottom, I looked behind and realized that we could not be seen from the path.

"How clever of you," I said as I sat down on the soft grass, François next to me. "When did you discover this place?"

"About a week ago in my wanderings."

Lest you get the wrong impression of me, I wish to make it perfectly clear that I am a lady and François was a gentleman. It was my desire and also his that I remain a virgin until our wedding night. Notwithstanding that, at times I have let him rub my bosom or my pleasantly plump bottom. We regarded it as innocent fun—nothing more.

François put his arm around me and pushed me back gently until I was lying down. Behind and above him I could see millions of stars twinkling in the cloudless sky. He kissed me, and I was immediately intoxicated by his manly scent and the nearness of his body.

After our lips met, his tongue began to explore my mouth, I reciprocated immediately, my tongue dueling delicately with his. While he kissed me, François unbut-

14

toned my blouse deftly, exposing my breasts. "Danielle, my sweet Danielle," he murmured as he smothered my globes with hungry, wet kisses.

Then he ran his tongue around the circumference of my large rosy aureoles, making me arch my chest upward as he took as much of my breast flesh into his mouth as he could.

Was it then that I was doomed? Was François a seducer? A devil? Or did he somehow manage to reveal something about me that even I did not know? Why do I continue to torment myself with questions to which I have no answers?

Once my nipples were hard, he sucked on them and nibbled on them gently. I took his head and moved it to my other breast, to distribute equally the pleasures which purled outward in waves of increasing passion.

Then he reached under the folds of my skirt, swiftly pulling down my knickers. François's eyes gazing at my naturally blond sexmound. He kissed my rounded stomach before he made his way down to my groin.

"No, you mustn't!" I panted.

But François chose not to hear me. He positioned his head between my legs, his fingers spreading my cunnylips apart, revealing my inner pinkish flesh. Then he ran his tongue up and down the length of my slit before he started to suck on me, sticking his tongue as far as he could up into that most private of orifices.

Alas, the supreme intimacy of the kiss caused my

pants to become louder and more frequent as he worked on my clit, swirling his tongue around its base, making the ultrasensitive nubbin of cuntflesh rise and radiate with sublime pleasure. Never had I felt such bliss!

I surrendered and squirmed around, forcing him to scrunch his hands in under my soft bumcheeks so he could hold onto me, keep his lips pressed hard against my soft hairy mound.

My heart raced as I felt pressure begin to build up in my chest, my bosom rising and falling. Finally there was a tremendous release, the power of which I had never experienced before as my canal filled with hot juice. François swallowed thirstily and continued to suck on me, until I had no more cream to offer him.

And what of my resolutions, my vows to remain a virgin until my wedding night? Had I been deceiving myself? Had François deceived me? More questions that buzz around my head like stinging bees.

The next thing I knew, François was atop me, the head of his penis passing through the gates of my garden of love. Protest was out of the question as I was suddenly swept along by a current of passion so strong that I could not resist it. Little did I know that it would carry me to my eventual doom.

François penetrated deeply into me. When he broke through the thin wall of tissue, I cried out—not in pain, but in joy as he began to hump me rhythmically, his pelvis bouncing hard against mine. My eyes opened wide as I climaxed yet again. I panted faster and faster, encouraging François to maintain a steady pace. Love-cream trickled our of my hole, striping my thighs.

I spasmed again, writhing underneath him, love-juice flowing profusely down the length of my canal, coating his rod in the process, lubricating it, encouraging François to hump me even harder and faster. I confess freely that I reveled in the length and girth of my lover's manly instrument. Soon I climaxed again, covering his thrusting rod with my sweet liquids. François began to work harder and harder, managing to suck on hard nipples while he humped me, adding to my pleasure.

Then he spurted a thick stream of jism into me. The sheer joy of it made me cry out, the sounds exciting François to the point where he spent himself a second time. Loud sounds of joy and thankfulness filled our little nest as I expressed my ecstasy like a wild animal, free of all restraints.

François had transported me into a world where one pleasure built on another. Unable to restrain myself, I cried out louder and louder, holding onto François's strong shoulders as I squirmed under him, his magical organ continuing to elicit passionate responses from my more-than-willing body.

Unfortunately, I cried out too loudly. In doing so, I attracted the obviously unwanted attention of several men who just happened to be strolling by on the path above us. Thinking I was being assaulted, they rushed to my aid, scrambling down the steep grassy hill. They pulled François off me while yelling for more help. It soon arrived, but not before they had punched François in the face a few times. My protests went unheard and unheeded as I rearranged my clothing quickly.

The next thing I knew, two large blue-uniformed gendarmes arrived on the scene. One of them handcuffed François's hands behind his back while the other one attempted to calm me as I was still in a state of high excitement and extremely agitated.

"You don't understand—I wanted it!" I said to one of the policemen.

"Sure you did. That's why you were yelling like a stuck pig!" he scoffed.

The four of us trudged up to the path where a large crowd had gathered, drawn by the commotion. The men were boisterous and loud, shaking their fists, hurling insults at François. I heard one dowager say, "You can't even walk in the park anymore without having to worry that some animal is going to jump out of the bushes."

The gendarmes dispersed the crowd and escorted François and me to the prefecture, where we were separated. François was shoved rudely down a hallway and he was thrown into a filthy cell.

I was then questioned gently by a mustached senior officer in the privacy of his tiny office. He listened patiently to my explanations, occasionally making notes on a small pad but I knew he did not believe me. "It's a common reaction," he said from the other side of his battered dark wood desk when I had finished. "Many women are afraid that if they give testimony, their attackers will seek them out again."

"But he did not attack me!" I insisted.

"I understand perfectly," he said patronizingly as he brushed an imaginary bit of lint off the front of his well-worn black jacket. "One of my men will escort you home."

I had no choice but to give him my name and address. Upon hearing it, he raised his eyebrows and excused himself, leaving me alone in the sparsely furnished room for several minutes before he returned, accompanied by a muscular young gendarme. "Officer Lechamps will see you safely to your door."

"What will you do with François?" I asked.

"So *that's* the name he used. Interesting," said the senior officer softly, rubbing his chin. Then, in a louder voice, "We'll take good care of him. Don't trouble yourself over it, mademoiselle." He bowed slightly, a cue to Officer Lechamps to steer me gently out of the prefecture.

We walked for several blocks before I had the courage to ask the officer what would happen to François, hoping he would give me an honest answer. "He will be arraigned before the magistrate tomorrow morning, mademoiselle. You're lucky that your father is a prominent member of the legal profession. The chief inspector recognized the name immediately. The swine who attacked you will get everything he deserves."

How had it changed so quickly? One minute I was in

the arms of sublime bliss. The next, my lover was being assaulted and then imprisoned. Was there anything I could do or say to ease his plight?

My head swam with such thoughts. Only when we saw a gendarme bicycling toward us was I jolted back to reality. The chief inspector had obviously sent the man ahead of us to alert my parents. Officer Lechamps waited until my mother opened the front door before he saluted and walked away. All the lights in the house were on, a sign that everyone was up and waiting.

"My baby. Are you all right?" Maman blubbered as tears flowed freely down her cheeks.

"I'm fine," I replied.

"Your father wants to see you in his study."

I slowly climbed the blue-carpeted steps that led to the second floor and entered the study, where Papa often worked far into the night, sitting behind his ornate Louis XV desk. There were bookcases on every wall and I always felt uncomfortable in the room, regarding it as a sanctum where the presence of a female was tolerated, not welcomed.

Papa stood behind his desk wearing one of his expensive well-tailored suits. He invited me to sit on an ornate tufted red velour chair. He then turned and went over to the high windows, his back to me.

"I realize that you are probably still in shock, but there are certain details of this unfortunate incident that must be clarified immediately," he said after he turned to face me. "I have been informed that you declined medical attention. Needless to say, you will be examined tomorrow morning by Dr. Turvinel. As you know, he is an old friend and an excellent physician." He cleared his throat. "There appears to be a rather glaring discrepancy as to exactly what happened. The chief inspector, whom I happen to know quite well, by the way, was kind enough to confide in me. Naturally, I will be taking appropriate action against your attacker. However, before I do so, I have to be absolutely positive that I am in possession of not only the facts, but also the truth. I'm sure you can understand that," he said gently.

"Yes," I whispered.

He took a deep breath. "Were you attacked?" he asked bluntly.

"No."

"I see. Did you know your…"

"Of course I did! It was François!"

"The chief Inspector's position is that you were, in fact, assaulted and naturally I have to respect his professional opinion. This is a most awkward situation." He sighed. "As if I haven't got enough on my mind as it is. Let me see if I have this straight. Am I to understand that you encouraged François?"

"It just *happened*. How many times do I have to tell you?"

"And you chose a public park?" he exploded in a rage that sent his spectacles tumbling off the bridge of his nose. "Doesn't François have a place of his own? Go to a hotel! Anywhere! But no, that would have been too easy. You had to do it right out in the open. In a public park, of all places!

"Do you have any idea of the scandal that would result if this became public knowledge? My reputation would be ruined! And your mother's! You have behaved like a five-franc *poule*! My own daughter! It's unbeliev-able." Then he took several deep breaths in order to calm himself. "The truth must never leave this house. The chief inspector will find a way to see that it never gets in the papers. He owes me a favor anyway.

"You will be confined to your room until I decide what to do with you. Those newspaper people would give their eyeteeth to get me on something like this. You will communicate with no one. Have I made myself clear?"

"You can't treat me like I'm a child!" I protested.

"I can when you act like one. Look, I'm not as narrow-minded as you might think. I don't necessarily object to what you did, just the way you did it. Now leave me. I've got to do some thinking. With luck, I'll be able to nip this thing in the bud."

"How could you?" sobbed my mother, who had been listening at the door.

"I enjoyed it!" I spat, sending poor Maman into a paroxysm of sobs.

After being locked in my room, I lay on my bed, reflecting on what had happened. Being discovered in the Bois was an unfortunate accident, one that could not have been predicted or anticipated. Father was right: the truth must never leave the house.

But something much more important occupied my thoughts. François had liberated me. I knew I was no longer the same person I had been prior to losing my virginity.

I also felt that I was being punished for doing something that was quite natural. I doubted that I would ever see François again, and the thought made me sad. But I made up my mind then and there to assert my sexual independence as soon as the opportunity arose, for I knew I had barely scratched the surface. The problem that faced me was how to go about it.

I was already a prisoner of the bliss which François had blessed me with. But searching for it would damn my soul for all eternity.

Entry № 2

May 17, 1867

I remained under what amounted to house arrest for two weeks, receiving no visitors, save for the maid who brought my meals. The well-intentioned Dr. Turvinel concluded that I was still in shock. The old fool! I was in a state of jubilation! Nothing I said should be taken seriously. The only comfort I had was in the memory of the pleasure François had given me.

More importantly, the long-dormant longings awakened by my lover increased my resolve both to satisfy and to increase my knowledge of all the various forms I was sure they took. Did I consider myself a rebel, going against the moral standards which form the fabric of our society? Or was I a weak-willed woman given to indulging herself wantonly in the baser acts of sexuality?

I answer no emphatically to both questions. A woman's body was a most wondrous thing, and I would surely be remiss if I did not investigate its potential thoroughly.

Those resolutions were the result of many lonely hours during which I carefully weighed all the possible ramifications of such actions. Having done that, my resolve was strong and my conscience clear. How brave I was then! And how foolish!

After dinner one evening, Papa visited me, the first time he had done so since my incarceration. I wore a long skirt and high-necked blouse in an effort to give him the impression that I had reformed myself.

"I have come to a decision," he said sternly, standing in the doorway. "It was not an easy thing to do. Unfortunately, your irresponsible actions have graphically demonstrated a lack of consideration for the other people who also live in this house. Although I have managed to keep your name out of the press, at least for the time being, frankly, I do not trust you. Your mother, whose salon you also jeopardized, and I discussed what should be done with you. We reached a decision that we hope will benefit all of us. This is your punishment. I am sending you abroad. "I have managed to secure employment for you in the household of Lord Francis Parkinson-Smythe. He is a wealthy barrister whom I know both professionally and personally. We studied together at Cambridge. His wife's name is Gertrude. I believe he has a son, Wilfred.

"More to the point he has agreed to allow you to become a member of his household staff, another favor I now owe because of you. You will remain in his service either at his London home or his family estate for a period of not less than one year. It should take that long for this whole messy business to blow over and forgotten about. You have no idea of the strings I've had to pull."

I gasped. "You're exiling me."

"That is *precisely* what I'm doing. I'm sorry but I have no intention of allowing a reckless young woman whose judgment is suspect at best to ruin in one hour what has taken me twenty years of hard work to establish and maintain."

"You can't do this to me! It's not legal."

"You're both right and wrong. It is somewhat illegal, but I can do it, and I will do it. You are my daughter and I love you dearly, but I simply cannot afford either professionally or personally to allow this scandal to go any further. There are too many repercussions. You will leave Paris in three days' time from the Gare du Nord. A private cabin has been reserved for you on the ferry which departs from Calais. Upon reaching Dover, you will be met by one of His Lordship's servants. No reasonable courtesy shall be denied you. You will be paid the standard wage that all English maids receive. If you need additional monies, I will send them to you. Should you have any thoughts about behaving in any manner other than that of an educated, sensible young woman, I strongly advise you to forget about them. I assume you are wondering what will happen to François. I had a long talk with the presiding magistrate. He has generously agreed not to press charges. We saw no sense in ruining what promises to be a productive and fruitful life. I'll say good-bye now." He bussed me lightly on the cheek and left the room.

Exile.

I could think of no other word that described what was being done to me. And for what? A careless indiscretion, an unfortunate discovery. It was unfair, but the weeks of solitude during which I spent many introspective hours enabled me to realize that my body was a wondrous instrument. No one—not even my revered father—had the right to tell me how I should or should not use it.

Strengthened by these thoughts, I accepted my fate—even welcomed it.

Of course, now I can see now that it was lunacy—total madness—but that is in hindsight. I was rebellious, eager to explore the world François had given me but a glimpse of. And Papa was providing me with the opportunity. What irony! How bittersweet it seems now. If only I could tell him to his face—but that of course is impossible.

Entry № 3

June 7, 1867

Less than a week later, my clothes were packed, Maman bade me a tearful farewell, and I was escorted to the Gare du Nord. Papa had said a private compartment had been reserved in my name.

How fickle fate is. How quickly one's circumstances change. When I first boarded the boat train, I was depressed. Gloomy thoughts filled my head. But now, in the space of less than half a day, I could not believe my good fortune, for I believed I had a suitor on the train that is taking me to Calais.

He was tall and fair, and sat facing me, one table removed, in the dining car. Although unchaperoned, one of the porters—no doubt hired by Papa—always positions himself at the end of the car, where he can observe my every movement.

My admirer's finely cut coat, waistcoat, and trousers, which I recognized as being made of expensive fabric, clearly established his status as a gentleman. When our eyes met I felt my cheeks redden. The warmth traveled down into my loins. I have discovered that squeezing my thighs together as tightly as I can produces the sweetest of sensations that flow outward with a heat that is far greater than the apparent one in my cheeks.

I did not know how to go about making further contact with him; my abilities in these very subtle matters are woefully inadequate. I could only hope that my gentleman was more experienced than I.

A fortuitous accident gave him the opportunity he needed. After lunch I was sipping my coffee when the car lurched suddenly, causing me to spill it. Seizing upon the chance that fate had offered him, my suitor immediately came to my aid, moving the rolling cup out of the way and mopping up the coffee with several linen napkins before the waiters could come to my assistance.

"Mademoiselle, I would consider it a great honor if you would allow me to buy you another coffee," he said, bowing politely.

"I accept your offer," I replied demurely. "A single woman traveling alone cannot be too careful. I would be most grateful for your protection."

Please allow me a small digression. The warm weather

allowed me to choose outfits that did not overly conceal my pleasingly plump bottom or ample bosom. I did so confident that I am compromising neither my taste nor my morals. Evidently, my somewhat amateurish ploy had worked.

I will not bore you with the details of our conversation. It had the full attention of the porter, who was powerless to do anything save watch. My admirer's name is Jacques Rambeau, a gentleman in his late thirties. He is on his way to London, where he has business with a coal exporter.

"A profitable business, as you might imagine," he explained. "Would it be too brazen of me to inquire as to your destination?"

"Not at all, sir. I am going to London, where I shall be employed in the household of Lord and Lady Francis Parkinson-Smythe."

"The name is familiar. Is he not one of England's most influential barristers?"

"That is my understanding."

We lingered in the dining car for as long as we dared, making idle conversation. When it became obvious that our continued presence in the deserted car might arouse gossip, Jacques said, "Please allow me to escort you back to your compartment."

As he helped me on with my shawl, I was very aware of Jacques's most attractive facial features, his straight black hair and light gray eyes. Although I am fairly tall for a woman—five feet, seven inches, to be exact—Jacques was taller by at least a head.

Fate looked kindly upon me a second time. In order to negotiate the length of the carriage, we were obliged to walk down a narrow passageway that ran between the window side of the car and the doors to the individual compartments. One person can pass freely, but two encounter much difficulty.

As we slowly made our way toward my compartment (followed at a respectable distance by the watchdog of a porter), the train pulled into some nameless station. In an instant, the corridor was packed with people. Some were getting off while others were getting on. All of them were encumbered with luggage, which added to the confusion.

Jacques and I were literally trapped by the unruly mob and could not have moved even if we had wanted to. My back was against the brass rail that ran below the windows, while Jacques was facing me.

Our bodies crushed together as I held onto both the rail and one of Jacques's arms, fearful of being carried away by the swarm of people whose rudely manifested determination either to get to their seats or to disembark left little time for common courtesies.

My admirer's face was close to mine as my bosom pressed against his chest. Then I felt him begin to rub one of my bumcheeks, and then the other. I also felt a stiffness press against my thighs. He investigated my cleft as well, making me shiver with delight.

"Your beauty has intoxicated me from the moment I saw you. I am enthralled by you. Please, I beg you to come to my stateroom so we can converse under less stressful circumstances. I must know everything about you. Please tell me that you will," he whispered into my ear.

"It is impossible, for I am locked in my compartment. If that were not so I would fly to you in an instant. You must think of another way."

At that point, we were interrupted by the impertinent porter, who coughed before he said in a pompous, officious manner, "No lingering in the corridor, please. Company rules."

I looked around. To my amazement, we were the only ones left. The narrow aisle had emptied as quickly as it filled. "Trust me, *mon amie*. I will think of something," Jacques said as he bowed and kissed my hand.

Lest you think I behaved like a common *poule*, let me assure you that Jacques was a very handsome man. Fate had brought us together, but the agony of not being able to consummate our mutual attraction was almost unbearable after my jailer had locked me in my compartment. How cruel circumstances can be; how little control we have over them. Nevertheless, I accepted the fact that I would never share the most intimate of pleasures with Jacques. I took strength in the knowledge that he was just the beginning of a long journey I was about to embark upon. Sleep came slowly that night, for my very soul was being tortured.

I might also add that my dim-witted guardian had somehow managed to sense that something was afoot. Taking every precaution lest he lose the generous tip with which Papa had no doubt bribed him, he delivered my remaining meals directly to my compartment, thus dashing the few remaining slight hopes I had about meeting Jacques again. When we arrived at Calais, the porter escorted me to the waiting ship.

Resigned to my fate, I prayed that the crossing, which was to take all night, would be a smooth one, as I have a delicate stomach. The following morning, I would be met by Lord Parkinson-Smythe's emissary, who would then chaperon me on the train that would take us to London. I understand now why Papa is such a good barrister: he leaves nothing to chance. Every contingency has been thought of and resolved in a manner that satisfies Papa's desires. My own desires have thus been thwarted, but I am confident that I shall soon be able to rectify matters in a way that is appropriate to my own wishes.

By the time we disembarked from the train and boarded the ship, it was nearly nine o'clock in the evening. In all honesty, I must confess that, although understandably small, the accommodations Papa had arranged for me were undeniably first class.

There was an adequately sized closet, washbasin, commode, *bidet*, a soft mauve upholstered chair, a small writing table with a matching chair, and a firmly mattressed bed.

Frustrated and tired, I changed from my traveling costume to a white silk nightgown over which I wore a pink dressing gown, intending to read for an hour or so before retiring for the evening. Through the small porthole, I could see the harbor where lights from other ships twinkled like man-made stars.

Just as I was about to turn off the light, I heard a soft tapping on the door. Apparently Papa had concluded that once I was aboard the ship, I would be protected from any ill-advised adventure, for the steward had not locked the door to my cabin. Naturally, I had. I tiptoed over to the door, my bare feet silent on the beige carpet, and put my ear to it.

"Who is it?"

"C'est moi, Jacques," was the urgent whispered reply.

I knew I had but an instant—at most, seconds—to decide if my resolutions were as strong as I thought they were. If I did not open the door, I knew I would be consigning myself to a sheltered, almost spinsterish life, one devoid of any of the pleasures I was so eager to reexperience.

On the other hand, if I did allow Jacques into my cabin, there was no turning back. I would have only myself to blame should there eventuate unforeseen, unfortunate circumstances. Should I open the metaphorical door to a new life that promised much, or would it be wiser to deny myself those very things I had wished for so fervently?

I took a deep breath and willingly assumed full responsibility for my fate. Jacques quickly, almost furtively, brushed past me, letting me close and lock the wooden cabin door.

He produced a bottle of champagne which he had hidden under his coat, while I went to the basin, where I found two tall, clear glasses. He eased the cork out carefully, cleverly coughing as it popped in order to mask the sound. After he poured the bubbly liquid, Jacques raised his glass to me.

"To us, *mon amie*," he toasted.

The effervescent wine tickled my nose as I sipped. My heart pounded in my bosom. I knew what was going to happen, but not exactly how I was going to be affected. I do not drink much; a glass of wine with lunch or dinner is more than sufficient. The combination of the champagne and anticipation quickly made me feel quite giddy, in and of itself a not unpleasurable sensation.

Jacques took our nearly empty glasses and put them on the table while I remained standing, not knowing what to do, for I had never been in such a position before.

It soon became apparent that my suitor had.

"Forgive me, my dear but your beauty has enslaved me. The champagne is excellent, but I must taste your lips for I know they will be sweeter than anything man has ever produced."

Then he embraced me, pressing his lips gently against

mine. My tongue met his as we kissed. Again I felt a hardness press against me which served to fuel my hunger. He cupped my bottomcheeks and pulled me hard against him, my bosom pressing against his chest.

"And now I must see you for I am sure your beauty is a testament to the power and glory of our Creator," he said as he led me gently over to the bed. After he removed my robe, he pulled the wide neckline of my nightgown over my shoulders, and it slithered to the floor. "*Mon Dieu!* Never have I seen such a wondrous bosom."

The bedside lamp was turned down, creating a most romantic atmosphere. I lay on the white-coverleted bed as Jacques removed his clothing quickly, his eyes roving over my body. I relaxed, trusting to both his experience and gentleness. I am a natural blond, and this quirk of nature had much attraction for him as his eyes lingered there before he lay down beside me.

Jacques lavished kisses upon my globes, causing my sensitive buds to flower. Then he suckled on them like a babe in arms, his ministrations increasing my desire and passion. I was soon panting as he moved down between my legs, kissing my soft, furry mound before he favored me with the most intimate of kisses.

His tongue entered me, probing and eliciting gasps of delight which soon intensified as he prodded my clitoris with the tip of his tongue, causing that most sensitive of appendages to rise and radiate pleasure to every part of my body. I was now Jacques's prisoner of love. When I spasmed, I regarded the sweet juice that flowed into his mouth to be a tribute to the power he had over me.

But it was a power more given than taken; for I willingly let him make free with me, curious how the next pleasure would manifest itself. My clitty pulsed with delight. I panted faster and faster as I was overcome with yet another spasm. Was there no end to the joys which he heaped upon me once I had surrendered, giving my body and soul to his care? To what distant realms of passion would my lover carry me?

"Your love-juice is unlike any other," Jacques panted when he finally disengaged himself. "And now you must pay me what many regard as the most ultimate of compliments."

"I will do anything, my love—anything you ask of me."

He moved up on the bed so that his pelvis was opposite my face. Then I understood what he wanted me to do.

I had never sucked upon a man's member before, nor had I given it much thought. But now that the moment of truth was upon me, I must confess to a certain amount of anxiety. The idea, in and of itself, did not repel me. Of greater concern was what, if any, pleasure it would bring, both to myself and to my lover.

Fortunately, Jacques's oral affections which he had bestowed upon me with an abundance surely born of passion had put me in such a state of fulfillment that I was hungry for more.

Had I sunk to the level inhabited by the bawdiest of

sluts? No, that was most assuredly not the case. I had been liberated and was in the process of venturing into unknown places where I was confident my body would respond pleasurably.

His member was most impressive—dare I use the word intimidating?—in both length and girth. I pulled down the foreskin gently, exposing his helmeted head. Acting upon pure instinct, for I had no practical experience to draw upon, I slipped my lips over him and lowered my head, trying to take as much of him as I could into my warm, wet cavern.

After I moved my mouth up and down several times, I felt a great relief. Although at first the act gave me an odd pleasure, I was not yet aware of the power it would hold over me—a power that would all too soon manifest itself as both a blessing and a curse.

The relief fortified me with the self-confidence I needed in order to swirl the flat of my tongue around his head, marveling at how smooth it was. Growing surer of myself by the second, I became bolder and ran the tip of my tongue up and down his underside before I delicately traced the swollen veins with the tip of my ever-active tongue. I marveled at how the smooth head contrasted with the rigidity of the shaft; and as I applied myself, these differences produced in me a deeply felt, not clearly understood desire that demanded to be satisfied.

Jacques's moans convinced me that my actions met with his approval. Thus encouraged, I took him into my mouth once more and began to move my head up and down, squeezing his girth with my lips. He reached down so he could pay exciting attention to my breast buds, pinching them, which caused pleasure to run through my body.

Then a most unexpected thing happened. As I sucked on him, a profound hunger invaded the most private of my parts. It revealed itself in the form of a shortening of breath accompanied by a heightened awareness and appreciation of what I was doing. These things were quickly followed by a powerful spasm whose warm cream lined the walls of my cunny. Soon I felt droplets of my love-juice seep out as Jacques continued to manipulate my pleasure-hardened buds.

And that was how I came to know that sucking on a cock excited me to the point of orgasm.

It was a most marvelous discovery. Even then, in my naïveté, I knew it was a gift which, in many ways, was to change the course of my young life. The resulting bliss was almost unbearable, and it came from a totally unexpected source. Never have I been more in touch with my innermost passions than I was at that moment when my cunny first contracted while Jacques's cock was in my mouth. It elevated me to undreamed-of heights of sexual pleasure. Admittedly, I am only nineteen years of age and there is still much to be learned and experienced but I knew I had already been blessed infinitely more than most females, and for that I was most grateful.

I sucked harder and harder, almost demanding another orgasm from myself. My efforts were interrupted only when Jacques reached down and lifted my head off his tool.

"*Sacré bleu!*" he panted. "Never have I seen such a hungry sucker."

"It brings me great pleasure," I confessed with as much modesty as I could muster under the circumstances.

"Indeed it must," Jacques agreed. "Now I must have you completely, for never before has my passion been so aroused. I must possess you!"

I lay on my back, spreading my legs and drawing my knees up to my chest. The seconds passed like minutes as Jacques positioned himself, looking down at my blond garden whose gates glistened with overflowing love-juice.

He entered me slowly and, considering the length and girth of his rod, most considerately. At first I wondered whether I could accommodate him, for François was not nearly as well endowed. But it soon became apparent that I was able to take everything he had to give me.

My tight but well-lubricated canal was soon completely filled by his magnificent tool. He began to give me a good humping, rearing back and thrusting his mighty rod up into me as far as he could, eliciting the sweetest gasps of pleasure from me as I wrapped my legs around his waist and began to move my pelvis upward, meeting him halfway in hope of increasing both our pleasures.

Within minutes Jacques dispelled any doubts I might have had, for even though my knowledge is limited I feel safe in assuming that not all men are equal when it comes to matters concerning the cock and cunt.

He brought me to orgasm in no time at all, lunging in and out of me faster and faster, his manly member penetrating deeply into the upper regions of my cunny, the head hitting places never before touched. Trust me when I say that my spasms rendered me breathless. Soon the room began to spin, forcing me to hold onto his shoulders. My most private juices coated his tool and thus made it easier for him to continue his breath-taking assault upon my cunny.

Save for François, I had no one to compare Jacques to. Even so, I knew instinctively that he was a cocksman of the first order, displaying remarkable stamina and endurance.

Crying out in delight, I was overtaken by yet another powerful orgasm, which made my entire body tingle. Then Jacques picked up speed, and I sensed he was going to spend himself. The anticipation was delicious. His head swelled slightly before he spurted a long, thick stream of virile juices into me. Either by chance or design, his timing was excellent, for it enabled me to extend my orgasm and thus be elevated to greater heights of passion.

"My love," he panted as he withdrew his still-hard rod, "get on your hands and knees, for I have not yet had my fill of you."

I sat up and caressed his wondrous instrument with

my fingertips before bestowing dainty kisses upon the head. Then I assumed the desired position, resting my forehead on the pillow, my large bosom grazing the white linen coverlet as my stallion mounted me from the rear. I had not been taken that way before and found it to be somewhat awkward at first. I had to turn my head and look around to see what he was doing.

"A derriere such as yours is worthy of only the greatest of painters," he said admiringly as he caressed my soft, round cheeks. Then he started to enter me.

"Jacques, Jacques!" I panted as I felt inch after inch of rockhard penis pass into me. He didn't stop until his groin hairs were pressing against my bumcheeks.

"Never have I experienced such passion," he grunted as he withdrew his tool from me, leaving only the head inside. He began to give me a most vigorous humping, holding onto my hips as I moved them from side to side, causing his deeply penetrating head to rub against the sides of my tight sheath.

Never in my wildest imagination could I have dreamed of the ecstasy the female body is capable of if it is properly stimulated. Needless to say, Jacques was more than able. He soon had me in the thrall of a mighty orgasm, whose sweet cream seeped out from between my lips, trickling down my inner thighs.

I do not know how many times I spasmed; the number is unimportant. Suffice it to say that I was avalanched by one pleasure after the other which left me gasping for breath. I could feel Jacques's balls bounce off my clitty, which produced a subtle but immensely stimulating variation on the pleasure to which I was already a slave.

After what seemed an eternity of bliss, my cocksman finally spent himself, bathing my cunny with his copious manly jism. He stayed in me so I could feel his cock subside. My body shuddered as more joy darted through me, rekindling the passion I had just experienced.

Then we collapsed into each other's arms and remained there until I finally regained most of my composure. Jacques went over to the desk, where he refilled our glasses, his limp member bobbing between his legs. The mere sight of it conjured up images of intense satisfaction.

"Never before have I had such a night of bliss," he exclaimed.

"Nor I. How long will you be in London?" I inquired, barely unable to keep my eyes off the instrument which had provided me with so much joy.

"Several weeks. Forgive my audacity, but would it be possible for us to rendezvous? It is my most fervent wish."

"And mine as well, *mon ami*, but I do not know the address of my employer."

Jacques took a sip of his champagne, got up, and returned with a small business card. "I can always be reached at this address," he said as he handed it to me. "Send me a letter by private courier, for they are much faster and more discreet than the regular post. I will fly to your arms no matter where you are," he said gallantly.

"I shall do that within twenty-four hours of my arrival," I assured him.

"It is late, and while my desire for you beats strongly in my heart, I think it best if I leave, for I do not which to compromise your reputation in any way."

After he dressed, he held me tightly. "Till we meet again, *mon ami*," he said before he slipped out of my cabin.

Sleep did not come easily, for waves of pleasure continued to roll over my body. I was convinced that I had gone through a momentous metamorphosis, but a question nagged at me. Would I be able to figure out a way to continue receiving such joys without compromising either myself or my employers? Surely they maintained the highest moral standards.

It goes without saying that, once I had been made aware in a most direct and profound manner of the apparently endless variations of achieving such bliss, I would naturally seek them out. Knowing little about the English, I concluded that I would simply have to wait until I gained such knowledge as I needed in order to pursue my amorous explorations.

Naturally, I intended to contact Jacques as soon as I could. He was both a gentleman and a superb cocksman, and I had no intention of degrading myself by lowering my standards. Papa's influence was great and made me fearful that he would soon learn of any misdeed or *faux pas* I might commit, no matter how inadvertent. I would therefore have to use all my wiles if I were to successfully initiate and continue my explorations of the previously hidden world of sexual pleasures.

Exhilaration eventually gave way to exhaustion. I gladly fell into the arms of Morpheus.

Entry № 4

June 8, 1867

The passage was smooth. I got a good night's sleep, which I knew would be most beneficial as I began my first day in England. After having a hearty breakfast in my cabin, I carefully chose an appropriate costume: a light gray, ruffled, high-necked dress with generous folds that managed to conceal the size of my breasts and therefore spare me the indignities of unwanted attention. The ship was docked and I had just finished pinning my shoulder-length hair on top of my head when there was a knock on my cabin door.

Editor's Note: The records of the ferry company indicate that a one-way, first-class passage, Calais to Dover, for

*one was indeed purchased on June 3, 1867. The records
do not indicate the identity of the purchaser. In any
case, Danielle's father (or, more than likely, an assigned
agent) made the actual purchase. However, the manifest
list does indeed include the name Danielle Appleton.*

"Entrez" I replied while I put a wide-brimmed hat on
my head.

A short, stocky man entered, bowler hat in hand. He
wore a black-and-white checked wool suit, low boots,
and a stiff collar around which was a poorly tied cravat.
"Miss Appleton?" he asked.

"*Oui*, I am *Mademoiselle* Appleton."

"My name is Peter Quigmire. I have been sent by
Lord Parkinson-Smythe to escort you to London. I have
a letter for you."

The clearly written note was from His Lordship,
authorizing the bearer to act as my chaperon.

"Lord Parkinson-Smythe has made arrangements so
we can leave the ship without having to fight our way
through the mob. Is this all your luggage?" He looked at
my large brown leather bag and a matching smaller one.

"Yes."

"If you'll follow me then…" He took the luggage.

Although he wore gentleman's clothes, I had a vague
feeling that there was something of the ruffian about
him. I also thought he smelled ever so slightly of horses.
Not being familiar with English society, I dismissed my

observations as being irrelevant and followed him down the corridor.

Had I but known of the abasements and indignations which were soon to follow, I would gladly have thrown myself into the sea. Drowning would have been a far kinder fate than the one which was about to befall me.

We disembarked via a smaller, separate gangplank which allowed us to avoid the crush of passengers who were slowly being funneled down the exit. A short walk brought us to the waiting train, where we soon found ourselves ensconced in a first-class compartment.

Of the ride to London I shall say little, save that my escort did not make any attempt to engage me in conversation. The day was sunny and warm; so as you might imagine, I spent most of the journey looking at the verdant English countryside.

The train made numerous stops, which gave me my first opportunity to observe the English people. We lunched in the compartment and arrived at Victoria Station at approximately six o'clock that evening.

It was large, crowded with people representing every social class; and noisy, not unlike the Gare du Nord or Gare du Sud in Paris. Eschewing the services of a porter, my escort easily carried my bags himself. The lower classes and suspicious-looking travelers made me glad of the protection he afforded me. We made our way quickly through the cavernous depot, our destination a black hansom which was waiting for us at the curb.

After my luggage had been stowed, oddly enough inside a closed compartment as opposed to the normal way of attaching them to the top of the carriage, we were off.

As I look back, I had numerous chances to escape. However, it serves no useful purpose to dwell on what might have been. Exhilarated by the sights of this most modern of metropolises, I paid attention to little else. In hindsight, that was a fatal mistake.

Editor's Note: Danielle's observations were correct. The normal custom was to stow the luggage on the rear of the carriage. However it would have done her little good to protest or even question the act. She was unfamiliar with local customs and exhilarated by finally arriving in London. Even if she had protested, the sly Quigmire could have easily manufactured a plausible response. Although she did not know it, Danielle's fate was sealed the moment the carriage door closed.

Our horses, whose rhythmical trotting provided a familiar, reassuring sound, soon delivered us to the residence which was going to be my home for the next year. Even to a complete stranger, the area in which the house was situated was indeed quite elegant. Unlike some of the other neighborhoods we had passed through, the streets were clean and well paved, and I did not see any rough-looking people. Tall gas lamps provided sufficient illumination, but I was most impressed by the towering elms whose leafy branches formed a most pleasing canopy over the street, creating a verdant living archway through which we passed.

A formally attired butler emerged from the four-story red brick house with its dark window shades and fetched my luggage while I admired the wide expanse of the classic Palladian residence, dominated by a colonnaded porch.

"I will show you to your room," he said as the carriage—from which Peter had not emerged—drove away.

Editor's Note: Tax records show that Lord Francis Parkinson-Smythe owned a house in the fashionable section of Mayfair. The house was bought three years before Danielle's arrival and descended in the family.

After ascending a sweeping staircase, we walked down a broad hallway, passing several rooms whose thick dark wood doors were closed. I would have to learn what lay behind them. Several landscape paintings, which did not attract my interest, adorned the walls. What did intrigue me, if ever so fleetingly, was the silence. Although the house was well-lit, I could not discern any sound of people.

At the far end of the hallway, the butler stopped and opened a door.

Editor's Note: For obvious reasons, in most large homes, the servants' quarters were usually placed near the kitchen.

However, for reasons that will become apparent to the astute reader later on, it seems that Lord Parkinson-Smythe was an innovator. He had put the maids' rooms on the second floor. Thus the arrangement in his London home was as follows: first floor—large foyer, butler's quarters, kitchen, sitting rooms, entrance to garden; second floor—formal dining room, cooks' and maids' rooms; third floor—office, study; fourth floor—His Lordship's and Her Ladyship's private quarters.

"This will be your room," he said after he turned up the lamps and set my luggage down. "My name is Rufus. I'll have Cook prepare a dinner for you." Then he left, closing the door behind him.

The room was rather large. It contained a large coverleted bed, a small, obviously mass-produced pine table with a matching chair, a thickly padded brown leather easy chair, a freestanding maple closet, and a chest of drawers on which sat a large round mirror and a white porcelain pitcher and basin. Parting the heavy black floor-to-ceiling draperies, I could discern the bulky shapes of thick, trimmed shrubbery which I assumed were part of a larger garden.

Presently there was a soft knock on my door. As I started to walk toward it, it opened. A snaggletoothed white-haired woman, who was sixty if she was a day, entered, carrying my dinner tray. She put it on the table and wiped her hands on her apron.

"This should hold you," she said cheerfully. "I'm Maggie. You just get some rest now. Charlotte—she's the other maid—will fetch you in the morning."

I ate my dinner of mutton, potatoes, and green beans slowly, as if every bite would reveal something new and different. Then I unpacked. The closet had more than enough room for my clothing.

I settled into the comfortable bed, for the journey and the stimulating but somewhat-discomfiting experience of being plunged into a different environment had tired me considerably. As I remember, my last thoughts before drifting off to sleep concerned themselves with how eager I was to see what awaited me in the morning. How innocent I was! How gullible! The signs were all there, but I could not see them. I have no one to blame for my subsequent misfortunes but myself. Little did I know that I was about to enter a hell on earth from which I fear there is no escape.

Entry № 5

June 9, 1867

Bright sunlight streamed into my room, awakening me. Attracted by the melodious sounds of birds, I went over to the window and looked out upon the large garden where the little creatures flitted between the trees and thick bushes. Presently there was a gentle knock on my door and Maggie came in, setting a tray down upon the table. "I've brought you your breakfast. When you've finished, come down to the kitchen, it's on the first floor. Charlotte will tell you what your duties are," she said cheerfully.

I must confess that after I lifted the lid off the large tray, I was greatly taken aback. An English breakfast, consisting of eggs, potatoes, sausages, and toast is more like a French dinner. Nevertheless, I managed to eat most of it—I was hungrier than I had first thought. Then I looked in the closet and found a maid's black uniform, which I put on. Amazingly, it fit me rather well.

I had no difficulty in finding the kitchen. I met Rufus on the way downstairs and he instructed me, obviously sensing my hesitation lest I accidentally enter a room where I was not supposed to go. There were so many of them—all with their doors closed.

"There you are at last!" Maggie said cheerfully, turning around from the large table where she was chopping vegetables. There was also a huge oven, pantry, many cupboards, and a long rack where pots and pans hung from copper hooks. Next to a cupboard was a row of small brass bells. Above each one was a label indicating the room of the house. I was introduced to Charlotte, who was sitting at a bulky table where she sipped a cup of coffee. Like me, she wore an ankle-length black uniform with a frilled white apron and matching round cap.

I am five feet seven inches tall, and Charlotte was able to look me in the eyes. I could see her scarlet red hair under her cap, but it was her eyes that caught and held my attention. They were a most unusual green, and had I known of the evil that lay behind them, I would have fled for my life. But alas, I did not know, nor did I have any way of predicting the sinfulness that was to come.

Of the introductions I shall say little, for they are of little consequence, and served only as a prelude. They seduced me further into a feeling of well-being. Charlotte was cordial—nay, she was friendly. I must have been like a child. So easy to manipulate.

I was given a brief tour of the house, for there were many rooms we did not enter. When I questioned Charlotte, she replied in a vague manner. Naturally, it was not my place to query her further. The house was quiet, which I thought to be somewhat odd, but again I remained silent.

So many clues! Had I but listened to one of them, perhaps I could have averted the cruel fate which awaited me as surely as the sun rises in the morn.

After the tour, we went to my room, where I was taught how to make and turn down a bed, light a fire—for all the rooms had fireplaces—when to replenish the supply of coal, and how to lay out clothing. I practiced curtsying and the proper way of addressing His Lordship and Her Ladyship.

Three days after my arrival, I was summoned by Charlotte, who found me in my room making up my bed. She knocked twice, and then entered. "His Lordship wishes to see you," she said solemnly. I carefully pinned my hair under my white ruffled cap and made sure my apron was on straight, then followed Charlotte up the stairs and down the hall until she stopped in front of a heavy oak door upon which she knocked three times rather softly. I heard a muffled reply, and she opened the door.

Lord Parkinson-Smythe was sitting behind a Louis XIV desk. He wore a high-collared white shirt, cravat, trousers, and leather shoes.

Unlike my father's study, the room was curiously devoid of bookcases. It contained only the aforementioned desk, several leather chairs, and a small console on which sat several cut-glass decanters of liquor with all the needed accessories. The floor-to-ceiling double windows were open to let in the fresh air and the charming sound of chirping birds.

"Pray sit down," said His Lordship, after Charlotte and I curtsied. Charlotte then left the study. My employer was a tall, handsome man with narrow, almost almond-shaped gray eyes, dark brown hair, and thick muttonchop whiskers. He looked strong and fit, a fine example of a man in his prime. I would be less than truthful if I did not admit that I was aware of his physicality in ways that were both intriguing and exciting. Lest you give me credit where credit is not due, I will confess that Papa had told me his age, which was forty. "I have received excellent reports about you," he said in a deep baritone. "Forgive my tardiness in not introducing myself to you sooner, but there were pressing matters I had to attend to. Do you lack anything?"

"No, Your Lordship. I have been treated with the utmost kindness and respect," I replied.

"Excellent. Your duties are not too strenuous?"

"You are most considerate to inquire. No, they are not. You are also most kind to take me into your household. It is an honor to serve you."

"When an old friend calls, I am duty bound to respond." He rose and rang a small bell on his desk, signaling Charlotte to come in. "Now, if you will excuse me."

I curtsied and left, accompanied by Charlotte. "When will I meet Her Ladyship?" I inquired as we walked down the stairs to the kitchen.

"Soon, I suspect," Charlotte replied, as we entered the kitchen where Rufus was eating his lunch, not even glancing at us as we sat down at the massive table where Maggie would serve us.

Had I known better, I would have realized that something was seriously amiss. Normally, it is the custom of the master and mistress of the house to meet new servants as soon as they are employed. Yet another clue that slipped by me. How obvious they all seem now. But alas, it is too late!

Charlotte's reply to my inquiry as to when I would meet Her Ladyship was very accurate. After I had finished my duties, it was my custom to retire to my room, where I read or simply stargazed. I was gradually making the adjustment to living in a foreign country, but I still needed more time before I would be completely comfortable.

I had taken off my maid's uniform and was in the

process of changing into my nightclothes when the door opened suddenly, startling me out of my wits, for I hadn't a stitch of clothing on. I had not heard any footsteps outside my room that might have given me some warning of an approaching visitor.

I knew immediately that it was Her Ladyship. She wore an expensive short-waisted, puffed-sleeved light green blouse with a straight jade-green skirt. Her low-cut bodice revealed a most impressive aspect of her sex. Her black hair was curled in ringlets that fell gracefully on either side of her round face, which was heavily made up, her painted mouth looking like a gash. I thought her breath carried the aroma of wine but I could not be sure. I estimated her age to be approximately thirty.

"Do you not curtsy when your mistress enters?" she demanded imperiously.

"Forgive me, Your Ladyship, but as you can see, I am not prepared." My cheeks reddened with embarrassment.

"You should *always* be prepared!"

"Yes, madam," I said humbly as I curtsied. Then I quickly pulled on my nightdress over my head. "Is there something you wish?" I asked awkwardly.

Lady Parkinson-Smythe ignored my question as she came over to me. I had been right—there *was* wine on her breath. Her eyes slowly raked me, adding to my discomfort. "Francis has chosen well this time. I must remember to compliment him."

"I do not understand, my lady."

"You don't have to." She walked around me slowly, inspecting me as if I were a prize cow. I felt a hand graze my bums before she faced me again. "Yes, very attractive indeed," she said in a low voice as if she were talking to herself. "Show yourself to me!"

"My lady!" I gasped. "I cannot do that!"

"Are you not in my service?" she asked sweetly.

"Yes."

"Are you not here to please me and His Lordship?"

"Yes," I conceded, my head spinning in frightening confusion.

"Then show yourself. That is not a hard thing to do, is it? After all, we are of the same sex. We possess the same bodies, do we not?"

"Please, I cannot!" I said on the verge of tears.

Then she stepped back. "Very well," she sighed.

She left abruptly, her perfume trailing behind her. I sat on the edge of my bed, confused, anxious. Her Ladyship had made a most unusual request. Was this another quaint English custom that no one had told me about? Had I offended her to the point where my position was in jeopardy?

Alas, I did not have too much time to ponder these questions which I asked myself silently. Soon there was an insistent rapping on my door. I hastily put on a dark blue flannel robe and stood up. "Come in," I said with as much courage as I could muster, fearing for what might be on the other side of the door.

It was His Lordship, resplendent in a paisley dressing gown with wide black silk lapels. Curiously, he was barefoot, although I could see that underneath his gown he wore what appeared to be a white nightshirt. I curtsied as he locked the door behind him, a most ominous sign, although at the time I was ignorant of its portent.

"I am sorry to bother you at this late hour, but a matter of some concern has come to my attention. May I sit?"

"Oh, please do," I said, pulling a chair over to the fireplace.

Oddly enough, His Lordship chose to sit on my bed. "You have greatly offended your mistress," he announced gravely.

"I am terribly sorry, but she came upon me suddenly," I said, still standing.

"Are you saying that had she not come upon you suddenly, you would not have offended her?"

"She made a request that I could not honor," I replied meekly, my eyes on the floor.

"Ah, I see," His Lordship said softly, nodding. "Come closer." He remained silent until I was standing in front of him, looking into his peculiarly shaped eyes.

Editor's Note: Several realistic paintings of Lord Parkinson-Smythe survive. Careful examination of them reveals that his eyes were in fact slightly slanted, suggesting that one or more of his ancestors was Oriental. However, an exhaustive examination of Debrett's Peerage *does not bear out this theory. Therefore we can only assume that his almond-shaped eyes were of little consequence, save for the fact that they gave him a mysterious and slightly threatening look.*

"This is very distressing. I simply cannot have maids insulting Her Ladyship. It sets a bad example. You have behaved in a way that demands disciplinary action," he concluded.

"I sincerely regret my behavior, sir but the mistress's request was—"

"Enough of your paltry excuses!" he shouted. "There are no excuses! None, I say! The mistress is your lady and I am your lord! Do you understand me?"

My knees were shaking. It was all I could do to remain under control. "Yes, Your Lordship," I replied in a whisper.

"Excellent, excellent," he muttered. "And now I shall have to do something that will ensure that you remember and understand."

Entry № 6

June 9, 1867

His Lordship moved with a speed and accuracy that took me completely by surprise. His left hand struck like a snake, grabbing my wrist and pulling me across his lap, while his right hand reached down and pulled up my nightgown, exposing my bumcheeks.

"Unhand me! You cannot treat me thus!" I protested.

"I shall treat you any way I want to. Ahhh, what nice cheeks you have," he said as he rubbed them. Then he raised his hand and smacked me as hard as he could, while his other hand held me by the back of my neck.

"No, no! Do not do this to me!" I begged.

"You must be taught a lesson!"

Another blow landed on my cheeks, followed by yet

another. I squirmed, but was pinioned across his lap. How quickly he raised and lowered his hand, raining blows on my poor bum. It felt as if a thousand bees were stinging me as he spanked me. Heat rose from my quivering flesh.

"Mercy, mercy!" I cried out.

Alas, my entreaties fell on deaf ears. Lord Parkinson-Smythe continued to administer a thorough tanning to my buttocks. I fought as hard as I could to free myself from his grip, but he was too strong for me. I fear that my efforts only encouraged him to spank me even harder. The smacks sounded like pistol shots and the pain increased greatly, becoming almost unbearable.

Or so I thought.

Then the pain was replaced by a softening, a moistness which crept into my cunny. It was a magical transformation, one that was totally unexpected but, needless to say, most welcome.

It was as if a heretofore-unknown inner power possessed me. I found myself spreading my legs slightly as the warmth began to move up into my viscera. Then Lord Parkinson-Smythe stopped spanking me and instead began to probe my cunny with his fingers.

My cries of protest had changed into moans of desire. I was being swept along on a wave of passion that I could not resist, especially when His Lordship slipped two of his fingers up into my hole and gave me a good reaming out.

"Ah, it seems that this appeals to you," I heard him say softly as he continued to minister to me, seeking out my most delicate tissues.

I was helpless, a captive of my passion. My desire spiraled upward, my mouth now open as I panted faster and faster until I finally climaxed. No doubt this pleased His Lordship greatly, for he released his hold on the back of my neck and leaned over so he could pull my flimsy garments over my head. My ample bosom rose and fell as I felt warm liquid trickle out from between my cunnylips. I also felt His Lordship's eyes on my bosom, a portent—unknown to me at the time—of all that was to come.

Oh, if only I had the gifts of the tellers of fortunes, the readers of cards, palms, and tea leaves. If only I had the strength that comes with insight into the human condition and all its attendant madness.

But I do not and fear I never will. I had desire, and that alone was enough to doom me.

"Your mistress was right," he said. "Your body is a marvel to behold, even though she could only guess at its full beauty. Then he shucked off his dressing gown and nightshirt, scarcely changing position on my bed. His stalk was hard and tall, intimidating. He reached down and held my head gently with his hands, drawing it close to his rod. Then—with one more little pull—he was in my mouth. "Ahhh, now you will favor me thusly."

As you know, I have had very little experience when

it comes to sucking cock. I was almost innocent, not even a novice. But yet somehow that was overcome by the stimulation that His Lordship had provided me with. I know I am not the most intelligent of creatures, but I believe that there is a connection between desire and the ability to learn a task quickly.

I got up onto my knees between his legs, holding his most manly organ by its base as I raised and lowered my head, while he lay on his back. The intimacy between us fueled my desire and I moved my head faster and faster, even daring to caress his balls.

Again there was that warmth that emanated from my cunny. Oh, that most treacherous of orifices, and yet the most blessed of orifices! I fear that I could not help myself, for I was a prisoner both of myself and of the rod upon which I was so hungrily sucking. They conspired together, and the result was inevitable.

"By Jove, I do believe you released!" His Lordship exclaimed after I had climaxed. He sat up and reached down, exploring my cunny with a hand. "Indeed you did. Bravo! Bravo! Now lie on your back, for my ardor is running hot and I will not be denied!"

"Gently sir, for I am small and you are large," I cautioned as he positioned himself over me.

"You mind your business and I shall mind mine!" he reprimanded as he entered me slowly.

Nature had been most generous, giving him a long, very thick rod, which he proceeded to bury in my tight cunny, his passage no doubt made easier by the love-cream which lined my walls. Nevertheless, there was very little room to spare.

"Ahh, delicious!" he grunted. "How tight you are!"

"You make me so, sir," I panted.

"And I shall make you other things, too."

Little did I know at the time what he meant, for I was curious and eager to explore my newfound passion. I did, but at what a price!

His Lordship vented his passion by giving me a furious humping, driving his rod as deeply as he could up into my tight cunny. He was relentless and soon I was helpless, his assault upon my senses reducing me to an almost animal state in which I wanted more and more. Each time I released, my appetite was whetted all the more.

And more I got. My master was a cocksman of the first degree. He demonstrated that not only by his staying power, which was admirable in and of itself, but also by the way he paced himself.

I would reach a crescendo and he would allow my passions to subside a little before stoking the fires of my desire once again. Thus did he control me and allow me to be visited by the most exquisite of ecstasies.

I was his slave and forfeited for the time being (or so I thought) all independence. I did so willingly because he was opening up a whole new world for me, giving me flashes of it which only made me want to see more.

My writhings encouraged him and he spent himself, filling up my cunny with a great hot gush of manly fluid. He remained inside me, allowing me to feel his shrinking tool until he finally pulled out, releasing my own sweet juices which his rod had plugged up.

"You are indeed a true credit to your country," he said as he slipped into his nightshirt and dressing gown.

I scarcely heard his words, so wrapped was I in the coils of passion. "Sir?" I asked softly as if my voice had become separated from my body.

"'Tis nothing. You have done well. Much promise lies between your legs, my sweet."

Then he left.

I know what you are thinking. I was nothing more than a five-franc *poule,* a cheap streetwalker who plied her trade in the dark, dreary back alleys of Paris, selling herself to anyone for the price of a dram of cheap brandy. But no, do not be so quick to judge me, I beg of you!

I was innocent and, save for two previous sexual encounters, was totally ignorant not only of the act itself, but of all its possible consequences. What woman who has ever lived has not wanted to explore her sexuality?

Yes, I grant you that there are some, but to me that is not normal and, if I was nothing else, I was normal. Perhaps too normal, too ordinary. And would you condemn me for that?

Don't bother. I have done so already!

Entry № 7

The following morning, I woke up a different person. I could hear the birds singing more clearly, I was more aware of my body as I performed my morning ablutions, taking more care with my bosom and other intimate parts. I dressed more carefully. My heart fairly sang, and when I sat down at breakfast, I most definitely had a better appetite. Could Maggie and Charlotte tell? Did they know what had transpired? I knew not and cared not!

I do not know what I was expecting from His Lordship, but in any case, nothing happened. I had duties to perform, and I carried out my responsibilities as best I could.

There was an endless quantity of silverware to be polished, enough to serve Napoleon's army—not to mention all the dusting. I shall spare you the mundane details of my chores. Suffice it to say that they were many and they were tedious and they were never-ending.

I did write Papa and Maman though, knowing that they would be anxious to hear from me. I said nothing of my adventures and kept the letter short and to the point, although I did make special mention of the fact that, in my humble opinion, His Lordship and Her Ladyship were fine examples of English propriety, and I sensed that their outstanding moral character was already beginning to have a positive effect on me.

I must also add that I did have some free time, which I used to explore the neighborhood. The weather remained fine, like the climate of my native Paris, and was conducive to taking walks.

Mindful of my position, I was careful not to engage in conversation with strangers and confined my excursions to the immediate area in which I lived. The population seemed to be wealthy, the ladies all dressed in silk, accessorized with wide-brimmed hats adorned with feathers and parasols.

The men were clearly gentlemen, identified as such by their silver-topped walking sticks and long swallow-tail coats and top hats, which were frequently raised in acknowledgment as I passed. For I, too, was dressed like a lady, even though I almost always wore a rather plain dress to which I added a sash of bright red or yellow ribbon, depending on the predominant color of my costume. Although the neckline was low, there was enough fabric to conceal the true size of my bosom, for I quickly ascertained that I was larger than the average Englishwoman. A hat, complete with floral trimming and the almost-obligatory parasol completed my outfit.

Editor's Note: Danielle is right in her assessment of Mayfair. It was a wealthy neighborhood. Had she ventured several miles to the south, on the other side of the River Thames, she would have seen quite a different London, the kind described so memorably by Charles Dickens. However, she was insulated from the lower classes who lived and died in abject poverty. It is interesting to note that Danielle, certainly no sociologist, does not draw wholesale conclusions, as some people are wont to do, but keeps her observations well within the obvious limitations of her immediate environment.

I found that such diversions were a pleasant and necessary break from my often-monotonous routine. I also found—or thought I found—that many gentlemen were looking at me. I have always been pretty, but it was only after my master had demonstrated his sexual expertise so vividly that I realized I had changed. Had the gentlemen I encountered also noticed the change?

Charlotte often accompanied me on my walks, for it was deemed that I should not go out alone. We strolled slowly, at times twirling our parasols impishly, giving vent to our youthful enthusiasm that always seemed to accompany the spring.

"Why do the gentlemen look at me so strangely?" I inquired as we made our way down a broad street.

"Because they know you are not English. You intrigue them."

"But I am no better or worse than an Englishwoman."

"In their eyes you are, for you have mystery."

My cheeks flushed red. "Surely you don't think that I—"

"Of course you're not doing it on purpose. It's just the way you are," Charlotte explained patiently.

"And do they also know I am a servant, these Englishmen with such keen minds?" I asked.

"Ah, that is part of the puzzle. They are not sure, and it makes you all the more desirable."

"Some of them are very attractive," I admitted, feeling at ease with Charlotte.

"Indeed they are, and they would make free with you in the twinkling of an eye if they could," Charlotte cautioned.

"I think I shall be able to resist them."

"You had better," she said in a sterner voice.

"What do you mean?" I asked as I bowed my head slightly, acknowledging a tall gentleman who raised his hat as he passed.

"Lord Francis has his ways. He is a good man, a fair man, but he can also be—shall we say, demanding."

I knew what Charlotte meant. "How long have you been in his service?"

"Five years. My parents were killed in an unfortunate accident. After I paid all the death and estate taxes, I was a virtual pauper. Fortunately, I had a distant cousin who knew Lord Francis. He was generous enough to employ me."

"You are in his debt, then."

"To an extent, yes. I think we'd better be getting back."

Editor's Note: Sir Reginald Hopkins, Director of the world-renowned Shaftesbury Institute for the Further-ment of Emotional Health offered his opinion, and we paraphrase with his permission.

Danielle was very impressionable. Her words also indicate a strong desire to explore her sexuality of which she was well aware. Unlike the repressed Victorians, Danielle had an advantage: her nationality and upbringing. Her father had successfully assimilated into French society, adopting all of its social mores. It is a well-documented fact that the French, especially the Parisians, were, sexually speaking, much freer than their London counterparts.

As a result, Danielle was not only susceptible to the perspicacious Lord Parkinson-Smythe but, more important, she had none of the innate repressions of English-women of her approximate age.

Danielle is absolutely correct when she observes— although she admits she does not know why—that immediately after her encounter with Parkinson-Smythe, men on the streets of Mayfair looked at her quite differently. Subconsciously, the gentlemen realized that she was unlike any woman they had ever seen, and they reacted accordingly while, at the same time, staying within their well-defined parameters of socially accepted behavior.

These English are a curious race, for there were many gentlemen, if appearances hold for anything, with whom I gladly would have exchanged pleasantries. But none of them approached me, save from a safe distance.

How unlike my beloved Paris, for there a man can make his attraction to a woman known. Of course, contrary to popular belief, we are not libertines, but there are subtle, romantic ways that one can express one's feelings. In contrast, I find that the English are cold and distant. Of course, I am woefully lacking in experience in such matters and perhaps it is unjust of me to make such a rash judgment based on so little social intercourse.

There is a large park nearby and it is here that I spend my free time, limited though it may be. It is very well kept and is a popular place for nannies pushing prams, ladies walking arm in arm with their gentlemen, and equestrians whom I must say are most considerate. The benches are plentiful and the lawns of gently rolling grass they border provide a relaxing vista that is not dissimilar to the Bois de Boulogne.

Editor's Note: Danielle is referring to Hyde Park, a popular park designed by Sir Andrew Crenshaw, one of Britian's most beloved landscape gardeners.

†††

One such day ended with a scene that will be etched in my mind forever. I relate it here in order to communicate some idea of the bestiality into whose depths I was slowly, unknowingly sinking. Forgive me, but my sole desire is to recount the event as clearly as possible.

Although I know that no one will ever read these pitiable words, I nevertheless feel compelled to scribble them down as best I can.

After spending three afternoon hours in the park, I returned home and, after washing up a little and changing into my maid's uniform, I repaired to the kitchen to eat my evening meal. Although Rufus and Charlotte were not there, I thought nothing of it. Their duties sometimes made them take their meals at odd hours.

Maggie served me a hearty meal of mutton, fresh green beans, and boiled potatoes. Maggie's chattering was such that I shall not attempt to put it down. Her words fell upon my ears like raindrops upon a roof and after a while I scarcely heard them anymore. She was a good woman and always treated me with the utmost kindness. However, I found her constant prattling to be a nuisance. I had learned to interject an appropriate comment from time to time without really having to listen to her, for I did not wish to offend her.

After dinner I lingered in the kitchen. Although it was large, I found it to be cozy and filled with cooking utensils that were of great interest to me, as I wished to expand upon my limited culinary skills and knowledge.

As you might imagine, Maggie was more than willing to share with me her impressive array of talents, and I listened with all the attention of a fascinated student.

So many gleaming brass pots, ladles, and spoons, all hanging from racks, all having a different use; so many knives and cleavers all with different lengths and widths, all honed to razor sharpness. It would take a lifetime to learn all of their applications. I found it to be educational and pleasant.

Then a bell rang.

"That'll be Her Ladyship," said Maggie, glancing over her shoulder. She was working at the butchering table, preparing a chicken for tomorrow's dinner. "Better get on up there."

I straightened out my dress and cap, for the mistress put much stock on the servants being presentable at all times, and climbed the stairs. I knocked softly at her door. "Come in," I heard her say.

She was combing her hair at her dressing table. She wore a long silk dressing gown, cinched at her waist. The room was large and dominated by a four-poster bed and a curved-back love seat upholstered in maroon velvet. There was a separate room which contained the toilet and a large porcelain lion's-claw-footed tub. She had enough clothes to outfit a regiment, kept in several oak closets. Thick green carpeting made my approach almost silent. The room was lit by several gas lamps, one by the bed and a large hanging lamp which could be lowered from the ceiling with a pulley. In addition, there were several candlesticks on the dressing table and on a small desk. The room was a combination sitting/ bedroom, an arrangement that I felt to be somewhat odd. But then again, there were many things about the English that I thought were peculiar.

"Your Ladyship," I said as I curtsied.

"Come over here and brush my hair."

She closed her eyes. It was not the first time I had ministered to her in this way. I found it to be relaxing, one of my more enjoyable duties. On the table were many different jars and pots, all containing different colored and scented powders, paints, and rouges. I counted at least a dozen finely cut glass vials of perfumes. A square, multidrawered satin-lined jewel box was open, its diamond and pearl necklaces, intricately carved jade and onyx brooches, and ruby-encrusted bracelets spilling casually out onto the table as if their owner held them in either disdain or disregard. A teardrop-shaped pair of diamond earrings and many sparkling rings caught my eye and made me wonder how Lady Gertrude could treat her jewels so casually, for they were clearly worth a small fortune. I regarded it as being yet another manifestation of Gertrude's eccentric nature.

"It is time for me to take you into my confidence." Lady Gertrude moved forward, signaling me to stop brushing her thick ebony mane. I carefully put the tortoiseshell brush on the table before she turned around so she could look up at me. "I am aware of what happened between you and my husband the other night."

My hand flew up to my mouth and I instinctively stepped back a few paces. "I—I had no choice. I—"

"I know, I know. His Lordship can be most demanding, especially in certain areas as you yourself no doubt found out. I trust it was an enjoyable experience?"

"I will not deny it." I blushed.

"Francis is very adept. His talents are many. I am on my way to see him now. But first I have to prepare. That is why I summoned you."

"I do not understand, Your Ladyship."

"You will very shortly." She rose and went over to the bed, taking me with her. She lay down on her back. "Untie my robe." To my surprise, she was naked underneath it. Her breasts were more than ample, the aureoles large. She had a slightly rounded tummy, her hips flared out slightly, and the hair that covered her most private parts was short, as if it had been shorn. "I want you to help me. It is such a bother doing it by myself, and Charlotte… Well, never mind about her. Begin with my breasts. Use your hands."

"I—I have never—"

"Oh, come now. Surely you must have felt your own breasts at one time or the other. Well, have you?"

"Yes, " I admitted.

She sighed. "It's no wonder your country is in such a shambles! You *do* try my patience. But, time is short, and it is not wise to keep His Lordship waiting for too long. Excite my breasts!"

I sat down next to her, reaching out tentatively and

caressing her flesh, which was very pleasing to the touch, her skin soft and warm. Then I played with her nipples until they hardened and rose.

"Very good." Now Her Ladyship was slightly out of breath. "Are you sure you've never done this before?"

"Upon my word, madam."

"Never mind. Now for my clit." She took her fingers and parted her lips, revealing her pinkish inner flesh. "Well? It will not bite you! We don't have that much time! Maybe you fancy getting your bum tanned, but I prefer not to have to sleep on my stomach for three nights! Get on with it!"

I used my middle finger to gently massage that most sensitive of female appendages. Lady Gertrude closed her eyes and spread her legs a little farther apart, surrendering to my amateurish ministrations. Apparently they had the desired effect. Soon she was panting, and I could feel a slight wetness upon my hand.

"Good, good," she said. "Bring me my rouge—the light red—and some lavender scent. They're on the table." I hurried over and thankfully did not have any difficulty in finding what she wanted. I brought them back to her hastily. "Rouge my nipples," she instructed. After I had done that carefully, she instructed me to sprinkle some of the perfume on her cunny. "But not too much. Otherwise I'll smell like a Poole Street tart and His Lordship will be very upset." A few drops here, a few there, and the job was done. Then she sat up. "Now we must hurry."

"*We?*"

"Yes, you're coming with me," Her Ladyship replied. She hurriedly dabbed a different perfume behind her ears and in the crook of her elbows. Then she tied her hair up in an exaggerated bun and cinched her dressing gown tightly around her waist. "I think you'll find it interesting."

Before I could say another word, she took my wrist and led me down the hallway. When we reached her husband's chambers, she did not bother to knock, but entered right away.

Nothing could have prepared me for what I was about to see.

Entry № 8

June 15, 1867

Heavy black velvet draperies hung over the tall windows. There was a large raised red-coverleted bed, a small padded bench whose purpose I could not fathom, and a small green hassock. Illumination came from a large candelabrum whose flickering candles cast dancing shadows on the cherrywood-paneled walls. Additional light came from a gas lamp that hung over the center of the bed. His Lordship was nowhere to be seen. As I had never been in an English lord's bedchamber, I wondered if this was a typical example. If so, it was very peculiar.

Editor's Note: Danielle displays her youthful naïveté and innocence, for the room Lady Parkinson-Smythe took

*her to was not her husband's bedchamber. Rather it was
a special room, used only for more carnal pleasures. In
Danielle's defense, she had no way of knowing this.*

"Stand next to me," Lady Gertrude ordered softly.

"Where is the master?"

"Shhh!" She put her index finger to her lips.

Then, as if by magic, part of the far wall swung open
silently. Lord Francis came into the room through a
hidden door which closed automatically on well-oiled
hinges. He had on a red silk nightshirt which hung to
his knees. I thought I could see movement between his
legs, but I couldn't be sure.

"Look and learn," he said to me as he stood in front
of us.

I curtsied, not knowing what would happen next. He
and Lady Gertrude engaged in a most amorous embrace,
their mouths glued together for quite a long time before
she disengaged, taking off her clothes while he did the
same. It was hard for me not to stare at his member,
which was indeed more impressive than the last time I
was fortunate enough to see it.

He sat down on the chair, his legs spread, as Lady
Gertrude got on her knees and without any hesitation
began to bestow the most intimate of kisses upon him
before she took him into her mouth.

Lord Francis looked at me as she sucked on him. My
knees felt weak as I watched her move her head up and

down hungrily and quite noisily. The transformation was remarkable. She was a respected lady, one who held a vaunted position in society—and here she was on her knees, behaving in an exceedingly wanton manner.

Was the power of Lord Francis's member such that it reduced her to such a sluttish level, or was it merely an excuse to behave as she really wanted to? Given the chance, would I react in the same way? More questions to which I had no answers then. But now I do.

"Paying attention?" he demanded in a loud voice as Lady Gertrude licked his balls.

"Yes, Your Lordship," I said in a quavering voice.

I stood there transfixed, my feet rooted into the floor. Never had I seen such an exhibition before, for Lady Gertrude was now running the flat of her tongue up and down the length of Lord Francis's tool, her breathing labored. My hand went to my throat as she fondled his testicles, and I fear that I began to lose all my color. There was no air in the room, and the candles and lamp were giving off too much heat.

"You may go now," the master ordered.

"Yes, Your Lordship."

How I managed a curtsy without toppling over, I'll never know. On my way back to my room, I had to stop and lean on the wall for support lest I faint. Such was my reaction to the shocking spectacle I had just witnessed. Just prior to reaching the haven of my room, I was intercepted by Charlotte. Seeing that I was in obvious distress, she said, "Come to my room. I have something for your nerves."

Her quarters, just down the hall, were like my own, with a comfortable bed, small writing table, ample wardrobe space, dresser, an easy chair, separate bathroom, and a view of the rear courtyard.

"Do sit down." She took off her maid's cap, set it down on the foot of the bed, and repaired immediately to her dresser, where she poured a generous dollop of brandy into a plain glass. "Here, drink this," she instructed.

I did as I was bade without hesitation, the liquor burning my throat at first but calming me down quickly. I finished half of it and Charlotte poured a little more before she pulled the chair away from the writing table and sat down in front of me.

"You have been with the master and mistress?"

"Yes. How did you know?"

"From the look on your face. You were quite pale. Loosen your collar and breathe deeply," she advised.

"I was summoned to Her Ladyship's room after dinner. She had me…prepare her for the master. I was ordered to watch as she…" I could not finish the sentence.

"Yes, I know." Charlotte reached over and patted my hand. "It always comes as a shock the first time you see it."

"The mistress was like a…my English is not that good. I do not know the word."

"A female animal in heat?"

"Yes, that is it. Is she always like that?"

"No, not always. But most of the time. You have to be careful with her, for she has many moods."

"The master told me to watch and learn. It is all very confusing." My head started to spin. "I think I'd better go to my own room. I feel faint." I stood up and, had Charlotte not caught me, I would have fallen. It was probably the combination of what I had witnessed, the brandy, and the heat. She led me over to her bed and I lay down, hoping to regain my senses.

I was helpless. You do understand that, don't you? I realized what Charlotte was doing when she removed my shoes and unbuttoned my dress halfway down. "The air will do you good," she explained. "Your dress is much too tight. I'll have the seams taken out tomorrow." Of course she was well-intentioned. They all were. That's the point!

In all honesty, I must confess that as soon as my bodice was loosened, I immediately felt better. I began to draw in the sweet-smelling night air. But I was still in a daze, and therefore vulnerable.

Charlotte's fingers worked with all the dexterity of a pickpocket, for I barely felt her pull up my camisole, exposing my bare bosom. My eyes were closed and the brandy was making my head spin.

But these are merely excuses, and I shall not stoop to offer them, for proud French blood runs in my veins. The tip of Charlotte's tongue ran round and round the circumference of one of my aureoles while her soft fingertips manipulated my other breast ever so gently.

Did it feel good? Did I like it? Yes! There, I've said it. And without shame or guilt either, for she was very experienced and drew my passions slowly to the surface, her tongue and mouth mesmerizing me.

Once I was in the desired state, the rest was easy. She crooked an arm under me and lifted me up slightly so she could remove my dress and camisole. I offered no resistance, for my nipples were hard from pleasure. Nor did I resist when she removed my knickers. As soon as I was naked, she again applied her mouth to my nipples, one of her hands between my legs, caressing my blond mound.

Thus did she increase my ardor to the point where she could leave me unattended for a brief moment while she removed her maid's uniform. Naked, she lay down beside me and embraced me, our bosoms touching. I felt her tongue enter my mouth, and my head cleared ever so slightly.

I was about to enter the forbidden realm of Lesbian love of which I knew little. "No, no!" I protested weakly. "I'm not sure...please."

But my words fell on deaf ears. Charlotte moved down on the bed, lying between my legs, kissing my love-garden all over before her tongue passed through its gates. What a marvelous instrument her tongue was as she worked it all around. How adept she was at finding my clitty and licking it until it rose to its full height.

I panted faster and faster as Charlotte pressed her lips

against mine, keeping them there, making sure the tension kept on rising in my body until there was but one inevitable outcome.

My release was powerful, but as I was about to find out, it was an enslaving release. I threw my pelvis upward, unable to control myself. Charlotte's strong fingers bit into my plump bumcheeks, holding me as I writhed, surrendering to my passion, passing over into the forbidden land where Sappho reigned supreme.

"How sweet your juices are!" Charlotte panted as she moved next to me, caressing both of my bottomglobes.

I was quivering with excitement, standing on the edge of a whole new world without boundaries. Then, Charlotte squatted over me, spreading her lips apart with her fingers. "Pleasure me," she panted.

I reacted instinctively for, as I have mentioned, I had no practical experience in such matters. However, I did have a women's intuition. I took as much of her flaming red-haired garden into my mouth as I could, and soon I knew that what I was doing was right. Charlotte's moans only confirmed this.

In all honesty, I must confess that I did not find the act to be repugnant, for the mutual giving and receiving of pleasure is a natural phenomenon and takes many different forms. That is not to say that I would participate willingly in every variation, but this particular one was most enjoyable.

Charlotte moved around as I found her most sensitive of appendages and soon I felt her love-juice trickle into my mouth. I swallowed, and thrust my constantly moving tongue up into her as far as I could. In doing so, I made her climax yet again. Perhaps more to the point, I climaxed, too.

Had I sunk to the depths of depravity? No, *au contraire*, I reached new heights of sexual elation. Another door to my inner being had been opened and I passed through the portal willingly, eager to explore every possible pleasure.

Charlotte must have sensed this as well, for she moved down and leaned over me, offering me one of her nipples. How eagerly I took it into my mouth! What hunger I had! I sucked upon it like a mewling babe, eliciting gasps of delight from her.

When I had sated myself, I moved my head away. My new lover lay next to me until our passions subsided. Then she rose and sipped some brandy before returning to the bed where I lay naked and unashamed.

"You are a talented woman," she said somewhat mysteriously, lying down next to me.

"It was my first time."

"Yes, I know. Did you enjoy it?"

"I did not come here of my own volition," I began, intending to explain the circumstances which made my father send me abroad.

"I am familiar with your circumstances," Charlotte interrupted as she caressed one of my thighs.

Another clue! How obvious they seem now! How blind I was then! "Yes, I enjoyed it," I replied simply.

"That is good! As you know, Lady Gertrude is rather fond of women. Mark my words. Serve her well or there will be the very devil to pay."

"I must confess I do not know what you mean."

"It is of little importance, for you soon will. Now it would be best if you return to your own room if your head is clear enough."

"It is." And I dressed.

Little did I know that I was about to embark upon a journey that would take me to the very gates of hell.

Entry № 9

In my innocence, I did not give Charlotte's words any more thought. They passed through my mind like the breeze through my room. Nor did I dwell upon the scene between Lady Gertrude and Lord Francis that I had been forced to witness. In my mind, everything between people is possible. Although I am capable of being shocked and repelled, I am not surprised.

Therefore, when the mistress rang for me one afternoon, I entered her bedchamber with an open mind. I had been busy polishing silverware all morning—a task that I find to be most tedious—and I welcomed the opportunity to do something different.

Besides, I had not seen much of the mistress and the

master lately. I knew they led busy social lives for they went out almost every evening, dressed invariably in formal clothes. But they did little entertaining at home. Of course, sometimes one of Lady Gertrude's friends would come over for afternoon tea, but I was given strict orders to remain in the kitchen while Charlotte or Maggie waited on them. The same thing held true when Lord Francis entertained his male friends in his study. Again, Charlotte or Maggie served them.

There was a reason for that, but at the time I did not know what it was.

I knocked on her door and entered. The mistress was in her bathroom, luxuriating in a huge copper tub filled with hot scented water. It was a most ingenious and modern device, for it was possible to draw water directly into the tub from the kitchen. I had never seen such a thing and was fascinated by it.

Editor's Note: Indoor plumbing, as we know it today, was not a feature of Victorian England. The normal way of filling a bathtub with hot water was to heat the water, carry it to the tub, and empty it into the tub. This presented several problems. Much wood had to be accumulated in order to heat the water, which was brought to a boil in a large caldron. Second, an effective method of carrying the water, usually from the kitchen to one of the upper floors, had to be devised because water is quite heavy. By the time the water arrived at its destination, it was usually lukewarm. To be brief, it was not effective.

Lord Parkinson-Smythe devised an ingenious method of solving that problem. Realizing that if cold water can be drawn from a well by a system of levers and pipes which create suction which forces the water upward, he realized that there was no reason why the same methodology could not be applied to a house.

Thus, between the walls he built a series of pipes whose origin was in the kitchen and whose terminus was in the bathrooms. Water was still heated the same way, in a large caldron over a blazing fire, but it was transported up, not by hand, but by the suction created when a large hand lever was pumped up and down vigorously. As a result, he and the mistress had the rare and uncommon comfort of being able to bathe in a tub filled with hot water.

Lady Gertrude, whose mammary endowments were quite impressive, handed me a sponge. "Do my back," she ordered. I rolled up my sleeves and proceeded to bathe her back, kneeling on the floor beside the long, wide tub. "Ahh, that feels good!" she sighed. Her hair was pinned to the top of her head, lest she get it wet. After ten minutes or so, she leaned back. "Now my front, but not as hard," she cautioned, glancing up at me.

"I will be careful, madam."

"You'd better be."

I rubbed her as gently as I could, beginning with her chest and moving my hand down her torso, over her slightly rounded tummy, between her legs and finally her thighs. The water soaked my rolled-up sleeve, for the tub was fairly deep. By leaning over, I was just able to reach her calves. Naturally, the mistress did not deign to raise her legs in order to make it easier for me.

"You've been practicing, haven't you?" she asked, her eyes closed, her body stretched out full length.

"Madam?" I asked as I rubbed her thighs.

She opened her eyes. "You heard me. You've allowed someone to make free with you. I can tell by the way you touch me."

"I assure Your Ladyship that…" My voice trembled a little.

"Don't lie to me, you little slut," she hissed. "Do you think I'm stupid?"

"No, Your Ladyship."

She stood up. "Rinse me off!" There was a bucket of warm water at the foot of the tub. It took all my strength, but somehow I managed to raise it over my head and pour it on her. "If you're good enough for them, I suppose you're good enough for me," she said, looking at me after she stepped out of the tub.

She unbuttoned my dress and pulled it off my shoulders, her eyes fixed on my chest. I stood there, transfixed by both fear and latent desire. Then she pulled my camisole up and my knickers down. "Giving it away, are we, to any one who asks?" She licked her lips.

"No, no. Let me explain, please!"

She grabbed my wrist and led me into her bedroom.

"I have no desire to listen to more lies." Then she sat on the edge of the bed and yanked on my wrist, catching me unawares. I fell onto her lap. "This will teach you to lie to me, you French whore!"

"Please, please!" I whimpered.

Lady Gertrude brought the flat of her hand down on my bum with such force that it took my breath away. I received blow after blow. The sadistic mistress alternated bumcheeks so that my punishment was doled out equally. She spanked me for ten minutes before, cruelly, she opened her legs and I fell to the floor. Then she reached down and held my head in her hands, drawing it closer to her love-garden. "Show me what makes you so desirable!" she hissed.

Before I had a chance to respond, she pulled me against her black-tufted mound, holding my face there. I stuck out my tongue instinctively, entering her. Then I licked her slit before turning my oral attentions to her clitoris.

"Ahhh. Yes, yes, that's the way to do it!" she panted.

By that time, there was no longer any need for her to hold my head, the enthusiasm and vigor which I was displaying indicating that I had more than warmed to the task.

Lady Gertrude strained and labored, but eventually spasmed, much to her relief. "Stand up!" she panted, her eyes lit with passion. She felt my cunny. "You're sopping wet, you trollop!"

"Forgive me, Your Ladyship but I could not help

myself." I averted my eyes from hers—they frightened me.

"Just the way I like it," she mumbled.

"What?"

"Nothing. On your back! Spread your legs!"

Fearing that a worse fate would await me if I did not obey her, I did as she demanded immediately. Lady Gertrude knelt between my spread legs, her large globes moving slightly as she lavished oral attention on me, her appetite obviously having been greatly stimulated by the feel of my cream-dampened cunny.

After I spasmed, she suckled on me hungrily while exciting me further by burying two fingers up into my love-canal. Then, her craving not yet sated, she kissed me, thrusting her tongue into my mouth and probing everywhere. She used her fingers with the same expertise as her tongue, and much to her satisfaction, soon I spasmed again.

"Use your fingers on me, wench," she panted and lay down.

I did so, causing her to moan with delight. Lady Gertrude reached up and gave my pleasure-hardened nipples a good pinching, adding greatly to my own pleasure. She soon climaxed, thrusting her pelvis violently upward.

Gradually her passion subsided.

"Go now," she ordered after having collected herself. "You have served me well," she complimented as I dressed as quickly as I could, my inner thighs lined with love-cream.

And that was one of the reasons for my downfall.

Entry № 10

When I wasn't polishing, dusting, mopping, scrubbing, washing, ironing, folding, brushing, or sweeping, my duties took me into the kitchen, where I assisted Maggie. The atmosphere was more relaxed, and I could sit down while I worked. My chores consisted of preparing food. To be precise, I cleaned and sliced vegetables, whipped cream, ground coffee, brought wood up from the cellar, made sure the fire was steady and to Maggie's liking, peeled and boiled potatoes, and dressed and cooked meat and fowl.

It was very educational and I liked it. I could see the practical applications of my knowledge when I returned to France at the end of my year's service. Alas, that was not to be. Nothing could have been farther from reality, but of course I did not know that at the time. I sailed onward, oblivious to the horrible fate which awaited me.

Maggie was just in the middle of explaining the correct seasonings to use with chicken when Charlotte entered, pouring herself a cup of tea and sitting down at the large table where I was peeling potatoes and dropping them into a large copper pot. Her cheeks were flushed, her hair slightly disheveled, and she had a familiar glow about her.

"I've been with the master," she said by way of explanation.

"I was with the mistress the other day myself," I confided.

"Yes, I know."

"May I ask you a question?"

"Of course. I'm your friend—you can confide in me."

"This house has few secrets," added Maggie, who was making a pie crust.

"Forgive me if I am being rude, but it seems to me that this kind of behavior is somewhat odd. Perhaps it is because I am a foreigner and not used to the ways of your country. Can you enlighten me?"

Charlotte and Maggie exchanged a quick smile. "You are right, it *is* odd," Charlotte said. "But do not let it worry you. The master and mistress are randy—that is all there is to it. Nothing more, nothing less. I cannot speak of other masters and their servants, but I would suspect that it is fairly common. Does it concern you greatly?"

"No, I would not say that. I have learned much."

"And do you find the master and mistress to be abhorrent in any manner?"

"I cannot say that I do. As you advised, they have their moments as we all do. But aside from that, they have treated me very decently."

"They are honorable, and you can't say that about a lot of so-called ladies and gents," Maggie interjected.

"This is true. As long as they are satisfied and you are satisfied, then I would consider myself blessed if I were you," said Charlotte.

"Oh, I do," I said as I dropped a potato into the nearly filled pot.

Damned would have been a better word!

It is strange how quickly we learn to recognize footsteps. In my case, the same thing could be said about knocks on my door. That evening as I was lying in bed composing a letter to my parents, I heard a tapping. Without thinking about it even consciously, I identified the sound as belonging to Charlotte and asked her in.

My friend closed the door behind her quickly. She had on a dressing gown, her feet were bare, and her hair was pinned on top of her head. I sensed the urgency of her mission even before she spoke.

"The master wants to see us," she whispered although I could not see the need for her to speak so softly.

"At this hour? It is nearly ten o'clock."

"He is eccentric. If we do not present ourselves quickly, I fear he will become angry. Hurry!"

I jumped out of bed, leaving on the gas lamp, and threw on a long robe over my nightgown. Then I followed Charlotte as we padded silently down the hall on our bare feet until we entered what I still believed was Lord Francis's bedchamber. Of course now I know better. Little good that it does me!

He sat upon his chair wearing a pale blue silk nightshirt. The only illumination came from flickering candles. "You took your time," he said grumpily.

"I had to wake her," Charlotte lied.

"A reasonable excuse." He rose and stood in front of us, hands on his hips. "Remove your nightclothes." We did, and he began to fondle our bosoms immediately. "Ah, my beauties. What shall I do with you? The choices are many." Then he licked his lips before he said, "Sweet Charlotte, favor me." Although he spoke softly—nay, even gently—there was something in his voice that frightened me. I did not understand it. But, in keeping with my vow of being completely honest, I freely admit that I was attracted to it.

Editor's Note: Lord Francis was more than eccentric, and the unfortunate Danielle was correct in her assessment, as far as it went. The eminent psychoanalyst Dr. Edmund Fitzgerald was kind enough to read the Diary and, in his opinion, Lord Francis suffered from a combination of obsessive-compulsive syndrome and the need to control and manipulate. Was he mad, insane? Not in the clinical sense. But of course these differentiations would have meant little to Danielle, as there was little or nothing she could have done to alter them, and the inevitable results they produced.

Charlotte obediently pulled Francis's nightshirt over his head and began to fondle his flaccid member while he kissed me and rubbed my plump bumcheeks vigorously. Was he preparing me for another dreadful spanking or just whetting his appetite? I knew that I would soon find out, and used my tongue to fend his off as he moved it rapidly around inside my mouth.

Once he was fully erect, Charlotte got down onto her knees and pulled back his foreskin, revealing his helmeted head, which she licked slowly before taking him into her mouth. Again I was amazed at the sight that my eyes beheld. Charlotte immediately lost all sense of appropriate decorum and became, in much the same way as Lady Gertrude had, a woman whose appetite and passion knew no bounds. Was Lord Francis's member so powerful that the mere sight or sucking of it changed women? Apparently so. Charlotte moved her head forward and backward, breathing faster and faster.

"This is for you, my dear, so observe carefully," Lord Francis instructed as he used his thumb and index finger to induce my breast buds to flower. "Ahhh, my sweet Charlotte, how finely you suck my cock. Excellent, excellent!" He rubbed his hands together. "Now lie on the bed, my treasure, and you will receive your reward." How ignorant I was of his ways, for I assumed that he was going to hump her. But no, he had something else in mind. "Danielle, favor her with one of your French kisses. But first, her breasts."

I knelt next to the supine Charlotte and took one of her nipples into my mouth, sucking on it while I caressed her other breast. Lord Francis's hands skimmed over my back and bum before he cupped my garden.

"How warm you are, and how soft!" he said, feeling my strip of blond hair. Charlotte's breathing became more and more labored as she reacted to my sucking. I reacted too, opening my mouth so I could take as much of her succulent flesh as I could, much to Lord Francis's approval. "Your appetite matches my own. Well, not quite, but almost," he corrected. "And now, the kiss!"

Charlotte's garden was protected by a flaming red mat into which I nuzzled my nose, inhaling her most womanly aromas, savoring them before I traced the length of her generous labial folds delicately with the tip of my tongue.

My lips met hers, my tongue entered her, and my mouth was filled with her essence. By now I was quite comfortable engaging in Lesbian love. No, forgive me— comfortable is not the right word. I liked Lesbian love for it afforded me pleasure that came in different textures, different ways.

"Sublime, utterly sublime," Lord Francis panted as he caressed my back.

Then he stood behind me. Then I realized my stallion was going to mount me from the rear. I felt his swollen head pass through my garden gates as he entered me in one slow motion, my well-lubricated sheath affording him easy passage. He did not stop until his groin was pressing against my bumcheeks.

"Your Lordship!" I gasped.

"How tight you are! You grasp me like a glove. Continue the kiss if you want your reward!"

"Pray be gentle, for you are huge!"

"You'll soon find out what else I'll be. The kiss! The kiss!" he demanded with an urgency that could not be ignored.

Not wishing to incur his wrath, for I knew that he was equally adept with his hands as he was with his tool, I resumed my oral ministrations upon the panting Charlotte. With all due modesty, my technique had improved to the point where I could quickly induce her to climax.

Seeing this triggered a most dramatic reaction from His Lordship. He reared back and began to give me a hard, fast humping. Alas, he spared me not one millimeter of his rod, and soon I was in the throes of deeply felt ardor. Once again he displayed his superb cocksmanship, his balls bouncing off my clitty, adding yet another dimension to the heat which threatened to consume me.

Charlotte was also in the grip of as-yet-unsated passion, her increasing desire evidencing itself most clearly when she bucked up into my face, almost spasmodically, encouraging me to favor her clitty with my tongue.

Lord Francis's admirable efforts enabled me to climax several times, the room echoing with my and Charlotte's cries of pure joy. Then, with a mighty gush, the master spent himself, bathing me with a steady stream of his manly fluid.

Uncharacteristically, he withdrew his still-erect member from the hot confines of my tight sheath. Sensing that our tryst was coming to an end, I lifted my head up from between Charlotte's legs, the love-juice that was smeared all over my lips and cheeks vivid evidence of the efficacy of my newfound prowess.

But I was wrong. The tryst was not at an end. What followed was the first time I was exposed to the true bestiality of Lord Francis's nature. Alas, the cruelty he demonstrated was, in retrospect, but a mere hint of what he was capable of.

"Sit up and you shall have your reward," he panted, his member still erect.

"But I have already received my reward, have I not?" I asked in all innocence, for my entire body was tingling with sexual gratification.

"You dare to argue with me?" he shouted.

"No, no, I only—" I stammered as I sat on the foot of the bed.

He reached out and pinioned my head between his hands. Then he slipped the head of his tool between my lips and started to inflict a most disgusting act on me. Somehow I managed to pull my head back. "This is most unnatural!" I cried. Alas, I pleaded in vain. "Please do not subject me to this!" I begged.

"Maybe this will shut you up, you babbling French strumpet!"

Once again he put his rod into my mouth and began to commit the act usually confined to my love-garden. I tried to wriggle free, but Charlotte, his companion in depravity, had cleverly moved behind me, pressing her chest against my back, cupping my globes from the rear, holding me prisoner so the master could have his way with me.

He slid his rod in and out of my mouth as Charlotte pinched my already-flowered buds. Then, sensing that my struggles were subsiding, she moved a hand around between my legs, rudely thrusting two fingers up into my cunny.

"Excellent!" Lord Francis grunted when he saw what Charlotte had done. "Make her spasm! I want to see it!"

My senses were being assaulted from so many directions! The room seemed to spin, and Lord Francis continued to engage my mouth. Alas, I soon succumbed to Charlotte's digital attentions and, as Lord Francis had demanded, I spasmed.

Upon seeing this, the unimaginable happened. Lord Francis spent himself in my mouth! I felt the head of his penis swell slightly, giving me scant seconds to steel myself for what I knew was going to follow. Viscous gobs of jism were spewed into my mouth. I swallowed, trying not to choke, and he spent himself again. Then he held himself there, breathing like a racehorse as his tool shrank gradually. Then and only then did he remove it. Charlotte also released me, allowing me to fall backward on the bed.

My body trembled. The taste of Lord Parkinson-Smythe's manly fluids was heavy in my mouth. I tried to regain my composure while he and Charlotte helped themselves to some brandy. When I finally opened my eyes, Lord Francis had disappeared and Charlotte had put on her dressing gown.

"I'll walk you back to your room," she offered.

"I do not wish your company!" I snapped. "You have betrayed our friendship, and I shall never forgive you for that."

Charlotte sat next to me and put a protective arm around my shoulder. "And what would you have me do instead? Resist? Disobey the master? You know as well as I do what would have happened. Has a man never spent himself in your mouth before?"

"Never!"

Charlotte shrugged her shoulders as she handed me my gown. "There are worse things."

As I was to find out only too soon.

Entry № 11

July 10, 1867

I soon recovered. There was no lasting damage. I realized that it was just another way Lord Francis had of taking a woman and that I should not fault him. After all, it was I who was inexperienced, not he. It was the suddenness of it that bothered me most of all. The act itself—of receiving his fluids—was not inherently unpleasurable. I knew that it would not be the last time I would engage in the act and was determined to extract everything I could from it, for I planned to experience as much pleasure as I could. In spite of his sometimes-harsh manner, the master was a cocksman of the first order and could teach me much.

I was becoming more and more comfortable with my

lust. Would it be too bold of me to seek out the master? Or should I seek out the mistress? Or both? I pondered this for several days until I finally decided that the only thing Francis could do would be to reject me. The chances of that were slim.

That was how I found myself walking toward his study one night after dinner. The master and mistress had gone out, as was their wont. Knowing their habits, I went to my room, assuring myself that I had made the right decision. At around eleven o'clock, I heard their carriage pull to a stop in front of the house. I waited, giving Rufus time to take their wraps. As good fortune would have it, they repaired to the study. Full of confidence, it was my intention to seek out the master. How bold I was! And how foolish!

I crept down the hallway like a thief, for I did not wish to be discovered by Rufus or Charlotte. I was just about to open the door when I heard my name mentioned. Pressing my ear to the door, I quickly recognized the voices of Lord Francis, Lady Gertrude, and Charlotte. Puzzled and curious, I remained stock-still, listening.

"I think she is ready for the next step," said Lady Gertrude. "She has displayed all of the necessary characteristics. Charlotte, what do you think?"

"I agree, Your Ladyship. She is curious, energetic, and responds well to discipline. She also regards me as a friend."

"Well, Francis, you have remained silent for too long," Lady Gertrude said.

"It is because I am considering all of the possibilities, my dear," I heard His Lordship say. "I agree with what you say. Your points are well taken. However, you will forgive me if I am more cautious."

"And may I inquire as to the reasons for your caution?" Lady Gertrude asked.

"Of course, my love. As you correctly point out, Danielle is curious, energetic, and very responsive to certain types of discipline. She has written her parents dutifully, extolling the virtues of our household."

"How do you know that?" asked Charlotte.

"Before Rufus posted the letters, he gave them to me. Naturally, I read them," Lord Francis explained.

"Ah, Rufus is a treasure," said Lady Gertrude.

"Indeed he is. Charlotte, I trust you have made sure she has met no one during your excursions?"

"That is correct, Your Lordship."

"Excellent. My caution is only natural. As you know, the next step is a large one. We must be one hundred percent sure that we do not falter. Our past successes should not cloud our judgment. If we make the slightest error, we will find ourselves in the dock at the Old Bailey. Trust me—we do not want to be there, for 'tis but a short distance to the Tower of London or, worse, Dartmoor Prison."

"Please Francis, you're frightening me!" said Lady Gertrude.

"You should be frightened, my dear, for our venture is

fraught with danger, as we all know the rewards are great."

"If I may be allowed to speak," Charlotte interjected.

"Please do," said the master.

"Danielle's beauty and charm do not go unnoticed during our walks. As you know, there are a great many handsome gentlemen in Mayfair. Although I have been successful in preventing them from speaking with her so far, I fear that there will come a time when one of them, emboldened by her charms, will break through the barriers I have constructed. As a woman, I know that Danielle is seeking friends. Eventually, despite my efforts, she will find them."

"The ungrateful wench!" Francis snapped.

" 'Tis not ungratefulness, Your Lordship, but rather her way. Alas, the forces of nature are at work,"

"She's right, Francis," said the mistress.

"Your argument has much merit. You have won me over. But again, and I cannot emphasize this point too strongly, we must proceed with utmost caution," Lord Francis said gravely.

"And with expediency?" Lady Gertrude asked.

"If the deed were done, 'tis better it be done quickly, my dear."

"In the usual manner?" Charlotte asked.

"Yes. Advise Peter of our plans. Have everything in place."

"Well, I'm glad that's settled," said Lady Gertrude.

"And so am I. 'Tis late and I am tired. Charlotte, you will see to things?"

"I will, Your Lordship."

"Then that concludes our meeting, unless anyone has something else to say," Lord Francis said.

I scurried back to my room, locking the door behind me. What did they mean? I heard the words but did not understand them. To my eternal misfortune, I then made one more fatal mistake.

Entry № 12

June 11, 1867

Sleep came hard to me that night, for I pondered the import of the conversation I had overheard, trying to make some sense of it. Were they talking about me? I was fairly sure they were, but not totally. Although my command of the English language had improved greatly since my arrival in London, there were still many words I did not understand. I tossed and turned. Eventually, Morpheus gave me an all-too-brief respite from my mental labors.

I resolved to confront Charlotte in a tactful manner, for I still thought her to be my friend. In my naïveté, I truly believed that she would give me an honest answer, thereby putting my troubled mind to rest.

We were in the main sitting room, finishing our morning dusting, when I suggested that we take a short stroll before lunch. It was another glorious spring day, and the fresh air and chance to stretch our legs beckoned irresistibly.

"I was thinking the very same thing myself," Charlotte admitted. "The mistress won't be back until this evening. I see no reason why we shouldn't take advantage of the opportunity. We'll change into suitable clothing and meet in the front parlor in fifteen minutes."

I wore one of my favorite dresses. It was green, its train fashionably long, the bustle just right. The ruffles that ran up the center from the waist helped minimize the size of my bosom, which often attracted undue and unwelcome attention. My accessories consisted of a pair of white gloves with pearl buttons, a fringed yellow parasol, and a wide-brimmed hat adorned with a white silk ribbon.

Charlotte was similarly attired. Together, we meandered down the street, joining and mingling with other couples who had the same idea we did. Our attire did not identify us as servants, nor did our demeanor. As a result, we played a game, pretending we were ladies presiding over a grand home, instead of being merely maids.

Presently we found ourselves in the park, which was abuzz with activity. Children were flying gaily colored kites, other couples were picnicking on the well-kept lawns, ladies and gentlemen were riding magnificent horses on the bridle paths, nannies were pushing prams, and other people strolled, like ourselves, under a pale blue cloudless sky. The sun was warm, and after walking for a bit, we saw an unoccupied bench that benefited from the shade of an ancient oak.

"Shall we rest a while?" I suggested.

"I would like that," said Charlotte.

A fat brown squirrel scampered toward us, stopped, and sniffed the air. Sensing no danger, it ran past us and ran up the tree, no doubt going to its nest.

"I heard voices last night," I began after what I thought was an appropriate silence had passed.

"Voices?"

"Yes, coming from the study. I went to investigate."

"You did?"

"I overheard what appeared to be a discussion. I couldn't make out everything that was said, but I thought I recognized the master's, the mistress's, and your voices."

"Oh? And what were we talking about?" Charlotte asked innocently.

"The dangers involved with taking the next step."

"I'm afraid that makes no sense to me at all."

"Charlotte, you are my true friend, are you not?"

"I am honored that you think of me in such a manner."

"And you would never lie to me, would you?"

"Never! I swear it."

"I heard my name mentioned. Naturally, it was a

matter of some concern to me. I need your opinion for if the master and mistress were talking about me, I have a right to know, do I not?"

"Of course you do." Then Charlotte chuckled softly.

"Do you think my predicament is amusing?"

"No, not at all. I just remembered what we were talking about. It was so late and I was so tired that it had slipped my mind."

"Well? Are you going to tell me?" I asked anxiously.

"On one condition."

"What is it?"

"That you never repeat what I am about to reveal, for if you do, we will be punished severely," she said in hushed tones. "Have I your word?"

"You do," I replied solemnly.

"As you know Francis collects Old Master paintings."

"He has excellent taste, and I have admired his collection greatly."

"One of his favorite artists is an Italian named Dannitelli. His Lordship is a frugal man. Like any other man, he likes to save as much money as he can."

"That is perfectly reasonable. He would be a fool not to do so."

"His Lordship conducts his business through a broker, with whom he has dealt for many years. And there are customs duties to be paid on any work of art that is imported."

"I understand that."

"Lord Francis and his broker have devised a scheme that enables them to bring paintings into the country without having to pay the duties—which are outrageously high, I might add."

"Ah, now I think I understand."

"Naturally, this is breaking the law."

"I would think so."

"His Lordship's social and professional standing would be severely compromised if his activities came to light."

"I would imagine so," I agreed.

"He had to proceed most cautiously, for one false step would bring scandal down upon him. For some time now he had been negotiating to buy another painting, which he has long admired. That was what the discussion was all about. I am sorry if it has caused you any distress."

I felt as if a great burden had been lifted from my shoulders. Suddenly the sky seemed bluer, the sun warmer, the air fresher. "I am greatly relieved and cannot thank you enough."

"Again, not a whisper of what I just revealed to you."

"I swear it upon my life."

"As long as we are exchanging confidences, what were you doing wandering around the house so late?"

"I wanted to speak to the master about something," I replied evasively.

"Will you confide in me? Perhaps I can be of help. After all, we are true friends, are we not?"

"Yes, we are. I wanted to ask the master if I could have some evenings to myself," I lied.

"And for what purpose?"

"I wish to meet some more people, to make some friends. As you know, my term of service is only for one year, and I shall be returning to Paris when it ends. I would like to make the most of my time here."

"That is admirable. I shall speak to His Lordship on your behalf. I think it would be better if I did it instead of you."

"And why is that? I am perfectly capable of speaking for myself."

"I am sure you are, but I know His Lordship better than you do. I have been in his service longer. I am more familiar with his moods. Trust me, I will approach him when he is in an excellent humor. That way the chances of his agreeing to your reasonable request will be greatly increased. Does that not make sense to you? Of course if you insist, you are more than welcome to speak to him yourself."

"No, no, what you say is right and proper. I am obliged to you for taking up my cause," I said.

"'Tis nothing. You would do the same thing for me if our positions were reversed, would you not?" Charlotte asked.

"Of course."

"I think we had better return to the house now. Sometimes Her Ladyship gets back earlier than she says she will. It would be very bad if we were not there."

We walked out of the park. At that moment, I embarked upon a journey from which I fear there is no return.

Entry № 13

July 13, 1867

Two nights later, it happened. Not even our most gifted novelists or scientists could have dreamed up a plot so monstrous, so cruel, and yet so ingenious. It was simplicity itself, evil distilled to its lowest common denominator. And I—an innocent young woman whose heart was pure—was the victim.

It is said that fate is sometimes cruel and fickle. I believe that, but never could I have comprehended the lengths to which Providence had gone to torture me. And why? Was I guilty of some terrible crime? Was I being punished? No, no, a thousand times no. Forgive me, but my heart is heavy, and the tears which flow down my cheeks drop upon the pitiable piece of paper upon which I scribble and threaten to blur the words I scrawl so hurriedly.

I must not allow that to happen, for even though I know that no one will ever read this I must nevertheless make every effort to record, as faithfully and as truthfully as I can, the events which befell me.

Editor's Note: Danielle was obviously wrong; for her words and thoughts, many of them expressed simply but nevertheless eloquently, have finally come to light and are being read.

During the early part of World War II, London was subjected to massive bombing raids called "the Blitz" by the powerful German Air Force, the notorious Luftwaffe. Most of central London was destroyed. Most of us are familiar with newsreels of buildings in flames, huge piles of debris, and the inevitable scenes of brave young pilots running to their Spitfires and Hurricane fighter planes in an effort somehow to stave off the numerically superior enemy. It was a period of terrible suffering, and many innocent people were killed.

Among the dwellings leveled in the spring of 1940 was the house in Mayfair that still remained in the family of Lord Parkinson-Smythe. Like many others, it was reduced to a huge pile of rubble.

The owners of the house, Lord Geoffrey and Lady Judith, direct descendants of Lord Francis Parkinson-Smythe, had taken refuge in the country at the time,

Lord Geoffrey had been declared unfit for military service because he was legally blind, although with the use of powerful magnifying lenses he was capable of reading ordinary-sized print.

Upon their return to London at the end of the war, they decided to rebuild their home. During the course of construction and restoration, a worker installing water pipes in the basement, which also would eventually contain a wine cellar, found a battered steel strongbox in which was a tattered, obviously old, but still-legible book. He brought the book to his foreman who, believing it to be valuable, delivered it to Lord Geoffrey. His Lordship, in turn, realizing the historical value of the manuscript, turned it over to his solicitor, Sir Reginald Hodges, who subsequently made contact with our London affiliate and colleagues. And that is how the Diary, as we refer to it, came to be found, saved, and published.

Charlotte had relieved my anxieties concerning the conversation I had overheard, and I left it to her to act on my behalf. It was only natural that I seek out people my own age, and I considered my request to be a reasonable one. Of course, I would not shirk my duties.

I knew that under different circumstances my request would be most improper. But, considering the close relationship that my father enjoyed with His Lordship, I felt that certain formalities could be overlooked as long as I did not compromise the master or the mistress or their household. I had no intention of doing so, for I did not wish to offend Lord Francis or Lady Gertrude, nor did I wish to upset my beloved parents. Although I felt they had overreacted to my all-too-brief affair in Paris, that was irrelevant and did not enter into my line of reasoning.

Maggie had prepared a delicious dinner of kidney pie and blood pudding. Charlotte, Rufus, and I said little as we ate in the kitchen after the master and mistress had departed for an evening at the opera. After we finished, Rufus served us all a small glass of port, "To help the digestion," I remember him saying.

How delectable the wine was! How smoothly it went down. How deadly it was! Even though the kitchen was well ventilated, I remember feeling very drowsy and light-headed.

"Are you well?" Maggie asked.

"I…I'm not sure."

Then I fainted. Of course now I know that my wine had been drugged.

Editor's Note: According to Dr. Alfred Hillingsby of the Royal Society of Chemists, the drug of choice would, in all likelihood, have been laudanum, a mixture of opium and alcohol. Opium, as we are sure the astute reader is aware, is a bitter, yellowish-brown, strongly addictive narcotic drug prepared from the dried juice of unripe pods of the opium poppy. It contains such alkaloids as morphine, codeine, and paparverine.

The good doctor was kind enough to explain that opium could be ingested in several different ways. It could be smoked in a pipe, and we are all familiar with images of "opium dens" in which barely conscious smokers lie on mats, drifting off into a comatose fantasy world. It could also be combined with any alcoholic beverage, whose taste could be used to mask the drug's telltale bitterness.

Laudanum was used frequently during surgery because the patient was rendered unconscious and thus spared unnecessary agonies. However, in the unfortunate Danielle's case, it was utilized for quite a different purpose.

Many addictive drugs were freely available in Victorian England. A few of them were not legal, but still could be procured easily from an understanding chemist. Arguably the most famous detective of all time, Sherlock Holmes, was addicted to cocaine, a drug he thought helped to improve his mental acuity.

When administered properly, laudanum had no ill aftereffects, save for a slight hangover. Nor did the opium have an identifiable taste when used in combination with a stronger-tasting beverage. It could also be administered in food although the desired effect would have taken longer to be attained. Colorless and odorless, laudanum dissolved easily in liquid, making it the ideal drug for various nefarious purposes of which this is but one example.

†††

I do not know how long I was unconscious. When I started to awaken, I was aware of a severe jostling sensation not dissimilar to a ship being tossed about on the high seas during a violent storm and the rhythmic drumbeat of steel-shod hooves upon the earth.

I struggled to regain my senses, fluttering my eyelids, forcing my mouth to work, although I am sure I only babbled at first. "Wha...where...Help! Help me, someone... no... no...please don't..."

No doubt the cold air upon my face greatly assisted me in coming around, for I was finally able to comprehend the circumstances in which I found myself. It was dark. I was riding in an enclosed carriage. I was sitting between Rufus and Charlotte. I was bundled up in a heavy wool coat, my head wrapped in a shawl. Rufus and Charlotte leaned against me as I labored to hold my head up. I heard the crack of a whip periodically as the driver urged the horses to even greater speed.

Editor's Note: England had a very well developed system of roads and highways that connected larger cities and smaller towns to one another. Serving both the commercial and pleasure traveler, these roads were used by a variety of coaches, the largest of which would be an approximate equivalent of the American stagecoach so often seen in countless western films.

The Honorable Peter Pockington of the Royal Historical Society assures us that the type of carriage the unfortunate Danielle found herself in was a landau: a four-wheeled carriage with front and back passenger seats that faced each other. Thus it could carry six people in addition to two liveried footmen who rode standing on the rear of the carriage where the luggage was strapped. There were also a driver and a guard, adding up to a total of ten people.

The canvas roof of the carriage was in two sections and could either be lowered or detached altogether. Sometimes the canvas roof was replaced with a sturdier one made of wood in which there was a small oval rear window and two side doors with windows whose shades could be raised or lowered. The carriage could also be equipped with brass candleholders that were attached to either side of the driver's seat, in effect being a Victorian equivalent of our modern-day running lights on automobiles. When traveling at night, they were an important safety factor, as accidents involving carriages were not uncommon.

Pulled by four strong horses, a landau, especially if not hindered by the additional weight of luggage, could maintain an excellent speed; twenty miles per hour was the average. A driver who was not afraid to apply the whip liberally could generate even more speed out of the horses, although often to their detriment.

I tried to open the door—a foolhardy endeavor—but the brass handle would not move. As I tried to clear my head, a horrible possibility slowly entered my benumbed brain. I was being kidnapped. But no, it could not be! Such things did not happen in a civilized country like England.

"Where are we going?" I asked weakly.

"To the country," Charlotte replied tersely.

"But why? Why have I been treated in such a way? You have no right to do this to me!"

"Right?" Rufus snorted. "You'll find out about your rights, my lass!"

"Charlotte, what is happening to me?" I cried out.

"You shall soon see. Now keep silent, or we will be forced to do something very unpleasant."

As the landau's shades were drawn, I could not tell how close to morning it was. I sat silently; Rufus and Charlotte flanked me, making it impossible for me to move, although the idea of escape did not enter my mind. My wits were still fuzzy, and I did not fully comprehend what was happening.

After what seemed like an eternity, I heard cocks begin to crow. A faint light appeared around the edges of the window shades, indicating that another day was about to begin.

The carriage slowed in order to make a turn. The panting horses now trotted along a smoother road. Charlotte pushed the shade up, allowing a cold gray light to enter the confines of the carriage. We were proceeding down a long, narrow lane lined on either side with tall oak trees and thick evergreens. Beyond this verdant passageway I could see vast tracts of wild forest that looked most inhospitable and forbidding.

"Where are you taking me?" I asked.

"We'll soon be there," replied Charlotte.

The sun rose slowly, stronger light filtering through the trees. Some of it reached our carriage, warming us a little. Alas, I was woefully unfamiliar with the geography of England and was thus unable even to guess at where we might be. Also, I had been comatose for most of the journey and did not know if we were headed north, south, east, or west. It was extremely disconcerting as I tried to grasp something—some bit of knowledge that would quell the panic I felt bubbling in my stomach.

After what seemed like hours, eventually we slowed to a walk. When the carriage came to a halt, Rufus took a key from his vest pocket and unlocked the door, exiting first, holding out a hand for me lest I falter on the two steps down from the carriage. I refused his assistance disdainfully.

In front of me loomed the fortresslike facade of Lord Parkinson-Smythe's baronial estate. It was an immense rectangular structure and my eyes were drawn immediately to the four cupolas that dominated the corners, rising into the sky like crowns. The bricks were dark brown and the front of the building was reinforced with concrete at different levels as if to make the structure stronger, enabling it to support more weight. There were additional towers, a profusion of flying buttresses and pinnacles that rose around the upper part of the edifice which was decorated with elaborate sculptures depicting various Greeks and Romans in classical poses. A multitude of shaded windows looked like blinded eyes. I dared not guess what lay behind them.

Charlotte took my arm firmly, amazing me with her viselike grip, as Rufus retrieved our luggage from the rear of the landau. She unlocked the door with a huge steel key she retrieved from the depths of her purse. Then we entered. Rufus closed and locked the door behind us. The sound reverberated in my ears.

"Welcome to Mastiff Manor," said Charlotte.

In front of us sprawled an immense dining hall, dominated by an oak table which could easily sit fifty people. A suit of full armor which no doubt belonged to some knight of yore stood silent guard, while at the far end of the room was a fireplace in which I could have stood without difficulty.

Over the mantel was a pair of lethal-looking crossed pikes, ominous representations of His Lordship's family's martial past, between them a coat of arms and motto whose words I could not make out. Other instruments of war—maces, broadswords, daggers, and shields—adorned the dark wood-paneled walls. Light filtered through stained-glass windows, situated high above the ribbed arch of the great dining room and hall, creating distinct patterns on the slate floor.

"Your room is this way. Follow me," Charlotte ordered.

We ascended a narrow, steep stone staircase that was located on the side of the hall. The coldness of the place seemed to pervade my very soul. Up and up we went, the staircase twisting and turning, causing me to become disoriented. I tried to get my bearings, but I could make little sense out of the place, for it was quite unlike any other house I had ever been in. My leather boots echoed within the narrow confines of the passageway as we continued to ascend like intrepid mountaineers.

Editor's Note: Records confirm that Mastiff Manor did indeed exist. Located in the country, a distance of approximately forty miles from London, it was on the edge of the great Binnes Forest, one of the last standing tracts of wild land in England.

The house was no doubt designed in a slightly adulterated Gothic style of architecture which had been fashionable for many centuries. There are many excellent reference books on this subject, and the reader is advised to consult them if additional information is wanted. We, the editors, have decided to remain true to the essence of the Diary in the respect that Danielle was less than erudite when it came to matters involving detailed descriptions. However, her observations are correct for the most part, and we will interrupt her narrative only when we feel that a glaring mistake on her part changes the tenor of the Diary substantially. Otherwise we chose not to interfere and let Danielle's words speak for them-selves.

By the time we reached the uppermost floor I was quite winded and grateful when Charlotte stopped and retrieved yet another key from her purse, which she used to open a plain oak door.

"You will stay here," she said, as Rufus put my pitiable belongings on the foot of a smallish bed against the far wall of the tiny square room. He then lit a coal fire. "A meal will be sent to you shortly," Charlotte said curtly as she took off her gloves and warmed her hands by the flickering flames. "As you can see, there is ample coal. However, should you have difficulty, you will notice the sash by the side of your bed. Pull it and someone will come to your assistance."

"I demand to know what you are going to do to me!" I said as defiantly as I could, thrusting my chin forward.

"You demand nothing!" Charlotte wheeled around. "You will do as you are told! If not, well, there are ways…"

Then she and Rufus left. The locking of the door sounded like a pistol shot. There was a crude bureau, a water closet, dresser, a small table with chair and a porce-lain pitcher and basin. Black curtains covered narrow barred windows. I parted them and looked out onto a vast lawn. I could see what appeared to be stables and a small cottage, wisps of smoke rising from its chimney. The walls of my room were of roughly cut stone, cold to the touch.

Slowly, inevitably, I accepted the dreadful truth. I had been kidnapped! But as I lay down on my bed, I resolved to fight with all my strength, taking solace in the fact that my beloved father was an important, influential man. Once he knew the truth, he would surely rescue me.

How wrong I was!

Entry № 14

July 15, 1867

For two days I have remained in my room—or my cell, to be more precise, for that is precisely what it is. Rufus brings me my meals but does not answer any of my questions. I pace up and down like a caged animal or look out of my narrow window. Stable men lead fine thoroughbred horses out of the barn, but then they turn a corner and I cannot see more.

Aside from Rufus's footfalls, which I have come to recognize, I have heard no other sounds even though I press my ear against the door, listening as intently as I can. My heart is heavy, for I do not know what is to become of me, and I am terribly fearful. A profound sadness has entered my heart and I shed many tears. I have taken to wearing simple, rather out-of-fashion, shifts, there obviously being no reason why I should bother with anything else. They are ankle length with low-cut bodices and I have several of them. I have become quite adept at keeping my cell warm at night, knowing just the right amount of coal to be added to the fire so that it will burn steadily, eliminating the need for the heavy woolen blankets I discovered in my wardrobe.

On the second day of my imprisonment, I was served a lunch of cold chicken, cheese, apples, and freshly baked bread by the taciturn Rufus who, as always, wore a severely cut black jacket and trousers. Apprehension had been replaced by boredom, so I took a short nap after lunch. I was awakened by the sound of different footfalls in the corridor outside my room. Hearing the key in the lock, I sat bolt upright in my bed, instinctively drawing the sheet up to my throat in a meaningless posture of self-defense.

Lord Francis entered, wearing riding breeches and boots and a white shirt. He brandished a leather riding crop. After he locked the door behind him, he walked over to me as I shrank against the headboard.

"I trust you have been well looked after?" he asked pleasantly.

"I have been kidnapped, sir. What are your intentions?" I demanded.

He ignored my question and instead asked, "Do you

know why this place is called Mastiff Manor?" He reached out and stroked my chin delicately with the end of his crop. "Come over here," he said as he walked to the window. I did as he asked, fearful of what might happen should I refuse. Nevertheless, I stood slightly behind him. "See?" he asked excitedly, pointing with his brown leather crop, "There's one of them now. Look! There he goes." I peered down and saw a massive, short-haired, jowly brown dog trotting across the field toward the tangled mass of wild forest. "We have six of them. They patrol the grounds night and day. They're vicious beasts, capable of tearing a man to pieces. Oh, we feed them of course, but they're always hungry. Loyal, though, if they know you. Sometimes we even let them in the house. I think they're quite beautiful myself. Don't you?"

"You're mad!" I said disdainfully, turning away.

My back was to him and, like the coward he was, he took the opportunity to take advantage of me. With surprisingly little effort, he pushed me facedown onto the bed and in a flash had pulled up my shift and yanked down my knickers.

"Your insolence is intolerable!" he yelled.

Then he began to spank me, the palm of his hand ravaging my poor bumcheeks. Although my efforts to escape were valiant, alas, they were in vain, and served only to increase his perverted appetite. He increased the severity of his blows until I was begging for mercy.

"No more, no more!" I cried.

Amazingly, he stopped. "If you insist. You must show your gratitude, though."

"Yes, yes, anything," I whimpered, my bum glowing red.

Francis stood up and dropped his breeches, tapping the top of his boot with the end of the leather crop. "Well, would you sooner have a taste of the lash?"

I sat on the edge of the bed and took his flaccid tool into my mouth, keeping it there as it grew slowly to its fullest size. Then I pulled back the foreskin, exposing his helmeted head to which I administered the tenderest of kisses before I began to suck upon him.

The continuous tapping of the crop against his boot served as encouragement and also as a reminder. I ran my tongue up and down his sensitive underside, fondling his high-riding balls before I took him into my mouth once more and moved my head back and forth. Wetness began to fill my cunny and with it came a shortness of breath and an increased application of my oral ministrations. Much to his pleasure, I soon spasmed.

"Admirably done," he grunted as he moved my head back, his rod shining from my saliva. "I've missed you. On your back!"

I drew my knees up to my chest as he mounted me, his large head passing through the gates to my garden of love, going up my tight path until he could go no farther. When he did not move, I began to squirm slightly.

Then he started to hump me, the springs on the bed squeaking loudly as he drove himself in and out of my cunny, bringing me quickly to orgasm. I threw myself upward shamelessly, extracting as much pleasure as I could, for it was an escape from the misery which had been my constant and only companion ever since that fateful night when I had drunk the drugged wine.

Please, do not be so quick to judge me. You must remember that His Lordship was a cocksman of the first order, and I, in spite of my sorrow, was still a woman and responded as such. What woman would not have? None, I say, for Lord Francis wielded his tool like a magician, eliciting from me the most exquisite of pleasures.

Time after time I bathed his penis with my love-juice as I spasmed, my stallion increasing his speed almost demonically. Then he spent, spouting an effusion of his manly fluids into the depths of my cunny. He removed himself, straddling me, his tool magnificent even as it was shrinking. Then I showered his head with dainty kisses.

"That's better, my pet," he said as he rose and hitched up his breeches. "No doubt you are wondering what shall become of you."

Again, another cruelty but a much subtler one, for my head was still spinning from the humping I had just received, my emotions roiling in a wonderful turmoil of pleasure and fulfillment. How mercilessly he jolted me back to reality, wrenching me from the haven of my sexually induced state.

"Yes, naturally…" I mumbled.

He strode over to the window and looked out. "No harm shall come to you. You are possessed of great charms. In due time, they will bring an excellent price for there are people—powerful, rich people—who will gladly pay a fortune for someone like yourself. However, admirable as your skills may be, they do need improving. Look! There goes one of the dogs. By Jove, he's caught a rabbit! Tearing it to pieces he is. Jolly good show! Where was I? Oh, yes, improving your skills. Consider yourself to be at school, my dear." Then he turned and faced me, once again tapping his boot with his riding crop. "You will also have some company."

"When my father hears of this, he will have you arrested," I said boldly, for now my head was clear.

"But he never *will* hear of it," He put a foot onto the chair and leaned on his thigh, looking at me as I pulled up my knickers and straightened out my shift, having regained some of my composure.

"Have you forgotten about the letters I write to him? Once he does not hear from me, he will become suspicious and will make inquiries."

"Ah, the letters!" Lord Francis nodded. "Before Rufus became my all-around man, he was an artist. Well, to be more precise, he was a forger and an excellent one, too. Unfortunately for him, he lost sight of his limitations and tried to counterfeit five-pound notes. The Bank of England has many secrets, some of which Rufus did not know. In short, it was a very ill-advised venture and one that did not last very long. Fortunately, I was able to get him off with only five years in Dartmoor Prison. Men have been hanged for less. As you might assume, he's been very grateful to me ever since. Letters?" he scoffed. "They will be child's play for Rufus. Besides, he likes to keep his hand in, if you'll forgive the play on words. Now I must be off, for duty calls."

With that he left me, whereupon I began to sob uncontrollably. Although I could barely comprehend the meaning of his words, I knew in my heart of hearts that they were true. Lord Francis Parkinson-Smythe, respected barrister, admired member of the British aristocracy, whose credentials and moral standing were unimpeachable, was nothing more than a white slaver, a trader in human flesh.

But how could this be? This was modern England, one of the most socially and industrially advanced countries in the world, where personal freedom was valued as much as it was in my sweet France. I had heard stories— fanciful imaginations, nothing more—of pirates who preyed upon hapless travelers, often selling females to the harems of the Far East but those acts took place far from civilization, not in England.

Alas, to my eternal sorrow I was wrong. Those nefarious deeds did in fact occur right under the noses of those who were least suspicious. But how could such a thing go unnoticed for, as the evil Lord Francis had said, I was not the first.

†††

Editor's Note: Although slavery was outlawed in England in 1772, it nevertheless existed de facto, and on a far broader scale than one might imagine. Lord Francis Parkinson-Smythe was a typical example of those sinful individuals who practiced this most heinous of crimes.

He was not the type of person to kidnap prostitutes, illiterate immigrants, or other such poor souls, for in doing so he would have had to expose himself to a greater possibility of discovery. His method was more or less typical. Hiding behind his wealth, social standing, and all its attendant influence, he was able to prey upon women who were only slightly below his own social status.

Insulating himself and his victims by distance, specifically Mastiff Manor, and also by social class, his deeds went undiscovered, for he was a discreet man who selected his quarry carefully. The fact that the unfortunate Danielle fell into his clutches was an act of pure happenstance. Seeing an opportunity, Parkinson-Smythe took it. As we have seen from several of the Diary entries, he did so most prudently.

As a result, when the final act was committed—namely, the kidnapping—it was a fait accompli. Not only was he intelligent, but he also had the aid of several accomplices, namely his wife Gertrude, the manservant Rufus, whom he had saved from the gibbet, the maid Charlotte, the silent driver Peter, and the simple-minded cook Maggie. Together, they formed a circle of conspiracy and mutual cooperation that was impenetrable.

My sorrow at what appeared to be my doom soon gave way to hatred for this betrayer of trusts, this human vulture. I vowed to do everything in my power to resist his evil efforts to sell me to the highest bidder.

But what could I do? I was incarcerated in what amounted to solitary confinement, isolated in a huge mansion protected by vicious dogs, in the middle of what appeared to me to be a wilderness, sparsely populated and far from any town where, should I manage to escape, I might find help.

Thus did my questions heap more sorrow upon my poor soul and confound me with a bewildering array of possibilities, all of which added up to a life of sadness, if not worse. I knew only too well that influence and money wield much power. *Mon cher Papa*, though a quiet, soft-spoken man, had demonstrated that fact of life many times in his subtle ways. Never in my wildest nightmares did I think that I would be the victim of such power.

Entry № 15

I have grown accustomed to my cell and I imagine it is not unlike those in the Bastille where so many of my countrymen languished during the Revolution and Reign of Terror. Nor it is dissimilar from the Tower of London, where many of England's nobility suffered a similar fate. Of course, I have not been threatened with death. Mine is a subtler torment, and there is no doubt in my mind that Lord Francis is greatly pleased by this. It is apparent that he takes great pleasure in the suffering of others.

I have received a most unexpected but nevertheless extremely welcome surprise. The ever-silent Rufus had removed the remains of my lunch and I was standing by my barred window, feeling like a prisoner in a medieval castle. Outside I could see birds flitting about, their merry chirpings and warblings weighing heavily on my heart. How I longed to be free like them! How little I had appreciated my freedom and now I had lost it! Bright sunshine made the day tease me with the glory of freedom. Presently my reverie was interrupted when I heard heavy footfalls coming toward my room, prompting me to reach for a shawl which I draped instinctively over my bare shoulders.

The key rattled in the lock and Lord Francis entered, followed by two young workmen who carried a bed similar to mine which they deposited on the far side of the room.

"Now get the rest. Hop to it, lads." For emphasis, he snapped his riding crop against his thigh. The men, whom I estimated to be in their early twenties, were ruggedly handsome, but their eyes dared not meet mine. With all possible dispatch, they brought in another wardrobe and dresser, then bowed to Lord Francis and took their leave.

"You're getting a companion," he announced as he stood by the door. "I imagine it must get a bit lonely in here all by yourself."

"Swine!" I hissed, still standing by the window.

"Be that as it may," he said dismissively. "I hope you won't be too cramped." Then he opened the door and shouted, "Charlotte, bring her in now!"

All this activity was most perplexing. I confess that all I could do was to stand perfectly still, for I did not trust Lord Francis. His devious ways were many and mysterious to me. Anything was possible.

Presently Charlotte ushered in a female figure whose appearance was concealed by a voluminous hooded black cloak. Rufus followed with two threadbare satchels, which presumably contained articles of clothing. These he dumped unceremoniously at the foot of the newly placed unmade bed before he and Charlotte left.

"I'm sure you'll become great friends," Lord Francis sneered just before he strode out of the room.

As soon as the door had been locked, the woman, who had been thrust in upon me so rudely, dropped her cloak onto the bed. "I'm Angela," she said, as she opened her bags and started to store her pitiable belongings in the dresser. "And you are...?"

"Danielle," I replied as I sat in the single chair. "Forgive my lack of manners," I stammered but it has been so long since..."

"I understand," said Angela as she placed her bags on the floor so she could make her bed. She had a mane of chestnut hair, was almost as tall as I, her skin was ruddier than mine, and her bare shift, although loose fitting, indicated that she was indeed very much a woman.

Once she was finished and had stored her few belongings in the dresser and wardrobe, she sat down on her bed, for we had but a single chair, crossing a leg and, revealing a well-turned ankle. "How long have you been here?" she inquired sweetly.

"A week or so."

"And before that?"

"I was employed as a maid at Lord Francis's home in London." I then proceeded to reveal the sad facts concerning how I came to be exiled from my beloved France, omitting nothing.

"Ah. I understand," Angela said with a maturity in her voice that belied her years. "It is a typical trick of his."

"Would it be rude of me to inquire how you came to be in his power? Forgive me, but naturally I am curious."

"It would not be rude at all. My story is a simple and an all-too-familiar one. I was born and raised in Liverpool. My parents are poor but proud. I have two brothers and three sisters. Lord Parkinson-Smythe advertised in the *Liverpool Daily Gazette* that he was in need of a scullery maid. I applied and was hired. About three weeks after I arrived at his home, where I was given a room and treated most courteously, I might add, I was drugged and brought here. I have been living in a small room on the other side of the house."

"And we are prisoners—is that not so?"

"Indeed it is. You mean you don't know what Lord Francis is going to do with us? Has he not told you?"

"He said that there were people who would pay handsomely for someone who possesses my...my..."

"Charms?" suggested the blue-eyed Angela with admirable tact.

"Yes, charms. He also told me that I would have to perfect them and that eventually I would be sold into slavery."

"He did not lie," Angela said calmly. "But there is more."

"More? What could be worse? Oh, I do not think I can bear to hear it!" Tears rolled down my cheeks.

"Oh, my poor child! It is not as bad as you might think," Angela said gently.

"What could be worse than being in the clutches of this monster?"

"There are many things. What you say is true. Lord Francis is a monster and he is a trader in human flesh. But not all who come to Mastiff Manor go on."

"You mean there have been others? Before us?"

"Oh, yes. Francis has plied his despicable trade for many years. Let me explain. Most of the young women who come into his clutches do so as we did. If someone has sufficient charms and abilities, Francis deems them suitable for—to be blunt, forgive me—export to distant lands."

"And if they are not suitable?"

"Then he dismisses the young women, gives them a generous present for their silence, of course, and places another advertisement. Alas, there are many who answer, for there is much poverty, and people will do almost anything to improve their lot in life. Has the master mentioned the amusements he hosts?"

How such an innocent word, which usually conveys a feeling of merriment and joy, could made my flesh creep I do not know—but so it was. "Amusements?" I asked in a whisper.

"If Lord Francis takes a particular liking to you, he will not sell you into slavery, as such. Rather, he will keep you, either here or at his London home, to entertain influential friends and guests. As long as you satisfy him and his guests, you will be relatively safe."

"I think I understand. Are *you* safe?" I asked boldly.

"For the time being. Lord Francis has instructed me to tutor you, for he is of the opinion that you have great potential, if you will forgive me for being so forward. It is common knowledge that Lord Francis comes to his decisions first by himself and then he seeks the guidance of his wife, who is equally adept at the vicious forms carnality unfortunately takes."

My cheeks flushed red. "So I am to be a slave here in England! How cruel the fates are! Ah, the irony of it all. But why does he not use common streetwalkers? Would that not be easier?" I inquired. "And safer, for surely what he does deserves the severest of punishments."

Editor's Note: Danielle was quite right. The penalties for slavery were indeed severe. According to English law, those found guilty were sentenced to between ten and fifty years.

In addition, the presiding judge could order the

convicted slaver to make financial restitution to his victims, which often resulted in the sale of all assets, including property such as land, jewelry, horses, stocks, bonds, etc. In extreme cases, the guilty could be transported to the British West Indies or to India, where they would be under the direct control of the local governor. For all intents and purposes, they would be slaves themselves for the rest of their lives. It is no wonder then that Lord Francis acted so cautiously when deciding whether the time was right to kidnap Danielle for, as a barrister, he knew how severe the penalties were.

"No, for Lord Francis has particular and well-defined tastes, as I am sure you know. He also has high standards. If you can convince him that you are worthy of participating in his little gatherings, there is always the chance of escape, no matter how remote. But, should you fail to do that, you will wind up in a faraway land and will vanish from the face of the earth. That is why I have applied myself with as much energy as I could muster."

"Because you dream of escape?" I asked.

"Yes," Angela admitted.

"But the locked doors, Rufus, the forest, those horrible dogs…"

"Formidable obstacles. But insurmountable? No, I refuse to believe that. I was born free, and free I shall die, or perish in the attempt."

"And will we meet the other girls?"

151

"No. The manor has sixty rooms, and although Lord Francis keeps only six to eight captives at a time, they never mingle—save for circumstances like the one which brought us together."

"And the others who are here?"

"Pray for them and their souls, for they are lost. But we are not lost—at least not yet. Strive to please the master. Yes, I know it is a loathsome business, but 'tis your only hope. No, 'tis *our* only hope, for should you fail, you will take me into the abyss with you." Then she turned even more serious. "I will do anything to prevent that."

"I do not blame you, and you have my word that I shall aid you in any way possible."

"That is most reassuring. No doubt you are blaming yourself, but do not judge yourself so harshly. Your love affair in Paris, followed by your father's reaction and subsequent action was most unfortunate. But he did not know of the black blood that flows through Lord Parkinson-Smythe's veins."

"Yes, but he *did* know of the passion that flows through mine," I admitted.

"And that will be the one thing that will surely save you."

"You must be tolerant, for I am young in the ways of such matters and do not always understand them. Pray, explain it to me in a simpler manner."

"Are we agreed that both His Lordship and Her Ladyship are despicable people?" Angela asked.

"We are."

"But yet Lord Francis is a cocksman of the first degree, is he not?"

"Most assuredly."

"Then use the very passion, which unfortunately and through no fault of your own caused you to become his prisoner, to your advantage. Apply it well, please and pleasure him, and he will not dare part with you, for such ardor is rare. Once you are secure in your position, then we can go about the business of finding a way to escape."

"And are you confident in your position?"

"I am, but much depends on you. That is why I beseech you with all my heart to use the talents nature has seen fit to bless you with. Now do you understand?"

"Yes, I do."

"That is good. Now you rest, for Her Ladyship has requested your presence in her private chamber in an hour's time."

Entry № 16

The appointed time rushed at me like a strong gale off a barren coast, battering my senses. I wondered what perversions awaited me and how I would deal with them. It was true that my passions ran deep, but I was normal in my desires, not like the devilish master and mistress. But cope I must for it was my only chance at salvation.

I bathed and powdered my most private parts before changing into a fresh cotton shift. Angela made sure the low-cut bodice was adorned attractively with blue and white ribbons. Then she made herself presentable.

The key turning in the lock startled me. Angela was brushing my hair, and she stopped immediately as

Charlotte stood by the open door. "Come with me," she said.

I looked at Angela, as if there was something she could say or do that would give me courage. But she merely turned her eyes away from mine as I walked through the door, waiting until Charlotte, who wore a plain gray maid's uniform, had locked the door.

She led me down the corridor whose wood-paneled walls were adorned with large oil paintings of landscapes. Down the narrow stairs we went, the stones cold and rough against my bare feet. One level below, we entered another, narrower corridor. There were no paintings here, and I suspected that we were in some kind of secret passageway.

Editor's Note: Danielle was quite correct in her assumption. Many of the large baronial estates of the time were a maze of stairways that led to false doors, hidden passageways, and cul-de-sacs. Although no architectural plans of Mastiff Manor have survived, it is safe to say that it was possible to go from the bottom floor to the top entirely by the use of the hidden corridors to various rooms.

This complex arrangement meant that a lover could enter and exit the chamber of his or her heart's desire easily, without running the risk of being discovered by servants or spouses. Thus, many an illicit rendezvous was consummated. Should the lovers be discovered, the hidden doors made for a quick escape. Many a roué owed his life to such devices.

However, love was not the only purpose served, for assassinations were relatively common, especially during the mid- to late sixteenth century when most of these buildings were constructed. Given proper directions by a jealous or power-hungry wife, husband, daughter, son, or niece, a murderer could navigate his way to his victim's bedchamber, fulfill his deadly mission, and make good his escape.

Lord Parkinson-Smythe wisely used these confusing connections to his advantage for, even if one of his captives did somehow manage to escape from her room, it was safe to assume that she would soon become hopelessly lost. This is another example of Parkinson-Smythe's cunning and intelligence.

We made many sharp turns, the smooth gray stone walls barren until we stopped suddenly. Much to my amazement, Charlotte pushed on a section of the seemingly solid wall and, miraculously, it swung open noiselessly, allowing us entrance to Lady Gertrude's private chambers.

The sight took my breath away, stunning my eyes and senses. The mistress lay upon a huge four-poster bed whose silk hangings had been rolled up. There was a curved-back chaise longue, upholstered in green velvet. Several wing chairs whose seats were of wine red velvet were placed near a massive fireplace in which embers glowed. Tasseled ottomans were placed throughout the room. Several still lifes of flowers adorned the walls, along with older masters whose pink-cheeked cherubs cavorting among white clouds and blue skies seemed slightly out of place. A life-sized statue of some forgotten Greek goddess demurely holding a vase stood by the side of the bed, against whose headboard the mistress rested, the purple silk sheets pulled down, revealing her bosom. Illumination came from several large candelabra which were suspended from the ceiling. Heavy black draperies were drawn across the windows. Incense burned from a brass cup that sat on a red velvet covered octagonal table whose bowed, carved legs ended in lions' feet. There was a matching coverlet on the bed, along with several huge green pillows with tasseled corners.

Was Lady Gertrude a sorceress who could turn day into night? Was she possessed of demonic skills which she could summon at any time and use for her vile and unsavory purposes? A sense of phantasmagoria pervaded—nay, dominated—the room and fairly made my head spin.

"You have arrived at last," said Lady Gertrude. "Come closer," she said softly, moving a beringed hand lazily toward herself.

"You must please her. It is imperative!" Angela whispered into my ear as I walked slowly over to the foot of the bed.

"Show her to me. I have forgotten." Angela and Charlotte pulled off my shift quickly. Gertrude's eyes raked my body, lingering on my bosom and the honey-tufted strip of light blond hair that framed the entrance to my love-garden. "Most pleasing to the eye, but there are more important things, are there not?"

"Yes, mistress."

"Have you been treated well?"

"Yes, I have."

"Then show your gratitude, or you shall be dealt with in ways I can guarantee you will not like. I assume that you want to show your gratitude. If you do not, then you may go. The choice is yours."

"I am most desirous of you," I said as I knelt alongside her. "I shall express my thanks in as many ways as possible," I murmured, as I began to kiss her perfumed globes.

"Ah, that is good," said the mistress as I suckled on her nipples, her hands running through my hair. "Help her!" she panted. "Encourage her!"

While I applied my oral attentions to her other, already flowered, breast bud, Angela, who had removed her shift, sat behind me, her fingers playing with my cunnyslit briefly before entering me.

The delightful intrusion spurred me on to lavishing even greater attentions onto Gertrude's breasts, lasciviously licking them before I moved my head down over her rounded belly, Angela's soft feminine hands caressing my plump bumcheeks before she stimulated my clitty with the tip of her middle finger, making me moist.

"Enough! Now she must show me herself!" Lady Gertrude panted as she flung off the sheet which had been covering her from the waist down.

The act of Lesbian love, in and of itself, is not repellent to me. By the same token, if given the choice, I would much rather make love with a member of the opposite sex. However, Angela's words were a enough reminder to make me apply all my talents to the task at hand, which I quickly warmed to, giving free rein to my ardor.

Lady Gertrude's fleshy pudendum was guarded by a veritable forest of coarse black hair into which I furrowed my nose, inhaling her most pleasant aroma. Parting her lips, I traced the length of her labia with the tip of my tongue, and when I heard her begin to pant and move around, I entered her.

In all honesty, her taste was not unappealing, nor did the act fail to excite me. Soon I, too, was panting, unaware that Charlotte and Angela were watching me closely, judging my every move, evaluating me.

Gertrude soon spasmed, filling my mouth with love-cream which I sucked up and swallowed noisily, much to her added pleasure. She showed it by bucking her pelvis up hard against my face. My tongue, which was submerged into her as far as it would go, continued to be active, causing Her Ladyship to spasm yet again.

"Is she wet?" she panted.

I felt soft hands explore my cunny briefly. "Yes, Your Ladyship," Angela replied as I continued to suck on her.

"Enough!" she panted as she moved away from me. "Now on your back, wench!"

I did as I was told immediately, spreading my legs as Gertrude's mouth hovered briefly over my heaving bosom before she sucked hungrily on my nipples while reaming out my cunny with three fingers, stretching my flesh.

"Mistress, mistress!" I panted, on the verge of having an orgasm.

The combination of the incense, flickering lights, and Gertrude's attentions caused my head to spin. When I felt her tongue enter my most private parts, I surrendered completely to my passions, boldly reaching down and holding her head tightly against my cunny as I generously dispensed my love-juices into her mouth and over her cheeks in a series of breathtaking orgasms.

"The harlot is as hot as any I have ever seen!" Lady Gertrude panted as she finally took her mouth away, licking her lips.

Then we embraced, our bosoms, groins, and mouths meeting in a passionate lock that increased my desire. Throwing caution and propriety to the winds, I reversed my position on the bed so that my face was opposite Her Ladyship's cunny.

Another embrace ensued, during which we pleasured each other mutually, our arms wrapped around each other's bums, our mouths pressing hard against each other's love-gardens. Thus did we exchange an effusion of juice which sprang from the innermost parts of our beings, a veritable spring of love which our tongues, acting as divining rods, tapped into and caused to flow freely to the surface.

I do not know how long this most passionate of embraces lasted. So engrossed was I with the giving and receiving of pleasure that time ceased to have any meaning. Eventually it came to an end, both of us lying on our backs, our bosoms heaving up and down, our cheeks and loins coated with the sweetest of liquids. When I finally opened and focused my eyes, I saw Angela, who had put on her shift, and Charlotte sitting in the wing chairs, looking intently at both me and Her Ladyship.

"Wine!" Lady Gertrude ordered wearily after she had propped herself against the headboard while I remained sitting by her side, ready—nay, eager, for I must tell the truth at all costs—to pleasure her again should she desire me to do so.

Charlotte brought two goblets over to us. "I am not thirsty, Your Ladyship," I said, refusing the red wine that filled the cut-glass goblet.

"Ah, as I remember, your last experience with our wine was not an especially pleasant one, was it?" I did not answer this rhetorical question. Instead, Charlotte sipped the wine after she had returned to her chair, crossing her legs and continuing to stare at me. "I shall forgive your insolence," Lady Gertrude with an obviously false magnanimity. "Now take her away. She has served her purpose."

I put on my shift quickly before Charlotte escorted Angela and me back to our cell, where I lay on my bed, pleasure still echoing throughout my body, the taste of Gertrude's love-juice still in my mouth.

Angela busied herself with the rearrangement of her clothing in the wardrobe. Obviously, she did not want to intrude upon the blissful state which I was desirous of maintaining for as long as possible. Alas, everything must come to an end. Nothing is permanent save our final destiny. When I sat up and yawned and took in a deep breath, as if to cleanse my lungs of the almost sickeningly sweet smell of the incense which had filled Her Ladyship's chambers, Angela saw that as a sign that I was ready to engage in social intercourse.

"You did well," she said simply, closing the wardrobe doors.

"I am ashamed, for my passions run deep," I said, feeling my cheeks blush.

"Do not judge yourself, my dear. You are what you are and your traits are, speaking as one woman to another, most admirable. More to the point, I believe you pleased Her Ladyship."

There was a pitcher of water, some glasses, and a bowl of fresh fruit on our small dining table. After I slaked my thirst, I turned to Angela and said, "It was hard for me to tell. Lady Gertrude is a powerful woman."

"Indeed she is, but she *is* a woman. If, in fact you *did* please her, you might very well have saved us from a fate that makes me shudder when I dare to contemplate it."

"But she shares certain traits with her husband, does she not?" I asked as I sat down on my bed.

"Unfortunately yes. As you have doubtless experienced, they are both cruel, demanding, capricious, and intrinsically evil. Their hearts are as black as the coal which burns in our fireplaces and there is not a living creature on the face of this earth that has lower morals than they do.

"But that is not to say they are not without their weaknesses and, as I have indicated, those deficiencies can be exploited by using our collective strengths. Also, it is our only hope. We have no choice."

"But even if we *do* please the master and mistress, there are still no guarantees that we shall not be sold to some other monster. Is that not so?"

"Alas, what you say is true," Angela admitted.

"I fear our hopes are rather slim."

"'Tis infinitely better to have a slim hope than to have no hope at all," corrected Angela, and rightly so.

With that my heart sank even deeper. Depression enveloped me like the coils of a huge snake, threatening to squeeze the life out of me. Nevertheless, I vowed to persevere until the bitter end; for to admit defeat, especially at the hands of the swinish Lord Parkinson-Smythe, was but another kind of death, a moral one, which I could not do, no matter what the circumstances.

"Is there a Master of the Hounds?" I inquired.

"I assume so, although I have never met him."

Editor's Note: The owners of many large estates allowed vicious dogs to roam freely on the grounds in order to protect them from uninvited guests and also to safeguard the property while they were not in residence. The preferred breeds were the Irish wolfhound or the Mastiff, as is the case here. They were large, strong, and trainable. They were kept in elaborate, well-tended kennels and, contrary to what the sadistic Parkinson-Smythe said to Danielle, they were not kept in a state of semistarvation. However, Parkinson-Smythe does not exaggerate when he says the dogs were capable of tearing a man to shreds. Unless they were called off by the Master of the Hounds, the unfortunate interloper was likely to suffer serious injury, if not death.

"We must endeavor to meet him," I suggested.

"I think I follow your reasoning, and it is sound. Let us make a plan to that effect."

"As you yourself said, Lord Francis can be reasonable."

"That is true. Although he is evil incarnate, he can be manipulated as long as we are clever enough. But should he suspect, our fates would be sealed instantly," Angela cautioned.

"I am willing to take that chance for we have nothing to lose."

And so we fell asleep.

Entry № 17

July 25, 1867

I shall not bore you with the details of what transpired over the course of the next week. Suffice it to say that I coupled twice and sometimes thrice a day either with Lady Gertrude, Charlotte, or Angela. Lord Parkinson-Smythe had returned to London, leaving us under the more than capable care of Rufus and Lady Gertrude.

During these couplings I pleasured and was pleasured, reaching new heights of bliss and, with all due modesty, bestowing heretofore unknown joy upon the recipient of my oral affections.

Thus did my education continue. My charms were refined and honed until I realized that I had finally met the high standards set by Lady Gertrude and, by extension, Lord Francis.

Was it my fate to be confined to the realm of Lesbian love? Would I never again experience the exquisite pleasure that only a man can give a woman? Did Lady Gertrude and Lord Francis have a diabolical plan that they would hatch when I least expected it? Only time would tell; and during the periods when I was not perfecting my Lesbian techniques, I gave it much thought even though I knew it was fruitless to dwell upon those things over which I had little control.

But was I truly so helpless? I began to think not, for Angela had spoken with great wisdom when she said that Lord Francis could be manipulated. Although I am young I nevertheless have, through what might seem ill-advised efforts to explore my passions, learned that all men are vulnerable to a woman's charms.

The more I mulled over this situation that was much too complex for my simple mind to comprehend, the more I realized that Lord Francis, ogre though he might be, was still a male. Thus did I resolve to make him the object of my most skillful affections.

The opportunity came sooner than I thought. Soon after I swore to be true to my oath, Charlotte entered our chamber after we had finished our evening meal. "The master has returned and wishes to have a private interview with Danielle," she announced. This prompted Angela to take a shawl from the wardrobe and drape it over her shoulders hurriedly while Charlotte waited impatiently by the door. "Make yourself ready, for the master is most anxious," she cautioned me before leaving me alone.

I bathed as quickly as I could, barely feeling the tepid water upon my skin. Rushing to my dresser, I selected a corset which I managed to lace up myself as tightly as I could, thus enhancing the appearance of my bosom, which I sprinkled with rosewater. I then put on a simple shift which was trimmed modestly and accessorized with red and white ribbons. Standing in front of the mirror, I piled my mane of blond hair on top of my head, securing it with long blue velvet ribbons. After I applied more rosewater to my elbows and inner thighs, I was ready to meet the master.

Presently I heard his heavy footfalls in the corridor followed by the lock being turned and the door opening silently, for the hinges were always kept well oiled. I had lit several candles and made my bed and although I am not a magician, I felt confident that I had managed to create an illusion that would well suit my purpose.

As the master approached, his cologne preceded him. I rose from the chair to greet him. My heart pounded in my chest for I knew I had to remain in control. My passions were running high, but I must rein them in until the time was right. Then I would unleash them upon him.

"I have missed you," I said as I closed the distance between us.

Lord Francis caressed my bare shoulders as I tilted my head up, eager for his lips to be on mine. He obliged.

Soon our tongues were dueling, the tempo increasing as I felt a hardness press against my thigh.

"Business obliged me to return to London," he said as he held me at arm's length. "I have had excellent reports about you."

I shrugged off my shift, letting it fall to the floor. As I had not put on any knickers, I was nude from the waist down. The sight of my honey-haired mound caught his eyes immediately.

"I have missed you," I repeated, untying the strings of my corset before I wriggled out of it. "Come to me," I said as I sat on the edge of the bed.

"Your figure drives me mad," he said as he shed his clothes and stood in front of me.

"And you have a member that drives *me* mad, master," I countered.

I leaned forward, nuzzling my nose into his groin before I held his limp rod in the palm of my hand, licking and kissing the head. Then I put him into my mouth and kept him there, thrilling as I felt him grow until he had achieved a full erection.

Exposing the helmeted head, I showered dainty kisses on it before I ran the flat of my tongue up and down his sensitive underside. Then I opened my mouth as far as I could so I could balance his balls on my tongue while I caressed his thighs.

"What new tricks have you learned in my absence?" he demanded.

"None. I am demonstrating the passion I have for you," I replied as I resumed sucking on him.

Was I making a pact with the devil? Was I condemning myself to the flames of hell for the rest of eternity? I did not know, nor did I care. My only salvation lay in pleasing the master and thus hoping to gain a small measure of freedom from my cell which might in turn lead to my ultimate liberty. I must also confess that I received much pleasure from what I was doing, for the strength of Lord Francis's tool inspired me.

His girth and length inspired me to even greater oral efforts, my cunny moistening as my ardor increased every time I moved my head back and forth, taking as much of his manly tool into my mouth as I could. I wanted to consume him, devour him and, most important, master him.

"Enough! You will suck me dry!" Francis cried out, stepping back. His eyes were open wide, fixing on my bosom. "Your globes, I must have them!"

I lay on my back as Francis opened his mouth wide, sucking on my tender flesh while he skimmed his fingers all over my rounded tummy. My nipples responded by hardening, causing pleasure to purl outward, encompassing my entire chest. Both my breasts were equally favored by the master, who seemed to be possessed of more hunger for me than usual.

After he had sated himself, leaving me breathless in the process, he positioned himself between my raised spread legs. "Your cunny is unlike any other I have ever seen!" he exclaimed, stroking the narrow band of fluffy blond hairs that bordered my slit.

Then he entered me, his upward passage made all the easier by the sweet cream which lined the walls of my sheath. When he reached the end and could go no farther, he held himself there, pressing his groin as hard as he could against mine.

"Master!" I gasped. "You are so large and long. You fill me up completely." Then he reared back and started to hump me, sparing me not a millimeter of his masculine tool. His repeated lunges caused me to contract several times, bathing his rod with my love-juice.

I could not control myself. Nay, I had no desire to control myself. I began to buck up against him, matching him blow for blow, my globes shuddering on my chest from the force of his deep penetrations. Thus encouraged, my stallion displayed all the attributes that made him a cocksman of the first order: staying power, expert use of his masculine asset, and a hunger known to only a few men.

"Master, master!" I gasped as I was overcome by yet another mighty spasm which sucked the very air out of my lungs.

The furious assault upon my very being continued. He propped himself up on his hands so he could penetrate even deeper up into me, his girth completely filling up my tight sheath. At last he spent himself, erupting, jetting a steady stream of hot jism into me, causing me to convulse once again in a veritable spasm of delight.

"You have improved," he said after we had both recovered from our exertions and lay side by side on the bed.

"You inspire me," I said as I glanced down at his flaccid member.

"As I have others."

"I have a favor to ask you."

"And what might that be?" he inquired as he toyed with one of my breast buds.

"I am in need of exercise. The continued confinement to my room is not good for my disposition."

"Oh? And what form might this exercise take?"

"Nothing more than your permission to walk about the lovely grounds. The air would do me good. Naturally, either Angela or Charlotte would accompany me, for I would not wish to wander about unchaperoned."

"A wise idea. I see no reason why I should not grant your request, for it is a reasonable one. Now that you mention it, you do look a little pale. Do you find Angela to be a suitable companion? Charlotte has other, shall we say, duties to attend to."

"Angela is most agreeable."

"Then it shall be so." He rose and put on his clothes, his eyes lingering on my naked body. "You may go tomorrow, if you wish, and every day following. I shall inform Rufus and Charlotte of my decision."

"You are most considerate." I rose so I could press

myself against him, slipping my tongue into his mouth, keeping it there ever so briefly.

"'Tis in my best interest," he said at the door.

After he left, I put on my shift and congratulated myself silently. For the first time, I felt that I had mastered him. And it had been so easy, too. But I did not fool myself into thinking that the rest would be as easy.

Angela returned some fifteen minutes after Francis had taken his leave and was thrilled when I told her the news. "Excellent!" she said as she paced up and down in front of the window through which a slightly chilling evening breeze was flowing.

"Are you familiar with the grounds at all?" I asked.

"No, but the weather will allow us to spend most of the day reconnoitering the terrain. You have done well."

"And what happens next?"

"That I do not know, but at least we have taken the first step."

I never could have imagined what was next, so improbable were the subsequent events.

Entry № 18

July 26, 1867

The following morning dawned sunny and warm. After a hearty breakfast of porridge, bacon, eggs, and tea, Angela and I put on ruffled dresses and sturdy shoes and pulled on the sash by the bed. Presently Charlotte, wearing her maid's uniform, opened the door. "I have been instructed by His Lordship that you are to be allowed to stroll on the grounds. Be warned though, your movements will be watched. And don't forget your parasols."

Then she led us down the winding stone staircase, light filtering in through narrow-slitted windows until we reached the bottom floor. Instead of continuing on toward the front, Charlotte guided us toward the rear of the house. As we passed by several rooms, I tried to get an idea of what they contained. But that was impossible, for all the doors were shut. After what seemed like an eternity, we arrived at the far end of the first floor, where an enormous door opened on to the great lawn which I had seen from my high window.

"Remember, you will be watched!" Charlotte cautioned sternly before she disappeared back into the house.

I inhaled deeply. Never has the air tasted so sweet and fresh as it did then. I realized it was the first free air I had breathed in such a long time. Overhead, puffy cumulus clouds hung motionless in a pale blue sky while the birds' merry chirpings and warblings filled my ears.

"Shall we walk?" suggested Angela.

"Indeed, let us walk," I agreed.

The lawn was bare and devoid of any ornamentation such as a fountain or a statue, of which I was told the English are so fond. By my reckoning, which admittedly is inexact, I estimated that it was approximately three hundred yards until we reached the beginning of the forest.

Editor's Note: This is indeed an exception from the norm, as it was the custom to have a large fountain as the centerpiece of the rear lawn. These were very ornate. Generally speaking, they consisted of a tall statue representing a Greek or Roman goddess, around which were placed at regular intervals cherubs or even fish, from whose mouths water spouted into a circular shallow pool.

Alas, the reasons why Lord Parkinson-Smythe did not have such a fountain are lost to history.

What is not such a mystery is why the rear lawn was so bare. Indeed, the English, although Francophiles might disagree, have elevated gardening to an art form, and many of the gardens took the form of mazes. Short of that, the upper classes prided themselves on the variety of their gardens, which they designed and cultivated carefully. However, as we know the wicked deeds that took place on the estate, it is little wonder that Parkinson-Smythe wanted to have as much protection as possible from discovery. Robberies were quite common, and even with the added protection of guard dogs, gardens offered excellent hiding places from which thieves might be able to spy on the goings-on inside the estate. If made public, such discoveries would have ruined Parkinson-Smythe instantly.

However, the absence of a fountain and garden also posed problems for him, and one can only speculate about the excuses he must have been obliged to invent in order to explain why he chose not to adhere to the conventional customs which predominated during the Victorian age.

I looked back and saw the rear facade of the house rising upward while the two sides that ran parallel to it were bordered by a thick ten-foot-high wall of seemingly impenetrable shrubbery that extended to a distance of nearly two hundred and fifty feet from the point of its origin before it ended abruptly. In front of us was the wild expanse of the forest toward which we ambled, swinging our parasols gaily. After a few minutes, I turned around and saw Rufus following us at a discreet distance.

"I think we should sit and rest," Angela suggested.

"Yes, perhaps Rufus will grow bored and return to the house." We reclined on the soft grass, the sun warming us. "How good it is to be free again!" I sighed.

"We are not free yet," Angela reminded.

"Yes, but at least we are out of that wretched room."

"That is true, thanks to your charms which you obviously applied to Lord Francis's satisfaction," she said.

"And also to my own," I added.

"That goes without saying. Don't look, but I think you were right. Rufus thinks we are going to remain here. He is returning to the house."

"We will give him time."

"And then enter the forest?"

"Yes, but only for a short distance, for I do not want to do anything that would compromise us."

"Neither do I."

Apparently satisfied that we were going to remain where we were, Rufus trudged back to the house. Angela watched him out of the corner of her eye until she finally saw the door swing shut.

"Let us wait a little longer, for Rufus is a wily rogue. He might be watching us from the window at this very moment, hoping to catch us."

"Are you familiar with the terrain?" I inquired as I lay

on my back, the grass soft, the sun warm upon my body.

"No, for I was drugged as you were, and brought here in the dead of night," Angela replied.

I sighed. "That is most discouraging, for as you know, I lived in Paris. Although I have an appreciation of nature, I have never spent any length of time in close proximity to it."

"Do not let that worry you."

"Why not, pray tell?"

"I had an uncle who was a sheep farmer, and in my youth I used to spend many a happy month assisting him during the lambing and shearing periods. I love nature as you do, and do not fear it for it is a familiar environment. It may take several excursions, but I am confident that I shall soon get the lay of the land."

"And then we can make our plans to escape?" I asked hopefully.

"Precisely."

"Then let us begin immediately, for every hour I spend under the control of these wicked people is an hour stolen from my life."

"Well said!" Then Angela rose to her feet.

Such was my desire for freedom that my first impulse was to run madly into the forest. But that would have been madness. Instead we ambled slowly, no longer laughing, the minutes feeling like hours as we crept toward the dense forest.

In my anxiety, I swore I could feel eyes from the

house burning into my back, but I knew it was only my imagination. Had either Charlotte or Rufus seen us, our intentions would have been obvious. They would have stopped us immediately and forcibly returned us to the stifling confinement of our cell. After what seemed like an eternity, we reached the edge of the thick, seemingly impenetrable woods beyond which I was sure safety lay.

"Are you ready? Be sure of your answer, for once we enter, we will be committed to a course of action from which there will be no turning back."

"I am resolute," I said firmly, "for already I feel the succor of Mother Nature, and it gives me confidence."

Editor's Note: Maps generously provided by the Royal Geographical Society suggest that the great Binnes Forest was a tract of land that measured approximately thirty square miles. It was not, as the overly hopeful Danielle says, a place of arcadian refuge.

The smaller woodland creatures such as squirrels, moles, woodchucks foxes, and mice presented no danger nor did the numerous species of birds which called the forest home. However, the larger mammals such as stags and especially the wild boar, armed with two large tusks, could be formidable adversaries, especially when cornered or otherwise threatened.

Nor were the dangers confined to four-legged creatures. While an organized network of roads did not exist, there were numerous shortcuts and rough trails that led through the forest. Since time immemorial, these paths were used primarily by poachers. These criminals would not hesitate to murder anyone who happened upon them as they were committing their nefarious acts because the penalties for poaching were severe: public flogging and imprisonment. Indeed, records from the offices of the warden who was responsible for maintaining law and order within the confines of the Binnes Forest (an admittedly almost-impossible task) reveal that in 1860, a scant seven years prior to the beginning of Diary of a Slave Girl, twelve men were apprehended and convicted of poaching. Of the dozen culprits, three were jailed, eight were flogged and one was fined heavily.

In addition, there were numerous organized gangs who held up coaches that traveled on the well-known roads that encircled the forest. These wanted men would not hesitate to kill in order to save themselves from dancing at the end of a rope.

If the unwary interloper did not get lost among the maze of faint trails, most of which were nothing more than animal tracks, danger still lay in being beset either by poachers or by organized gangs of thugs.

Fortunately the naïve Danielle was unaware of these risks, although it is reasonable to assume that the more experienced Angela knew of their existence and, for reasons that are obvious to the astute reader, chose not to share them with her intrepid but nevertheless innocent companion.

Much to my astonishment, I soon found that the forest was not as hospitable as I imagined it would be. Large oaks towered over us, their exposed gnarled roots greatly impeding our progress. We either had to crawl under them or go around them while other great trees all made it impossible for us to walk in a straight line. As a result, we continually had to make detours, which served only to confuse me.

Nor was the mossy, leaf-littered ground flat. Instead it rolled ever so slightly, our progress hampered by thorns that grabbed at our voluminous dresses. After we had traversed down a small dale and had labored up the opposite hill, I suggested we rest for a minute as we had been walking—if that is the proper word—for nearly thirty minutes.

I confess that this was the first time I had been in a forest since that ill-fated rendezvous with Jacques. How long ago it seemed! Memories both bitter and sweet flooded into my bosom, making my heart swell. For although the Bois du Boulogne bore little resemblance to the Binnes Forest, they nevertheless were both sylvan environments. In that respect, both had certain characteristics which made it impossible for me not to recall the bliss Jacques gave me. However, I forced myself to concentrate on the present and not dwell in the past which, in spite of all the joy, was nevertheless a source of great unhappiness.

"I fear my legs betray me," I confessed, trying to catch my breath.

"'Tis hard going," admitted the equally out of breath Angela.

"Do you know where we are?"

My companion, in whom I had all the faith in the world, looked up at the sky for several minutes as if taking her bearings. "There should be a road in that direction," she said finally, pointing to the west.

"But how far?"

"That I do not know."

"How can you be so sure?"

"If you remember, when we arrived at the manor, the sun was rising on our right," she said.

"That is true."

"Therefore, the road we traveled must lie somewhere to the west of where we now sit. The problem lies in the fact that the road is curved, and I do not know the shortest way to it."

"But remember, this is only our first excursion. There will be others."

"As long as you continue to please Lord Francis," Angela reminded me.

"Of that you can be sure."

"Shhh, I think I hear something," Angela whispered, putting her right index finger to her lips.

I listened intently, but heard nothing for several seconds. Then the sound became clear. Apparently a large animal was running through the woods. We could hear twigs and branches snapping. I became alarmed instantly and stood up as the sound grew louder and louder. It was apparently heading in our direction. Our eyes strained to pierce the dense undergrowth in an effort to discover what was making such a clamor.

Then—to our horror—we saw a huge mastiff racing down the dale and starting to ascend the hill on whose summit we were resting. Its huge white fangs were bared in an extremely threatening manner. Foam dribbled from its open mouth, and its broad chest knocked everything in its path asunder.

Were we about to be chewed to bits by this ferocious dog? What should we do? We could not outrun it, nor were there any nearby trees we could climb. Our only protection was in the form of our parasols, puny weapons when faced with such a formidable adversary.

"Angela! The beast is almost upon us!" I cried.

"Use a rock! We'll bash its brains in!" she cried frantically.

Oh, if only I had stayed in my cell instead of going on this mad adventure! It surely was going to end in tragedy, for the dog would certainly rip out my throat. If only I had been content to continue to pleasure Lord Francis. If only, if only.

My knees trembled as I held the rock I had picked up, prepared to put up as good a fight as I could, for my very life was at stake. Just as the beast was preparing to leap on us, we heard a loud voice call out, "Brutus! Brutus! Off! Off, I say!"

Miracle of miracles, the creature came to a sudden halt and sat down, panting, foam and saliva dripping in a disgusting manner from its wide-open mouth. We could see its dreadful, enormous fangs, which were more than capable of tearing through our tender and defenseless flesh.

Its master walked up the hill slowly. The young man wore a narrow-brimmed blue wool cap, a gray-and-white wool jacket, soiled white cotton shirt open at the neck, rough black pants, and scuffed but sturdy knee-high brown leather boots. He carried a stout walking stick in one hand and a rifle in the other, while a long sheathed hunting knife was suspended from his belt.

Angela and I sank to the ground. I was fearful that I was going to faint. My heart was palpitating, tearing along at a fearful pace. My legs were drained of their ability to support my weight.

"Thank you, good sir, for you have saved us," Angela said in a barely audible voice.

The man, whom I guessed to be in his early thirties, was not unattractive, although somewhat rough looking. He was tall, nearly six feet, his hands were callused, wisps of brown hair peeked out from under his cap, and he carried with him the not-unpleasant odor of dog.

"We are truly indebted to you," I said, having regained my composure.

"I am Percy, Master of the Hounds," he said, politely taking off his cap.

"And I am Angela. My companion is Danielle. We are house guests of Lord Parkinson-Smythe."

"Here." Percy reached into his jacket pocket and brought forth a small tin flask. "Drink some of this."

"You are most kind, sir," said Angela as she tilted her head back and swallowed before handing the flask to me.

I took a sip of the raw-tasting brandy, somehow managing not to cough as I handed it back to its owner. "Indeed, most considerate. We were sure the dog was going to attack us," I said, looking at the still-sitting beast.

"Aye, he would have had I not been along. Lucky for you I was." Then to the dog he said, "Brutus! Go play!"

"Play?" I inquired politely. "What is there here for him to play with?"

Percy sat down in front of us, putting his rifle and walking stick next to him. "Oh, he likes to catch rabbits and eat them. He's good at it, too. Gets a squirrel every now and then."

"How charming," Angela said with as much sincerity as she could muster. "How many dogs are you master of?"

"Six at the moment. All mastiffs."

"And do they roam freely at all times?" Angela asked.

"I bring them in at night. That's what I was doing when I heard Brutus come after you. You're a bit far from the manor, aren't you? It's rough country hereabouts, not fit for ladies."

"You are correct, sir, but we became so enamored of your arcadian wilderness that we could not help ourselves. I fear we are lost," said Angela.

"I'll see you safely back to the manor," Percy said as he rose. Then he whistled and Brutus crashed his way through the low-lying greenery, joining us.

"And the dog?" I asked. "Will he…?"

"No need to worry, miss. He's as gentle as a lamb."

"Yes, I'm sure he is," Angela agreed. We walked for a while before she said, "We are in your debt, sir."

"Guests of His Lordship, did you say?" Percy asked.

"That is correct," I responded.

"I've heard about what goes on up there in the house."

"Oh? And what exactly might that be?" Angela inquired boldly, for she could tell that Percy was clearly taken with us.

"I cannot repeat it in front of ladies such as yourselves."

"I see. In that case, you must allow us to present you with a proper reward from saving us from being ravaged by your dog," said Angela in what I thought was a most brazen and forward manner. "We will be taking another stroll in several days' time and shall be on the very hill where we were today. Assuming—that is—that we are in no danger from your dogs; for, as you can see, we are not highwaymen nor interlopers. Your charges, noble beasts though I am sure they are, are incapable of making that distinction."

"I just might be at the same place myself. Don't worry your pretty heads about Brutus or the others. I'll make sure they'll not harm you. What you say is true. They are admirable animals, but their job is to attack and that they do." Then he stopped and parted the low-lying branches of a young tree. "There's the manor just ahead—you can see it through the trees. I'll go another way." He tipped his cap and walked away. "Brutus! Come!"

"I think we may have found an ally," I said as we walked toward the house.

"He prefers you to me—that was clear. I could tell by the way he was looking at you. Were you taken with him?"

"I could be," I admitted, "for he was most handsome."

"I am glad to hear you say that, for you may have to kiss him."

"Can he be compromised?"

"There will be but one way to find out. I think our excursion was a great success," said Angela as we opened the rear door of the house and began to climb the stairway that led to our cell.

The door was open, and our somewhat frivolous demeanor changed instantly when we saw the stern-faced Charlotte sitting in our chair. "Did you enjoy your walk?" she asked.

"It was most restorative," replied Angela as we stored our parasols in the wardrobe.

"I hope it did not fatigue you." She looked at me.

"Lady Gertrude wishes the pleasure of your company tomorrow night." She rose and left, locking the door behind her.

Had I known of the horrors that awaited me, I gladly would have surrendered to Brutus's fangs. The fate he would have dealt me would have been infinitely more merciful.

Entry № 19

Fortunately, there was enough to do to keep my mind occupied lest I think of the rendezvous I had with Lady Gertrude later on in the evening. Surprisingly, our clothes were none the worse for wear as a result of our excursion into the forest. The only damage was a few tears in our petticoats, which we could sew easily. My experience in dear Maman's shop came in handy, as my fingers were nimble and quick when it came to the use of the needle and thread. I could mend the slight rips so that they were virtually undetectable.

"We shall have to return to the place in the forest where we met Percy as soon as possible," I said as I held a petticoat at arm's length, examining it.

"Yes, but do not fear. He will be there every day until we come," said Angela, who was polishing our leather shoes.

I folded the petticoat before I replaced it in the bureau. Then I said, "Now that I have satisfied His Lordship, there remains only Her Ladyship. I am sure we shall be safe and not sold into slavery."

"Do not count on that, for their minds can change in an instant," Angela cautioned. "That is why we must meet Percy again as soon as possible, for I fear there is precious little time to waste."

"But how can we bribe him when we have no money or jewels?"

"You will use your charms, silly goose, for he is enchanted with you. That will be worth more to him than coin of the realm. Unless, of course, you find him repulsive."

"You know I do not."

"Well, then, the question is settled. Allow me another word of caution. Do everything you can to please Lady Gertrude. As you know, she and the master are of similar minds."

"I have pleased her before. I see no reason why I shall not be able to do so again. It was not an unpleasant experience either, even though Her Ladyship is untrustworthy."

"I fear your resolve might be tested."

"What do you mean by that?"

"I have heard rumors," Angela said softly as she put our shining shoes in the wardrobe.

"What kind of rumors?" I asked, alarm rising in my voice.

"I cannot repeat them, for I scarcely believe them myself. But I am sure there is nothing to worry about."

Nothing could have been farther from the truth!

I had on one of my finest dresses, my hair had been coiffed, and I was waiting patiently when, at long last, Charlotte unlocked the door and came in.

"You look lovely," she complimented me. I rose from the chair I had been sitting in while Angela remained standing by the window. Outside, the last rays of the sun were fading into twilight, and the birds whose songs had delighted us were beginning to settle into their cozy nests for the night.

"Thank you."

"But I am afraid your efforts are for naught, for you shall not need your prettiest dress."

"I do not understand," I said honestly.

"Then let me speak more clearly," she said, exasperated. "Take off your clothes!"

"Am I to be paraded about naked?" I asked fearfully, my hand rising to my mouth. The very words I had spoken filled me with dread, lest the answer be yes.

"No, no. Not at all, We are civilized here," Charlotte's gentle voice was meant to reassure me. "A simple negligee will do," she said as she went to the wardrobe. "Ah, yes, this black one is most attractive, is it not?" she asked, taking out the garment and putting it on the foot of the bed. I began to take off my dress, my eyes downcast, apprehension rising in my throat. "Come come," said Charlotte. "It will not do to keep Her Ladyship waiting."

I made the exchange as expeditiously as possible as Angela assisted me. Although the negligee was long and loose fitting, it nevertheless accentuated certain parts of my body, as might be expected.

Charlotte took out a black silk blindfold from a pocket in her skirt. "I shall have to put this on you."

"Am I to be like a sheep led to slaughter?" I cried in horror.

"No," Charlotte said as she tied the blindfold around my eyes. "More like a lamb."

I crooked my arm into Charlotte's as she led me down the corridor, the stones cold upon my bare feet, drafts going up my legs, chilling me, but alas, also having another effect, for the cool air made my nipples to harden and rise.

Unable to see, I was soon confused by the many turns we made in addition to the numerous ascents and descents, Charlotte guiding me carefully, letting me walk at my own awkward pace.

Editor's Note: This is but another example of the many false corridors and staircases that were a feature of the house. Charlotte's actions are meant to confuse the help-less Danielle, indicative of yet another safety measure instituted by the crafty Lord Parkinson-Smythe.

After what seemed like hours, we stopped. Charlotte opened a door. I immediately sensed the presence of other people, although I could not see them. What was infinitely more welcome was the rush of warm air that bathed my body, and I deduced that a large fire was burning.

We walked ten or twelve paces before Charlotte stopped and removed my blindfold. I blinked my eyes, trying to get them to focus. Gradually my surroundings became clear.

I was in a large, cherrywood-paneled, windowless room. On the far side was a large fire in which flames danced merrily. Chandeliers hung from the ceiling, producing bright beacons of light. In addition, there were half a dozen sconces in which thick tapers blazed. Had I been brought to a re-creation of Dante's Inferno? What kind of diabolical mind could have dreamed up such a setting?

In front of me sat half a dozen women all dressed in the finest dresses, all low necked, with puffed sleeves. It was a living palette of jonquil yellow, bright blue, and green, which were the most fashionable colors. Under-neath the skirts were acres of petticoats which rustled as the women moved slightly in their wing chairs. Lady Parkinson-Smythe, her hands clasped together in front of her, stood next to me dressed in a similar fashion while behind me was a comfortably padded backless black velvet chaise longue.

"Ladies," said Lady Gertrude, "this is our newest addition, Danielle. Charlotte, will you be so kind." Charlotte reached down and pulled my negligee up and over my head, causing my cheeks to flush red in my nakedness. "Danielle comes to us from France, and we all know what Frenchwomen are like." This produced appropriate titters from the audience, some of whom were smoking small, thin cigars. "Danielle is quite shy. However, she is brave and warms quickly to the task at hand. She does need a little encouragement, and I beg your indulgence. I assure you, though, that it will well be worth it. Charlotte, if you please, my dear."

The ladies' faces were middle-aged, unconcealed by wide-brimmed hats or veils. What kind of gathering was this? Who were these Medusas who came to witness the humiliation of an innocent person such as myself? What could their motivation be? What kind of devilment was Lady Parkinson-Smythe up to? I had assumed that her wish was to be with me alone. Oh, how terribly wrong I was!

Editor's Note: The International Society for the Furtherment of Women's Studies, headquartered in Geneva, Switzerland, has confirmed the fact that a group known as The Sisters of Sappho did exist. It was founded in 1856 and lasted, amazingly enough, some twenty-five years.

Based in London, its members, whose numbers varied from seven to approximately thirty, consisted of upper-class women whose sexual preference was for their own sex. Operating in great secrecy, for many of the members were married and also mothers, the group met in small numbers so as to better disguise the true intentions of their gatherings.

Although The Sisters of Sappho did not have a president or other officers, its acknowledged leader was Lady Gertrude Parkinson-Smythe. One of the inherent advantages of the organization was that its participants, all members of the landed aristocracy, had the use of large estates. Naturally, meetings were held when their respective husbands were not in residence. Because the penalties which would surely have resulted had the true nature of the group been discovered, the activities were of a highly charged nature.

The Sisters of Sappho was never exposed. It disbanded as quietly and as secretly as it had been originally formed. The group has been alluded to in several important monographs dealing with Sapphic love during the Victorian era, and the interested reader is encouraged to seek out these sources. They prove to be most revealing and interesting.

My first instinct was to claw Lady Gertrude's face and tear her eyes out of her head, for I felt that she had betrayed me. But I resisted, putting the prospect of claiming my freedom first. Some of the ladies leaned forward in their chairs, their eyes burning into my naked flesh, scrutinizing my every curve and fold, adding to my embarrassment.

"Charlotte?" I heard Lady Gertrude say.

Having unbuttoned the top of her maid's uniform and unlaced her corset, Charlotte stood behind me, her soft naked breasts pressing against my back as she caressed my rounded stomach and plump bumcheeks before turning her attentions to my bosom, which she cupped and caressed.

Then she gently pushed me onto my back on the chaise so she could shower dainty kisses over my belly. Alas, her affections soon began to have the desired effect. Please, I beg you, do not judge me too harshly. I reacted only as any woman would who was being so favored.

"Come, come, ladies, don't be bashful," said Lady Gertrude. "Edith, Sarah, Jane, I believe it's your turn to be first."

Through my half-open eyes, I saw the three ladies rise and unbutton their blouses and corsets, exposing their bosoms as they came over to me, kneeling on either side of me, the raven-haired Jane's head between my spread legs.

What followed was a passionate assault the power of which I had never experienced in my life. Nor could I have even dreamed of it. Edith and Sarah began to suckle on my risen breast buds while Jane rudely stuck her tongue up into my cunny and began to feast upon my love-garden, taking as much of it into her mouth as she could.

Their inhibitions were nonexistent, their behavior like vultures as they licked and sucked on my flesh. I confess that I responded in kind, reaching up so I could fondle their bosoms as I spread my legs farther apart, offering my sweet garden to anyone who wanted to partake of its pleasures.

I soon found myself sucking on Edith's large nipples, although I was careful to pay equal attention to Sarah's ample bosom as well. Jane used her tongue in a most expert manner and soon induced me to spasm, my love-juices trickling freely out of my cunny and into her ardent mouth.

Seeing that, Sarah and Edith then took turns on me while their places were taken by the remaining ladies who ravished me orally as I squirmed and began to thrash around, overcome by a series of powerful convulsions which produced exquisite bliss.

Dropping her knickers, Edith squatted over me and I immediately engaged her cunny with my mouth, bestowing upon her the most intimate of kisses. My active tongue soon produced a spasm which made her press her fleshy garden down upon my face as yet another lady drank from the love-juices which were flowing freely from between my lips.

After Edith climaxed a second time, her place was

taken by Sarah and I licked her eagerly, my passion and hunger rising to new heights. All the while, my throbbing nipples were being suckled upon constantly. Soft fingers ran over my stomach and thighs, and my cunny never lacked for oral companionship.

What bliss! What joy! How high I soared! There was no end to the abundance of soft bosoms and flowered buds upon which I sucked hungrily while producing spasm after spasm, love-juice flowing from my cunny into equally voracious mouths. Even Lady Gertrude participated, giving me the supreme pleasure of sucking on her clitty until she favored my mouth with her sweet effusions.

I was swept along in a torrent of passion and heat, a tongue continually in my cunny, lips clamped over my nipples constantly, soft, fleshy pudenda offering me their riches, hands everywhere on my writhing body, feeling, caressing, rubbing, extracting from me every bit of ardor I had to give.

Never could I have imagined that such ecstasy was possible, nor could I have envisioned that my body was capable of responding in the way in which it did. My clitty, the object of constant attention and the most intimate of affections, was a beacon of pleasure and delight.

How many times the ladies straddled over me, allowing me to suck upon them until they spasmed, I do not know. Nor do I know how many times I climaxed, for it became irrelevant. Everything blended together in a spectacular mixture of lustful desire whose appetite knew no bounds.

I was free, soaring like a bird high in the sky, elevated to undreamed-of heights of sexual liberation and knowledge by the ladies whose hunger matched my own. I shall be forever grateful to them. Yea, even unto this day, I remember that first fateful meeting with much affection.

Editor's Note: It is a matter of speculation and debate if the participants knew that, in effect, the unfortunate Danielle was a slave, for it was not uncommon for women to give themselves over, to place themselves at the mercy of a relatively large group, knowing that no harm would come to them and that they were under no obligation to continue should they feel uncomfortable for any reason.

What is not a matter of speculation is the fact that the group enlisted many young women who joined and participated simply out of curiosity. These women usually lasted only a few meetings and did not constitute what could be called the hard-core membership.

It should also be noted that it would not be uncharitable to say that even if the participants knew that Danielle was a slave, it would not have mattered to them. It is highly unlikely that they would have been identifiable, and even if they were, the power their husbands wielded would, in many instances, have insulated them from all but the most vigorous of prosecutions.

†††

Alas, the human body is capable of only so much pleasure. Eventually our ardor began to subside. One by one the ladies pulled up their knickers, retied their corsets, and rebuttoned their dresses, leaving me to lie upon the chaise, my sparse cunnyhairs wet through, my inner thighs striped with love-juice, my mouth full of sweet cream.

By the time I regained my composure and sat up, everyone was gone, except for Lady Gertrude and Charlotte. The latter had not participated in the proceedings and was glaring at me.

"Very well done," pronounced Her Ladyship as she rose from the chair she was sitting on. "Now I must join my guests. Charlotte, you may have your way with her if you wish."

I lay on my back, ready—nay, eager—to receive Charlotte. But to my surprise she stood over me, looking down. "No, not that way. I have something better for you." She pulled up her skirt and bunched it deftly around her waist before she withdrew a strange-looking instrument from the inner folds of her blouse.

"What...what is that?" I asked, my voice trembling.

"A new invention. I know you're going to like it."

I had never seen anything like it in my life. It was long and thick and had a tapered head. Could it be? No, the thought was too bizarre. But yes, it looked like a penis. Charlotte began to tie it around her waist with leather straps.

"No, please, do not use that instrument of torture on me. I beg you! Have mercy! Have I not pleased you enough?"

"Your point is well taken," Charlotte said, much to my amazement. "There will be another time that suits me better, for now you are ready to receive anything, you French slut. I shall derive much more pleasure when you are not in such a receptive mood." Then she unstrapped the instrument, returned it to the folds of her blouse, and pulled up her knickers before she let down her skirt and smoothed it out. "Now put on your negligee."

This I did, my knees quaking, for pleasure still ran strong in my body, making it weak. "Are you not going to blindfold me?" I asked as she led me toward the door.

"You'll not remember where you have been, nor how to return to your room," she sneered as she grasped my wrist and pulled me down the dimly lit, narrow stone-walled corridor.

It was true. Within minutes, I was hopelessly lost. We eventually arrived at the room—or rather the cell—I shared with Angela. Charlotte unlocked the door and pushed me in.

"I shall return when you least expect me and have my way with you when it suits me. Sleep well, French whore!"

Angela, who had been sleeping, was awakened rudely by Charlotte's loud voice. She struck a match, and soon our room was illuminated by a soft, glowing circle of light emanating from a large lantern that sat upon the desk.

"Is everything well?" she inquired sincerely, rushing over to me for I was teetering upon my feet and in danger of fainting.

"I—I am not sure," I replied weakly as Angela led me gently over to my bed, where I lay down.

"Have you offended Charlotte?"

"I have done nothing except please Lady Gertrude and her friends to the best of my ability," I replied.

"Think, girl, for it is of the utmost importance. The slightest detail might have dire consequences."

My brain was still reeling, but somehow I managed to force it to function in a rational manner. "Charlotte did not participate."

Angela, who had been sitting on the bed, rose to fetch me a glass of water, which I accepted gratefully. "That's it, then," she said.

"I fear I do not understand," I said, the water and urgency in Angela's voice reviving me, sharpening my senses.

"Charlotte is treacherous, as I am sure you know. Although she does not have the power of the master and mistress, she is nevertheless given much latitude. And she can be very cruel."

"I have seen that part of her nature, and it frightens me," I confessed.

"As well it should. Now you must rest, for you have

undergone a terrible ordeal. Tomorrow we will begin to make plans for our escape. I fear that time is running out," Angela said, as she turned off the lantern and got into her bed.

Little did I know that my tribulations were just beginning.

Entry № 20

August 1, 1867

It saddens me to report that for the past several days Angela has been taken out of our room early in the morning and has not returned until late at night. Her face is haggard, and when I tried gently to question her as to the nature of her absence, she refused most politely to answer. I shudder to think what she is undergoing, but I surmise it is a terrible trial.

As a result, we have been unable to make plans for our escape, the first step being a meeting with Percy. Without him—and I have every confidence that he can be bribed—we are surely doomed. How long will he continue to go to the small hill where we first met? Will he eventually be discouraged? Are we lost?

Alas, these questions burden me heavily but are not nearly as troublesome as the answers I do not have. They prey upon my mind and, try as I may, I cannot make them go away. They are like ghosts that haunt me.

This morning Charlotte fetched Angela after breakfast and took her away. My heart aches for my poor friend. She is probably suffering a fate that no normal human being could ever possibly imagine.

The English summer was in full bloom and I stood by the barred window, looking out longingly, knowing that a few scant miles away lay a highway that would lead us to freedom if we could ever find a way to reach it. So near and yet so far! How I envied the birds that could take wing and fly wherever their hearts desired, unencumbered by walls that blocked my own flight.

I am also fearful of Charlotte. Although she does not address me when she fetches and returns poor Angela, she gives me the most frightful looks, which send chills down my spine. Only the devil himself could envisage what evil thoughts she harbors toward me.

Alas, I was soon to find out. That very afternoon as I was staring out the window, I heard the key in the lock. I turned around immediately, thinking it was my dear companion Angela being returned to the relative safety of our room. But no, it was Charlotte, alone. She locked the door and thrust her hands deep into the pockets of her skirt.

"Admiring the view?" she asked sarcastically.

As was my wont, I wore a simple shift, for there was

no reason to put on anything more elaborate. My only justification for dressing up was a request to meet with the master or the mistress. A shift was comfortable and allowed air to circulate freely about my legs.

"I was just thinking," I replied innocently.

"Thinking can be dangerous." She advanced toward me, her very walk menacing me. "You're naked under your shift, aren't you?"

"Why, yes, I am. I saw no reason not to be, for it is stuffy in here."

"You have no morals at all! You're like a bitch in heat! And after the way we've treated you, too! You don't deserve the kindness we've shown you. Since you seem to have a desire to flaunt your wantonness, I shall oblige you. Remove your shift!" This I did, placing it on the bed as Charlotte stood in front of me. "Indeed, your figure is fine. I can see why both men and women desire you," she said as she hefted my globes brazenly. "Do you desire me?"

"I…I…"

"You hesitate? You don't know? Men have dueled to the death for my favors! Well, we'll soon find out." Charlotte tore off her clothing and lay upon my bed. Although her figure was certainly appealing, it did not produce any desire in me. "Please me, French whore, for Lady Gertrude has given me permission to have my way with you and please me well or there will be the very devil to pay."

"Why do you do this to me? Have I not done enough already?"

"You can never do enough! Now go about the business you are so capable of, for I am desirous of you."

As I was in the clutches of this wicked woman, I had no choice but to obey. I leaned over her and was about to kiss her breasts when she reached up suddenly, grabbed my hair, and pulled my mouth down against hers. I felt her tongue thrust into my mouth and move around, our bosoms crushing together as she kissed me, holding the embrace for a long time before she finally released me.

"Use your tongue well, French harlot!"

I ran the tip around the circumference of her aureoles until her nipples rose and became hard. While I sucked on them, I caressed Charlotte's stomach with my fingertips. Soon her labored breathing told me my efforts were not in vain.

Alas, they were not in vain for another reason. Though you might think me a shameless hussy, I must admit that I, too, was beginning to enjoy the act of same-sex loving. My cunny started to get wet. Thus was I twice a prisoner—first of Charlotte, and second of myself.

"Give me the kiss!" Charlotte demanded as she spread her legs and drew her knees up to her chest.

After I positioned myself between her thighs, I took my fingers and parted the lips of her garden, revealing her sweet flesh. Then I ran my tongue up and down her length, making her pant faster and faster. Her clitty rose, and when I massaged it with my tongue, she spasmed. I drank her love-juice eagerly, for she was most prolific in the way she dispensed that most precious and intimate of liquids.

I, too, climaxed, my ardor causing me to kiss her as hard as I could, endeavoring to reach as far up into her as I could with my tongue, prolonging her state of bliss, making her writhe and reach down so she could hold my head tightly against her until her passion finally subsided.

"With some training you could be an excellent prostitute," she panted as she licked my lips. "Kiss me, for I like to taste myself." This I did eagerly, our tongues fencing energetically, our torsos melding into one another. "Now for the surprise!" And Charlotte broke our passionate embrace.

She reached into the pocket of her skirt and withdrew the frightening instrument which I had seen the night I had pleasured Lady Gertrude and her friends.

"What is it?" I asked in a quavering voice.

"A substitute," Charlotte replied as she strapped it on.

Then the horrible truth dawned on me. It was a false penis, larger and thicker than any real organ I had ever seen. Charlotte made sure it was attached firmly, and tested it several times.

"Please, I beg you! Do not use that instrument of torture upon me."

"Silence!"

"No, no!" I cried.

"On your knees, slut!"

This I did, turning my head around as the sadistic maid positioned herself behind me, the false penis poised, filling me with dread. "Mercy, mercy!" I begged. "Have pity on me!"

"I'll have *this* on you, French bitch!"

Editor's Note: Sir Roland Featherstone, Senior Egyptologist at the Royal Historical Society, informs us that the first dildo was discovered in the pyramid tomb of Queen Nefertiti who reigned from the year 2600 B.C. to 2570 B.C. Although the shaft was fairly simple in shape, it was covered with a fine layer of gold. The handle was carved ornately and inlaid with precious jewels, indicative of its owner's wealth and status.

Over the course of the following centuries, the basic construction remained more or less the same although most dildos did not have jewels or valuable stones attached to them. Wood was the preferred material, and they were usually coated with a lubricant like beeswax.

The handle became less important. It was replaced by an increasing replication of the head of a real penis. Naturally there were dildos made of different lengths and girths, providing the buying public with a greater variety.

Although forbidden in Victorian England, dildos were nevertheless very much in vogue. Wood had been replaced by vulcanized rubber, and now it was possible to attach them to the body with an intricate system of leather straps, enabling one female to use it on another in much the same manner as a man would use his penis.

To someone like Danielle, who had never seen a dildo before, it must have indeed been a frightening prospect. One can only sympathize with her, especially when the wielder or user was of a somewhat sadistic temperament.

"No, no, do not torture me!" I implored.

As my eyes bulged in terror, Charlotte placed the huge head at the entrance to my garden. "I'm going to enjoy this," she grunted.

"I beseech you. I shall do anything you ask but not this! Not this!"

"Silence, harlot!"

Then she began to enter me, the head of her foul device parting the walls of my sheath, its girth filling me up. I feared she would do me a horrific internal injury as she continued to enter me until I felt her pelvis against my plump bumcheeks.

"I cannot take it!" I cried, wiggling around, trying to shake loose. But Charlotte's strong hands held me by my hips.

"You already have, bitch! But you'll soon be taking more—that I can promise you!" she snarled.

Upon saying that, the venomous creature started to torment me with the instrument she enjoyed wielding so cruelly. I thought my poor cunny would fairly burst, for the thing was so long and so thick. But to my amazement, my sheath somehow managed to accommodate the foul substitute for the male organ. I buried my face in the bedsheets, praying that somehow I would endure this trial of the flesh which was being inflicted on me.

The sadistic Charlotte obviously took much heart from my moanings and futile efforts to escape, for she began to hump me hard and fast, my wet sheath making it all the easier for her to commit the foul sin upon my poor flesh.

Then she reached around and began to stimulate my clitty with the tip of her middle finger. Oh, the pleasure it brought! How it became easier for me to accept what was being buried in my cunny I do not know, but it was surely so. I began to pant, reacting to the tension which I felt building up inside my body.

Charlotte spared me nothing of the rod which would never go soft, humping me with a vengeance. It shames me to the depths of my soul, but I must confess, I spasmed. Was I now married to the devil herself? Had this witch Charlotte joined me in a union that would damn my very being forever? Was she a sorceress who had cast a spell over me from which there was no escape?

Then, I climaxed again, for she was humping me hard and fast, displaying her proficiency at using this strange device in a manner which soon reduced my body to a series of racking convulsions. My sweet juices lubricated the false penis, making it all the easier for her to have her perverse, wicked way with me.

"Ahhh!" She moaned at last.

Then she quickly unstrapped the devil's tool from her waist as I lay on my back, exhausted from my labors. Quick as a cat, Charlotte pounced on me, squatting over my face, grabbing my head and pulling it up hard against her wet cunny.

"Finish it, finish it!" she panted.

I thrust my tongue up into her garden as far as I could and kept it there, moving it around as Charlotte continued to hold me tightly, grinding her cunny against my mouth, straining to spasm yet again.

And she did. When her convulsion had subsided, she released me and took up a position next to me, the two of us lying side by side, fellow conspirators in a passion that had no name.

"Still alive, are you?" she finally asked with her usual sarcasm.

I could barely nod.

"I think you liked my toy. In fact, I know you did. If you're a good girl, I'll let you play with it again," she said as she rose from the bed and began to dress.

"Why do you torment me in every way possible? Is there no end to your vile desires?"

She leaned over and felt my cunny, rubbing her fingers together. "From the juice that still drips out, I'd say you enjoyed being tormented."

"You are evil and shall be punished for your sins."

"Perhaps," she said at the door, "but not by you."

I then fell into a deep stupor, no doubt induced by

the violent spasms I had undergone. But yet how pleasurable they were, and how tormented I was by the bliss
I had derived from that artificial penis. I freed myself
from this inner conflict by realizing that I was only
responding in a most natural manner. How could I possibly be blamed for that, for a woman's spasms are one of
nature's most beautiful creations, no matter what form
they may take.

I twisted, naked, upon the bed, sensing that someone
was in the room—Charlotte returning to inflict more
anguish upon me. But no, it was Angela. And sunlight
still streamed in through the barred window.

"At last it is over," she said wearily, easing herself
upon her bed, wearing only a simple blue cotton shift.

"Over?"

"I have been pleasing Lord Parkinson-Smythe and his
peculiar tastes. I shall not insult your ears with descriptions of the abominations I have been forced to endure.
But at last he is sated, and I shall be left alone."

"Charlotte came here and used her—"

"I can tell by the expression on your face that something was troubling you deeply. Now I know what it is.
I, too, have been tormented by her rubber phallus. I
hope she did not inflict too much agony upon you."

"It was bearable."

"And perhaps a little enjoyable?"

"A little," I admitted.

"But that does not justify its use on helpless victims."

"Yes," I agreed. "That is why we must try and flee this place as soon as we can!"

"I see no reason why we should not take a stroll tomorrow."

"And meet Percy?"

"I hope so."

At long last I would finally be taking the first step toward gaining my freedom!

Entry № 21

"I see no reason at all why you shouldn't take a walk today. The weather is beautiful, and the exercise will do you good," said Charlotte the following morning after Rufus had removed the breakfast dishes. We had feasted on eggs, bacon, sausage, bread, jam, and tea. "I shall leave the door unlocked, but be warned: should you not go directly to the rear door, this will become known to us, and you will be punished most severely. Is that understood?"

"Perfectly," Angela replied. I nodded my head.

"Good. I think you know by now that my threats are not idle."

"Indeed we do," I said.

After Charlotte left, we lingered for a while, not wishing to appear too eager, for we knew we would be watched. "We are not the only ones who have tried to escape," Angela reminded me as we changed our clothes.

"And the fate of the others?"

"I do not know, but I can assume the worst."

"Then we must act with all dispatch."

"Indeed!"

We both wore simple dresses with few petticoats for ease in walking, mine in green and white, Angela's in yellow and tan, both outfits complimented with tiny white parasols. Naturally, we wore sturdy ankle-high boots. As we knew from past experience, our stroll would be strenuous.

We had no difficulty in finding our way to the rear exit of the house. The door had been unlocked for us. After ambling slowly across the great lawn, we stopped. Angela pretended that there was something in her eye so she could turn her head slightly.

"It is as I suspected. Rufus is watching us." She rubbed her eye several times.

"Is he following?"

"No. He is standing by the door with his arms folded across his chest. He is wearing an apron and no jacket."

"Then I surmise he is engaged in some kind of work within the house."

"That is probably correct. He will not stay there for long. Come, let us continue, for he has pressing duties that will prevent him from following us."

Angela's assumption proved to be correct; for when we turned and looked after we had walked for another ten minutes, we could no longer see him and the door was closed.

"Now we must hurry," she said as soon as we reached the edge of the forest.

"Do you know the way?"

"I will find it. Our very lives depend on it!"

We pulled up our skirts and rushed through the forest as fast as we could. Angela paused every now and then to take her bearings. It was hard for me, but I managed to keep up with her. The desperation of our situation gave me strength. After twenty minutes, during which we barreled through the vast forest, dodging branches and leaping over exposed roots, we finally looked down on the shallow glen, opposite which was the slightly rounded hill on which we could see the seated figures of a man and a dog, their dark shapes clearly outlined against the verdant background.

"You do try a man's patience," Percy said laconically as we sat next to him, trying to catch our breaths, our bosoms catching his eye.

"Is the dog…?" Angela asked.

"Brutus is fine. He'll not bother you."

"Please accept our apologies, but we were detained," I explained.

"Aye, I figured as such. I also know you are not guests at the estate."

"Oh? Then what are we?" Angela asked.

"Ladies of pleasure. Lord Parkinson-Smythe has a reputation for being a ladies' man."

"But he is married!" I said.

"Since when has that prevented a man from doing what he wants?"

"True enough," Angela agreed. "Then, if you know what we are, you must know what we want."

"I can guess." Percy took a swig from his flask, which he generously passed to us afterward.

"We no longer wish to be guests of His Lordship," Angela said after she and I had sipped some brandy.

"And you want my help."

"That is true," I said.

"I've always been one to help ladies in distress, but I run a risk. His Lordship is a powerful man, and work is scarce. Have you any money? Any jewels?"

"Alas, we have only the clothes on our backs," Angela admitted.

"Fine lot of good those'll do me. I don't mind sticking my neck out—I've done it before. But I've got to be paid. That's only fair. One service in exchange for another."

"And what service are you prepared to perform for us?" asked Angela.

"There's a coach that passes by not far from here twice a week on its way to London. I know the driver. I can flag him down. He'll take you aboard when he sees it's me. I'll also get you some food for the journey."

"That is most generous of you," I said.

"Kindness never filled a man's stomach, though."

"We do have something else that many men find quite attractive," Angela said.

"And what might that be?"

She unbuttoned her blouse and exposed her breasts, taking Percy's hands and placing them on her globes. "These. Men will do much to caress them. And there's more," she added. "Pleasures you have only dreamed of."

Angela pushed him onto his back, his hands still on her globes so she could kiss him, her tongue working hard in his mouth. Seeing that, I unbuttoned his breeches and held his flaccid tool in the palm of my hand, pulling back on the foreskin so I could lick the revealed helmeted head.

Although my cocksucking skills were far from being perfected totally, with all due modesty, I may say I was an excellent sucker for I truly enjoyed the act. Also, the gravity of our situation lent me added enthusiasm and energy.

To my surprise, Percy quickly rose to an admirable height which was complimented by an equally commendable girth. Angela leaned over him, running one of her hardened nipples across his lips, enticing him to suckle upon her while I raised and lowered my head, squeezing him with my lips, fondling his balls with my fingertips, feeling my cunny moisten.

Then Percy began to move his pelvis upward, humping my ardent mouth. Encouraged, I sucked as hard as I could upon him, my intimate, exciting noises soon causing the head of his rod to swell. Angela's hands found their way inside his shirt while she smothered his face with her large breasts.

My efforts were not in vain, for Percy ejaculated into my mouth, causing me to climax as well. Once I sensed he had shot his load, I lifted my head; Angela pulled down her knickers and squatted over him, guiding his still-hard, bared cock to her love-garden.

Percy sucked my nipples, displaying much hunger, while Angela propelled herself up and down, her pelvis meeting his as she leaned over. Then Percy took some initiative, thrusting upward hard and fast, giving my friend a fine humping, causing her to climax. Moving down, I caressed Percy's balls with one hand while I cupped one of Angela's breasts with the other.

Brutus sat, watched, and drooled.

Although somewhat rough in appearance, Percy proved to be a more-than-adequate cocksman and held himself back far longer than I thought he was capable of before finally spending. Angela timed her thrusting just right so that she climaxed with him.

It took us several minutes to recuperate from our exertions. Percy buttoned up his breeches while Angela and I laced up our corsets and pulled up our knickers. Brutus continued to sit, watch, and drool. I shuddered to think what unimaginably disgusting thoughts the beast might be having.

"You are ladies of your word, and I am a man of my word. Meet me here one week from today. If you cannot get away, be here three days after that. I shall speak to the driver of the coach and tell him to expect two additional passengers," said Percy.

"But we cannot pay him!" Angela cried.

"Lord Parkinson-Smythe is a son of the devil. Aye, if I knew I wouldn't hang for it, I'd use the dogs on him. Shooting is too good for a man like that."

"Bless you," I said.

"A man does what he can, when he can, and how he can. The coach will take you safely to London. I trust you to say nothing of our arrangement for if you do... well, you know what kind of man His Lordship is."

"We swear on it. We shall reveal nothing," Angela said, kissing him lightly.

"I'll walk you back. The other dogs are about, and without me, they would surely attack you. Brutus! Go play!" The dog ran happily off into the woods.

"Do you always let him do that, go play?" Angela asked.

"Aye, for he is especially fond of rabbits. Not that he gets one every day, mind you. They're quick little rascals!"

We walked in silence, my body quivering slightly from the intensity of the brief but passionate encounter. We could hear Brutus crashing around in the underbrush but could not see him. As far as I was concerned, it was just as well.

"There's the house," Percy said. "Remember, one week

from today at the same time. Don't be late. If you cannot be there, three days hence."

"We will be there. I swear it!" said Angela.

We reached the privacy of our room without incident and well within the time limit established by Charlotte. "I am giddy with excitement," I said as I removed my clothing, intending to change into a simple shift, for the air in our quarters did not circulate as freely as might be desired.

"The venture is fraught with peril," Angela said, standing naked by the window.

"Surely you are not thinking of remaining here?"

"And wind up even more of a slave than I already am? I would rather die first!"

"As would I. So it is settled then. We are agreed."

"I have never been surer of anything in my life, but we must exercise every possible caution for, as Percy said, others have tried to escape and I am sure many have failed."

"What if Percy is an agent of Lord Parkinson-Smythe?" I asked.

"Then we are doomed. Our fates will be sealed."

"But we still have to risk it, for it is our only chance."

"You are right. We have nothing to lose."

Angela was wrong. We—or, to be more specific, I—had a great deal more to lose. If anyone had described the abominations which were to be performed upon my poor flesh, I would not have believed them, for they would have seemed not of this earth.

Entry № 22

For six days now, we have been kept in our room. Charlotte refused our request to take another stroll and did not deign to give us an explanation. Both Angela and I have an uneasy feeling that something evil is brewing. It is a feeling—woman's intuition, if you will—that permeates our humble quarters. We do not speak of it, for we both know that it would only bring more worry and anxiety to our already-troubled minds. 'Tis best to be silent.

Our routine is simple: we rise early, breakfast at seven, mend our clothes and do any other mundane chores we can think of, lunch at twelve, nap for several hours during the afternoon, dinner at six, and are in bed by eleven.

We were one day from our appointed meeting with Percy and were becoming increasingly agitated. The tension was almost unbearable. However, an event occurred that was so vile in nature that it changed me forever. In keeping with my policy of total honesty, I must caution that it is not my intention to offend. However, if anyone who is reading this is of a sensitive nature, I respectfully suggest that they skip what follows, for they will surely be shocked and repelled.

One hour after we had finished our dinner, Charlotte entered our room. "His Lordship wishes the pleasure of your company," she announced after locking the door. "Choose your finest dress."

I had a beautiful large-bustled white linen dress that featured crosswise flounces, leg-of-mutton sleeves and was low cut, giving me plenty of décolletage. I laid it on the bed and was getting the necessary undergarments from the dresser when Charlotte stopped me.

"Just the dress. Nothing else. Oh, there is something else. That red bonnet will do nicely, the one with the poke brim and feathers. Don't forget the veil, either. Angela, help her to pin her hair up. I'm sure it will fit under the bonnet. And her love-garden—fluff up the hairs a little. Rouge her nipples—not too much now. Excellent, His Lordship will be pleased. Now, a few dabs of perfume. Use it sparingly— we don't want her smelling like a two-shilling tart, do we?" She surveyed me when the preparations had been completed. "Nice, very nice," she pronounced. "Come along then. Mustn't keep the master waiting—you know how he gets."

"Are you not going to blindfold me?"

"There is no need."

It was an odd—although not unpleasant sensation— to be nude under my dress. The absence of a corset made my breasts jiggle more than they ordinarily would have. We walked quickly, arriving within a few minutes at the entrance to the room in which I was to please the master.

Many candles and sconces provided more than ample illumination. The fire created a cozy warmth, and the furnishings had stayed the same. What had changed was the sex of the inhabitants of the room. They were all male, a dozen of them, ranging in age from middle thirties to early fifties. They sat in their chairs, sipping brandy, the air redolent of cigar smoke. All were in formal attire and had the air of gentlemen, as evidenced by the fine cut of their clothes. Some sported mutton-chops while others preferred walrus mustaches.

Lord Francis sat in a backless black velvet chair and rose when Charlotte and I entered. She then stood by the fireplace on the far side of the room while he rose.

"This is the reason for our little gathering, gentlemen. Allow me to present her to you." The audience remained motionless in their chairs as Francis began to unbutton the front of my dress. Was I to be exposed to these strangers in all my nakedness? When it became apparent that was his intention, my face flushed red with humiliation. He undid my sleeve buttons, his body shielding mine from the view of the others. Then he dropped my dress to the floor, rendering me totally naked.

"There!" he said proudly, standing aside so that all could view me. "My newest addition. Come closer, gather round." The men did, some still holding their brandy snifters. "Notice how quickly her buds flower," Lord Francis said as he gave my nipples a gentle pinching, causing them to rise. "More beautiful globes will be difficult to find," he said as he hefted them. "See for yourselves. Notice the plump bumcheeks, the sparse hair that guards her garden. She is a wonder of nature, is she not?"

Stranger's hands began to feel my breasts, rub my tummy, and explore the crack between my bumcheeks. The humiliation was complete. Or so I thought. "And she is most willing to please, as I shall now demonstrate. If you will return to your seats, gentlemen." Francis stripped off his clothes. "Well, are you going to make a liar out of me?" he asked as he took off my hat and veil. "Observe the full lips, the straight nose, the beautiful eyes that beg to serve her master."

"Please, do not make me do this!" I pleaded.

"On your knees! Now pleasure me!" he ordered.

I took his flaccid rod into my mouth, holding it there until he achieved a full erection. Then I ran the flat of my tongue up and down the sensitive underside of his tool, caressing his balls at the same time. Francis watched intently with a stern expression on his face as I began to favor him orally, moving my head forward and backward, squeezing his thickness with my lips.

"Charlotte!" Francis barked.

His sluttish accomplice came over and knelt so she could thrust three fingers up into my cunny, stimulating me into sucking on his rod even harder. With her other hand, she pinched my already-flowered buds. And thus she got me to spasm, holding up her wet hand for all to see. The audience murmured their approval as my sweet juice seeped out from between my cunnylips.

Then Francis held my head steady between his hands and began to fuck my mouth. I felt the head of his tool rub against the roof of my mouth as he performed this perversion on me. Alas, I was helpless to prevent it—I was still in the throes of my spasm.

When His Lordship removed his rod from my mouth, I thought, in my innocence, that he was finished, but no, he was just beginning. He began to masturbate and within seconds he spent himself, spraying gobs of jism over my face. When he was done, the evil Charlotte helped me to my feet only to place me on the padded chaise. Feeling his manly juices running down my cheeks, I spread my legs and drew my knees up to my chest ready—nay, although it may bring eternal shame upon me—eager to accept him.

"See how anxious she is, gentlemen," His Lordship announced as he prepared to enter me. "Her appetite knows no bounds."

The assemblage continued to stay where they were. Why did they not come closer as the ladies had? Why were they so aloof? It was as if they were judging me, making cold conclusions without regard to passion.

Editor's Note: The unfortunate Danielle is correct, but for reasons obviously unknown to her. The men who were witnessing these acts were middlemen, agents who represented rich and powerful Middle Eastern potentates. These representatives would regularly attend spectacles like the one Danielle is describing in order to find the most desirable women for their clients.

In this way, Lord Parkinson-Smythe protected himself; for, as far as anyone was concerned, Danielle was just a maid. As her employer, he could terminate her services whenever he wanted. But in fact, she was about to be sold to an agent who would then arrange transport and eventual delivery to her new master.

However, should His Lordship be questioned— which was highly unlikely, but he was clever enough to foresee any eventuality and prepare for it—he could claim that Danielle had gone into the service of another household that was represented by an employment agency. Once no longer in his employ, what happened to her was no longer his affair. Thus he managed to separate himself from the person who actually bought her—a most effective method of avoiding detection.

†††

His Lordship entered me, my well-lubricated canal providing him easy passage, enabling him to make that most pleasurable of journeys without stopping until his groin was pressing against mine. I squirmed impatiently, having surrendered unconditionally to the limitless bliss that a woman knows only when she is being pleasured by a cocksman of the first degree.

I was oblivious to the observing audience as he began to hump me, his long, thick tool filling up my canal, my sheath grasping him tightly. Charlotte stood near us and looked straight ahead, ignoring my moans which filled the room as Lord Francis's rod drove me steadily toward another orgasm.

It felt as if my body were exploding into a thousand pieces as I climaxed, my body producing an effusion of that sweetest of feminine secretions, bathing the master's tool, thus facilitating the bliss which he was bestowing upon me.

I wrapped my legs around his waist, unwilling to release him, refusing to separate myself from the joy which was being thrust into me. I no longer had any inhibitions, for they were erased by the tool which was being thrust in and out of my cunny. Like the most wanton of harlots, I threw my pelvis upward, want-ing—nay, demanding—that His Lordship give me as much of his wondrous instrument as was humanly possible, for I would settle for nothing less.

Love-juice escaped from my cunny and ran down my

bumcheeks, leaving a faint pearly trail behind. My whole body shook as Lord Francis made me the recipient of all the skills he had in applying that most manly of arts. I clung to him, holding onto his arms as well, my bosom heaving up and down as I sought in vain to satisfy my air-starved lungs.

Editor's Note: It is evident from Danielle's description of the scene that Lord Parkinson-Smythe is doing everything he can to demonstrate to the agents that Danielle would make an excellent slave. Knowing that the Middle Eastern potentates were very demanding, the clever Parkinson-Smythe was well aware that if he impressed the agents, he would be able to get a higher price for Danielle. Thus his efforts, although certainly rewarding for Danielle, are very self-serving in that they were designed to drive up her value.

Never have I made love with a man in such a way, for His Lordship elevated the art of cocksmanship to an almost spiritual level. His staying power was remarkable. Most men would have been unable to hold back for so long, especially in light of the way I was reacting, which would have been more than enough to make most mortals release.

I was amazed when he pulled his still-hard tool from the warm recesses of my cunny and began to use his hand on it. Was he not going to spend himself in me?

No, it was apparent that he was going to rain his sperm on me once again. This he proceeded to do, glops of his hot, thick jism splattering all over my stomach.

"On your knees!" he ordered, breathing hard. Anticipating that my stallion was going to take me for a third time, from the rear, I assumed the position anxiously. "Charlotte, prepare her."

In spite of the ecstasy which made my head spin, I was still able to hear his words. What did they mean? Alas, to my shame, I was about to find out. Charlotte stood next to me and spread my bumcheeks far apart, exposing my tiny ring. Then she applied a generous amount of almond oil to that most private of parts. It was impossible to contemplate the unthinkable, but when I felt the head of His Lordship's rod begin to nudge at my unyielding ring, I knew that the foulest of abominations was about to be perpetrated upon me.

"No, no!" I cried. "Do not subject me to this. Mercy, mercy!"

"She protests, gentlemen," panted His Lordship, turning his head so he could address the audience, "but she will soon be singing a different song. As you have seen, her appetite is boundless."

"I beg you. No, no, spare me this cruelty!" I pleaded.

But my supplications were in vain. I knew there was no perversity, no act so hideous or unnatural that the sadistic Lord Parkinson-Smythe would not gladly commit upon a helpless female.

"I beseech you, master, for you will do me a grievous injury."

The monster was deaf, interested only in satisfying his own aberrant lusts. He was worse than an animal, he was evil incarnate. He started to enter me as my ring expanded slowly. How would I ever survive. He was too long and too thick—surely I would burst! The gentlemen who were watching did nothing to help me. The beasts obviously shared Lord Parkinson-Smythe's disgusting tastes. My humiliation complete, I prepared myself for the worst.

To my amazement, I found that I was able to accept him simply by relaxing my muscles. 'Twas indeed a blessing. Having done that, I began to experience the most exquisite and unusual of pleasures which only intensified after he was completely buried in my bum.

Then he began to bugger me, holding onto my hips in much the same way as Charlotte had done when she used the artificial penis on me. Every thrust he made resulted in complete penetration and when I felt his balls hit my erected clitty, I began to race toward a spasm.

"Master, master!" I gasped, amazed at the depth and scope of the joy which fairly well consumed me.

"You see, gentlemen," His Lordship panted, turning his head without missing a stroke. "Is she not a treasure? Would not any man be proud to own her? She would be the jewel of his collection!"

Lord Francis buggered me hard and fast, droplets of my precious love-juice seeping out from between my cunnylips, encouraging him to even greater exertions. I spasmed yet again, my ring glowing from his continued deep penetration.

Then he left me, once more spending himself on my back, his fluids splattering over me as he turned to his audience. "Gentlemen," he panted, "I think I have demonstrated the value of my newest acquisition."

"Bravo," I heard one man say.

"Hear, hear," said another.

"Well done, old boy," added another.

"Please repair to my office. I shall join you shortly. Charlotte, you may take her away now."

Although I was still light-headed and feeling faint, the inconsiderate Charlotte pulled me rudely to my feet, grabbing my dress and hat. "No need to put these on. Come, your work here is finished! It's back to your cell, my little French bitch."

She half-dragged, half-pulled me down the corridor. I was fearful that my pleasure-weakened legs would not support me, but somehow they did, allowing me to reach my cell where I promptly collapsed on the bed. Charlotte threw my clothes on top of me in a most contemptuous manner. "An excellent performance. Your future owner will be most pleased!" she sneered before she slammed the door shut and locked it.

"What cruelties did they subject you to?" Angela asked anxiously. After I recounted them, she thought for a minute before speaking. "We must make our escape attempt tomorrow, for I fear that we shall be sold as soon as the arrangements can be made. Once that happens we are doomed."

"How can a man be so vile?"

"I do not know. Do you think you will have the strength? You have undergone a terrible ordeal!"

"I would crawl on my hands and knees!"

"Good. I shall make the request after breakfast tomorrow morning."

"Freedom! How sweet the word sounds," I murmured.

"We are not free yet, for there are many dangers."

More than I realized.

Entry № 23

August 9, 1867

"I see no reason why not. After all, you earned it," Charlotte said with a leer after we had asked her if we could get some air outside. "Besides, His Lordship likes his girls to have some color when they leave here. It makes a good impression. Both this door and the outside door shall be unlocked, but let me remind you. Do not wander— Rufus will be watching you."

After our breakfast dishes were removed, Angela said, "My instincts were right. The master intends to sell us. The tribulations we have both been subjected to were designed to show us off to potential buyers."

"But I thought you said that if we pleased him he would keep us."

"I did say that. But you know as well as I do that he is very unpredictable. If you have another opinion, you are welcome to it. You are also welcome to stay here if that is what you think best."

"Oh, no! Please forgive me, for I did not mean to offend you. I am prepared to make our dash to freedom. Once we reach London, I can contact my father. He will save us."

"Then let us prepare, for we will get only one chance. Let us wear another skirt under our dresses. We can hide it easily in our petticoats, along with another blouse, for we will need a change of clothing. Remember, we have no money, and London can be a cruel city."

"That is true. But we have another commodity."

"Pray let us hope we do not have to use it. Come, let us get ready," Angela said as she went over to the bureau.

By wearing one less petticoat, it was a simple matter to hide both a skirt and a blouse under our voluminous dresses. We checked each other to see if we gave anything away as we walked, but we did not and our confidence grew accordingly. The day was sunny and bright, justifying both a parasol and a bonnet.

Two hours before we were supposed to meet Percy, we made our way downstairs. I was fairly well trembling with a combination of fear and eagerness, but we did not rush. We walked slowly across the great lawn as we always did, putting a fair distance between ourselves and the house before we stopped, ostensibly to sit and relax, but actually to make sure we were not being followed.

"That is odd, " I said. "Normally Rufus would be by the door. But he is not."

"Perhaps he thinks we are incapable of such a subterfuge as we plan."

"Perhaps," I said.

We made good progress through the forest. As we drew nearer to the place where we were supposed to meet Percy, our confidence grew in leaps and bounds. Freedom beat beneath my bosom as surely as my heart did.

Alas, I am afraid that we were too overconfident. What happened next nearly made me faint.

"Just where do you think you're going?" boomed Rufus's voice as he stepped out from behind a large oak tree. Obviously, the rogue had been following us and had set up an ambush.

"Just…just…for a walk," Angela stammered.

"A walk? In these woods? It's back to your cell, my little sluts, and a good whipping!" he snarled as he grabbed our arms and started to drag us back the way we came.

After a short distance, I yelped with pain and slumped to the ground. "I fear I have twisted my ankle," I said, looking up at him.

"Blast! Now I shall have to carry you. Damn your French hide!"

As soon as he let go of Angela so that he could bend

over to lift me, Angela picked up a branch that lay conveniently among the forest debris and whacked him over the head with it. Rufus collapsed in a heap.

"*Mon Dieu*, have you killed him?" I asked as I stood up.

"No, he is only unconscious. Is your ankle all right?"

"Yes, that was just a desperate trick."

"Come, we must hurry."

We raced through the forest and, fifteen minutes later, met Percy. He led us immediately to the place where he would flag down the coach. "You were late," he said as we hurried along, taking what appeared to be a barely discernible path that led through the seemingly impenetrable forest. Brutus raced ahead.

"Rufus followed us," Angela replied breathlessly. "We had to dispatch him."

"Permanently?"

"No, he will live."

"Take heart. We're almost there."

Ten minutes later, we emerged from the forest and stood on the edge of the wide, rutted dirt road. Percy handed us a small parcel. "Food, a few shillings, and a small flask of brandy."

"You are too kind," I said as I kissed him lightly on both cheeks.

"I hear the stage now."

The thundering of sixteen horses' hooves grew louder and louder until the coach finally came into view, slowing so it could safely negotiate the curve at whose peak we were standing. Percy waved his arms and flagged it down.

"Got a couple of passengers for you, Jack," he called up to the driver.

"Get in then. Quickly."

"In you go," said Percy as he assisted us.

"Gee yap!" yelled the driver, slapping the horses' backs with the reins.

We settled back on the padded seat. There was one other passenger sitting opposite us, an older woman wearing a heavy veil. We paid little attention to her until she lifted it and looked at us.

"Fancy meeting you two!" said Maggie.

"What…what are you doing here?" I asked in a whisper.

"Been visiting relatives. I'm on my way back to His Lordship's estate. We'll be stopping there in about ten minutes. He won't be pleased with you. No, no. The master deals very harshly with ladies who try and escape. I can assure you of that."

Ten minutes! I must think of something! But what?

MASQUERADE

S. CRABB
CHATS ON OLD PEWTER
$6.95/611-1
A compendium of tales dedicated to dominant women. From domineering check-out girls to merciless flirts on the prowl, these women know what men like—and are highly skilled at reducing any man to putty in their hands.

PAT CALIFIA
SENSUOUS MAGIC
$7.95/610-3
"*Sensuous Magic* is clear, succinct and engaging.... Califia is the Dr. Ruth of the alternative sexuality set...."
—*Lambda Book Report*

Erotic pioneer Pat Califia provides this unpretentious peek behind the mask of dominant/submissive sexuality. With her trademark wit and insight, Califia demystifies "the scene" for the novice, explaining the terms and techniques behind many misunderstood sexual practices.

ANAÏS NIN AND FRIENDS
WHITE STAINS
$6.95/609-X
A lost classic of 1940s erotica returns! Written by Anaïs Nin, Virginia Admiral, Caresse Crosby, and others for a dollar per page, this breathtakingly sensual volume was printed privately and soon became an underground legend. After more than fifty years, this priceless collection of explicit but sophisticated musings is back in print—and available to the contemporary connoisseur of erotica.

DENISE HALL
JUDGMENT
$6.95/590-5
Judgment—a forbidding edifice where unfortunate young women find themselves degraded and abandoned to the wiles of their cruel masters. Callie MacGuire descends into the depths of this prison, discovering a capacity for sensual torment she never dreamed existed.

CLAIRE WILLOWS
PRESENTED IN LEATHER
$6.95/576-X
The story of poor Flora Price and the stunning punishments she suffered at the hands of her cruel captors. At the age of nineteen, Flora is whisked to the south of France, where she is imprisoned in Villa Close, an institution devoted to the ways of the lash—not to mention the paddle, the strap, the rod…

ALISON TYLER & DANTE DAVIDSON
BONDAGE ON A BUDGET
$6.95/570-0
Filled with delicious scenarios requiring no more than simple household items and a little imagination, this guide to DIY S&M will explode the myth that adventurous sex requires a dungeonful of expensive custom-made paraphernalia.

JEAN SADDLER
THE FASCINATING TYRANT
$6.95/569-7
A reprint of a classic tale from the 1930s of erotic dictatorship. Jean Saddler's most famous novel, *The Fascinating Tyrant* is a riveting glimpse of sexual extravagance in which a young man discovers his penchant for flagellation and sadomasochism.

ROBERT SEWALL
THE DEVIL'S ADVOCATE
$6.95/553-0
Clara Reeves appeals to Conrad Garnett, a New York district attorney, for help in tracking down her missing sister, Rita. Clara soon finds herself being "persuaded" to accompany Conrad on his descent into a modern-day hell, where unspeakable pleasures await….

LUCY TAYLOR
UNNATURAL ACTS
$7.95/552-2
"A topnotch collection"
—*Science Fiction Chronicle*

Unnatural Acts plunges deep into the dark side of the psyche and brings to life a disturbing vision of erotic horror. Unrelenting angels and hungry gods play with souls and bodies in Taylor's murky cosmos: where heaven and hell are merely differences of perspective.

OLIVIA M. RAVENSWORTH
THE DESIRES OF REBECCA
$6.50/532-8
Rebecca follows her passions from the simple love of the girl next door to the lechery of London's most notorious brothel, hoping for the ultimate thrill. She casts her lot with a crew of sapphic buccaneers, each of whom is more than capable of matching Rebecca's lust.
THE MISTRESS OF CASTLE ROHMENSTADT
$5.95/372-4
Lovely Katherine inherits a secluded European castle from a mysterious relative. Upon arrival she discovers, much to her delight, that the castle is a haven of sexual perversion. Before long, Katherine is truly Mistress of the house!

MASQUERADE BOOKS

GERALD GREY
LONDON GIRLS
$6.50/531-X
In 1875, Samuel Brown arrives in London, determined to take the glorious city by storm. Samuel quickly distinguishes himself as one of the city's most notorious rakehells. Young Mr. Brown knows well the many ways of making a lady weak at the knees—and uses them not only to his delight, but to his enormous profit!

ERICA BRONTE
LUST, INC.
$6.50/467-4
Explore the extremes of passion that lurk beneath even the most businesslike exteriors. Join in the sexy escapades of a group of professionals whose idea of office decorum is like nothing you've ever encountered!

ATAULLAH MARDAAN
KAMA HOURI/DEVA DASI
$7.95/512-3
"Mardaan excels in crowding her pages with the sights and smells of India, and her erotic descriptions are convincingly realistic."
—Michael Perkins,
The Secret Record: Modern Erotic Literature

Kama Houri details the life of a sheltered Western woman who finds herself living within the confines of a harem. *Deva Dasi* is a tale dedicated to the sacred women of India who devoted their lives to the fulfillment of the senses.

VISCOUNT LADYWOOD
GYNECOCRACY
$9.95/511-5
Julian is sent to a private school, and discovers that his program of study has been devised by stern Mademoiselle de Chambonnard. In no time, Julian is learning the many ways of pleasure and pain—under the firm hand of this beautifully demanding headmistress.

N. T. MORLEY
THE CONTRACT
$6.95/575-1
Meet Carlton and Sarah, two true connoisseurs of discipline. Sarah is experiencing some difficulty in training her current submissive. Carlton proposes an unusual wager: if Carlton is unsuccessful in bringing Tina to a full appreciation of Sarah's domination, Carlton himself will become Sarah's devoted slave....

THE LIMOUSINE
$6.95/555-7
Brenda was enthralled with her roommate Kristi's illicit sex life: a never ending parade of men who satisfied Kristi's desire to be dominated. Brenda decides to embark on a trip into submission, beginning in the long, white limousine where Kristi first met the Master.

THE CASTLE
$6.95/530-1
Tess Roberts is held captive by a crew of disciplinarians intent on making all her dreams come true—even those she'd never admitted to herself. While anyone can arrange for a stay at the Castle, Tess proves herself one of the most gifted applicants yet....

THE PARLOR
$6.50/496-8
The mysterious John and Sarah ask Kathryn to be their slave—an idea that turns her on so much that she can't refuse! Little by little, Kathryn not only learns to serve, but comes to know the inner secrets of her keepers.

J. A. GUERRA, ED.
COME QUICKLY:
For Couples on the Go
$6.50/461-5
The increasing pace of daily life is no reason to forgo a little carnal pleasure whenever the mood strikes. Here are over sixty of the hottest fantasies around—all designed especially for modern couples on a hectic schedule.

VANESSA DURIÈS
THE TIES THAT BIND
$6.50/510-7
This true story will keep you gasping with its vivid depictions of sensual abandon. At the hand of Masters Georges, Patrick, Pierre and others, this submissive seductress experiences pleasures she never knew existed.... One of modern erotica's best-selling accounts of real-life dominance and submission.

M. S. VALENTINE
THE GOVERNESS
$6.95/562-X
Lovely Miss Hunnicut eagerly embarks upon a career as a governess, hoping to escape the memories of her broken engagement. Little does she know that Crawleigh Manor is far from the upstanding household it appears. Mr. Crawleigh, in particular, devotes himself to Miss Hunnicut's thorough defiling.

BUY ANY 4 BOOKS & CHOOSE 1 ADDITIONAL BOOK, OF EQUAL OR LESSER VALUE, AS YOUR FREE GIFT

MASQUERADE BOOKS

ELYSIAN DAYS AND NIGHTS
$6.95/536-0
From around the world, neglected young wives arrive at the Elysium Spa intent on receiving a little heavy-duty pampering. Luckily for them, the spa's proprietor is a true devotee of the female form—and has dedicated himself to the pure pleasure of every woman who steps foot across their threshold....

THE CAPTIVITY OF CELIA
$6.50/453-4
Celia's lover, Colin, is considered the prime suspect in a murder, forcing him to seek refuge with his cousin, Sir Jason Hardwicke. In exchange for Colin's safety, Jason demands Celia's unquestioning submission....

AMANDA WARE
BINDING CONTRACT
$6.50/491-7
Louise was responsible for bringing many clients into Claremont's salon—so he was more than willing to have her miss a little work in order to pleasure one of his most important customers. But Eleanor Cavendish had her mind set on something more rigorous than a simple wash and set—dooming Louise to a life of sexual slavery! Soon, Louise is a slave to not only Eleanor, but her own rampant desire.

BOUND TO THE PAST
$6.50/452-6
Doing research in an old Tudor mansion, Anne finds herself aroused by James, a descendant of the property's owners. Together they uncover the perverse desires of the mansion's long-dead master—desires that bind Anne inexorably to the past—not to mention the bedpost!

SACHI MIZUNO
SHINJUKU NIGHTS
$6.50/493-3
A tour through the lives and libidos of the seductive East. Using Tokyo's infamous red light district as his backdrop, Sachi Mizuno weaves an intricate web of sensual desire, wherein many characters are ensnared and enraptured by the demands of their carnal natures.

PASSION IN TOKYO
$6.50/454-2
Tokyo—one of Asia's most historic and seductive cities. Come behind the closed doors of its citizens, and witness the many pleasures that await. Lusty men and women from every stratum of society free themselves of all inhibitions in this delirious tour through the libidinous East.

MARTINE GLOWINSKI
POINT OF VIEW
$6.50/433-X
The story of one woman's extraordinary erotic awakening. With the assistance of her new, unexpectedly kinky lover, she discovers and explores her exhibitionist tendencies—until there is virtually nothing she won't do before the horny audiences her man arranges. Soon she is infamous for her unabashed sexual performances!

RICHARD McGOWAN
A HARLOT OF VENUS
$6.50/425-9
A highly fanciful, epic tale of lust on Mars! Cavortia—the most famous and sought-after courtesan in the cosmopolitan city of Venus—finds love and much more during her adventures with some cosmic characters. A sexy, sci-fi fairytale.

M. ORLANDO
THE SLEEPING PALACE
$6.95/582-4
Another thrilling volume of erotic reveries from the author of *The Architecture of Desire*. *Maison Bizarre* is the scene of unspeakable erotic cruelty; the *Lust Akademie* holds captive only the most luscious students of the sensual arts; *Baden-Eros* is the luxurious retreat of one's nastiest dreams.

CHET ROTHWELL
KISS ME, KATHERINE
$5.95/410-0
Beautiful Katherine can hardly believe her luck. Not only is she married to the charming Nelson, she's free to live out all her erotic fantasies with other men. Katherine's desires are more than any one man can handle—and plenty of men wait to fulfill her extraordinary needs!

MARCO VASSI
THE STONED APOCALYPSE
$5.95/401-1/Mass market
"Marco Vassi is our champion sexual energist." —VLS

During his lifetime, Marco Vassi's reputation as a champion of sexual experimentation was worldwide. Funded by his groundbreaking erotic writing, *The Stoned Apocalypse* is Vassi's autobiography; chronicling a cross-country trip on America's erotic byways, it offers a rare an stimulating glimpse of a generation's sexual imagination.

MASQUERADE BOOKS

THE SALINE SOLUTION
$6.95/568-9/Mass market

"I've always read Marco's work with interest and I have the highest opinion not only of his talent but his intellectual boldness."
—Norman Mailer

During the Sexual Revolution, Vassi established himself as an explorer of an uncharted sexual landscape. Through this story of one couple's brief affair and the events that lead them to desperately reassess their lives, Vassi examines the dangers of intimacy in an age of extraordinary freedom.

ROBIN WILDE
TABITHA'S TEASE
$6.95/597-2

When poor Robin arrives at The Valentine Academy, he finds himself subject to the torturous teasing of Tabitha—the Academy's most notoriously domineering co-ed. But Tabitha is pledge-mistress of a secret sorority dedicated to enslaving young men. Robin finds himself the and wildly excited captive of Tabitha & Company's weird desires!

TABITHA'S TICKLE
$6.50/468-2

Once again, men fall under the spell of scrumptious co-eds and find themselves enslaved to demands and desires they never dreamed existed. Think it's a man's world? Guess again. With Tabitha around, no man gets what he wants until she's completely satisfied....

ERICA BRONTE
PIRATE'S SLAVE
$5.95/376-7

Lovely young Erica is stranded in a country where lust knows no bounds. Desperate to escape, she finds herself trading her firm, luscious body to any and all men willing and able to help her. Her adventure has its ups and downs, ins and outs—all to the pleasure of the increasingly lusty Erica!

CHARLES G. WOOD
HELLFIRE
$5.95/358-9

A vicious murderer is running amok in New York's sexual underground—and Nick O'Shay, a virile detective with the NYPD, plunges deep into the case. He soon becomes embroiled in the Big Apples notorious nightworld of dungeons and sex clubs, hunting a madman seeking to purge America with fire and blood sacrifices.

CHARISSE VAN DER LYN
SEX ON THE NET
$5.95/399-6

Electrifying erotica from one of the Internet's hottest authors. Encounters of all kinds—straight, lesbian, dominant/submissive and all sorts of extreme passions—are explored in thrilling detail.

STANLEY CARTEN
NAUGHTY MESSAGE
$5.95/333-3

Wesley Arthur discovers a lascivious message on his answering machine. Aroused beyond his wildest dreams by the acts described, he becomes obsessed with tracking down the woman behind the seductive voice. His search takes him through strip clubs, sex parlors and no-tell motels—before finally leading him to his randy reward....

AKBAR DEL PIOMBO
THE FETISH CROWD
$6.95/556-5

An infamous trilogy presented in one special volume guaranteed to appeal to the modern sophisticate. Separately, *Paula the Piquôse*, the infamous *Duke Cosimo*, and *The Double-Bellied Companion* are rightly considered masterpieces.

A CRUMBLING FAÇADE
$4.95/3043-1

The return of that incorrigible rogue, Henry Pike, who continues his pursuit of sex, fair or otherwise, in the homes of the most debauched aristocrats. Ultimately, every woman succumbs to Pike's charms—and submits to his whims!

CAROLE REMY
FANTASY IMPROMPTU
$6.50/513-1

Kidnapped to a remote island retreat, Chantal finds herself catering to every sexual whim of the mysterious Bran. Bran is determined to bring Chantal to a full embracing of her sensual nature, even while revealing himself to be something far more than human....

BEAUTY OF THE BEAST
$5.95/332-5

A shocking tell-all, written from the point-of-view of a prize-winning reporter. All the licentious secrets of an uninhibited life are revealed.

MASQUERADE BOOKS

ANONYMOUS

DANIELLE: DIARY OF A SLAVE GIRL
$6.95/591-3

At the age of 19, Danielle Appleton vanishes. The frantic efforts of her family notwithstanding, she is never seen by them again. After her disappearance, Danielle finds herself doomed to a life of sexual slavery, obliged to become the ultimate instrument of pleasure to the man—or men—who own her and dictate her every move and desire.

SUBURBAN SOULS
$9.95/563-8/Trade paperback

One of American erotica's first classics. Focusing on the May–December sexual relationship of nubile Lillian and the more experienced Jack, all three volumes of *Suburban Souls* now appear in one special edition—guaranteed to enrapture modern readers with its lurid detail.

ROMANCE OF LUST
$9.95/604-9

"Truly remarkable...all the pleasure of fine historical fiction combined with the most intimate descriptions of explicit love-making."
　　　　　　　　　　　　　　　　　—*The Times*

One of the most famous erotic novels of the century! First issued between 1873 and 1876, this titillating collaborative work of sexual awakening in Victorian England was repeatedly been banned for its "immorality"—and much sought after for its vivid portrayals of sodomy, sexual initiation, and flagellation. The novel that inspired Steven Marcus to coin the term "pornotopic", *Romance of Lust* not only offers the reader a linguistic tour de force, but also delivers a long look at the many possibilities of heterosexual love.

THE MISFORTUNES OF COLETTE
$7.95/564-6

The tale of one woman's erotic suffering at the hands of the sadistic man and woman who take her in hand. Beautiful Colette is the victim of an obscene plot guaranteed to keep her in erotic servitude—first to her punishing guardian, then to the man who takes her as his wife. Passed from one lustful tormentor to another, Colette wonders whether she is destined to find her greatest pleasures in punishment!

LOVE'S ILLUSION
$6.95/549-2

Elizabeth Renard yearned for the body of rich and successful Dan Harrington. Then she discovered Harrington's secret weakness: a need to be humiliated and punished. She makes him her slave, and together they commence a thrilling journey into depravity that leaves nothing to the imagination!

NADIA
$5.95/267-1

Follow the delicious but neglected Nadia as she works to wring every drop of pleasure out of life—despite an unhappy marriage. With the help of some very eager men, Nadia soon experiences the erotic pleaures she had always dreamed of.... A classic title providing a peek into the secret sexual lives of another time and place.

TITIAN BERESFORD

CHIDEWELL HOUSE AND OTHER STORIES
$6.95/554-9

What keeps Cecil a virtual, if willing, prisoner of Chidewell House? One man has been sent to investigate the sexy situation—and reports back with tales of such depravity that no expense is spared in attempting Cecil's rescue. But what man would possibly desire release from the breathtakingly beautiful and corrupt Elizabeth?

CINDERELLA
$6.50/500-X

Beresford triumphs again with this intoxicating tale, filled with castle dungeons and tightly corseted ladies-in-waiting, naughty viscounts and impossibly cruel masturbatrixes—nearly every conceivable method of erotic torture is explored and described in lush, vivid detail.

JUDITH BOSTON
$6.50/525-5

A bestselling chronicle of female domination. Edward would have been lucky to get the stodgy companion he thought his parents had hired for him. But an exquisite woman arrives at his door, and Edward finds—to his increasing delight—that his lewd behavior never goes unpunished by the unflinchingly severe Judith Boston

THE WICKED HAND
$5.95/343-0

With an Introduction by *Leg Show*'s Dian Hanson.

A collection of fanciful fetishistic tales featuring the absolute subjugation of men by lovely, domineering women.

NINA FOXTON
$5.95/443-7

An erotic classic! An aristocrat finds herself bored by the run-of-the-mill amusements deemed appropriate for "ladies of good breeding." Instead of taking tea with proper gentlemen, naughty Nina "milks" them of their most private essences. No man ever says "No" to Nina!

MASQUERADE BOOKS

TINY ALICE

THE GEEK
$5.95/341-4
The Geek is told from the point of view of, well, a chicken who reports on the various perversities he witnesses as part of a traveling carnival. When a gang of renegade lesbians kidnaps Chicken and his geek, all hell breaks loose. A strange but highly arousing tale, filled with outrageous erotic oddities, that finally returns to print after years of infamy.

LYN DAVENPORT

THE GUARDIAN II
$6.50/505-0
The tale of submissive Felicia Brookes continues. No sooner has Felicia come to love Rodney than she discovers that she has been sold—and must now accustom herself to the guardianship of the debauched Duke of Smithton. Surely Rodney will rescue her from the domination of this depraved stranger. *Won't he?*

GWYNETH JAMES

DREAM CRUISE
$4.95/3045-8
Angelia has it all—exciting career and breathtaking beauty. But she longs to kick up her high heels and have some fun, so she takes an island vacation and vows to leave her inhibitions behind. From the moment her plane takes off, she finds herself in one steamy encounter after another—and wishes her horny holiday would never end!

LIZBETH DUSSEAU

MEMBER OF THE CLUB
$6.95/608-1
A restless woman yearns to realize her most secret, licentious desires. There is a club that exists for the fulfillment of such fantasies—a club devoted to the pleasures of the flesh, and the gratification of every hunger. When its members call she is compelled to answer—and serve each in an endless quest for satisfaction.... The ultimate sex club.

SPANISH HOLIDAY
$4.95/185-3
Lauren didn't mean to fall in love with the enigmatic Sam, but a once-in-a-lifetime European vacation gives her all the evidence she needs that this hot, insatiable man might be the one for her....Soon, both lovers are eagerly exploring the furthest reaches of their desires.

ANTHONY BOBARZYNSKI

STASI SLUT
$4.95/3050-4
Adina lives in East Germany, where she can only dream about the sexual freedoms of the West. But then she meets a group of ruthless and corrupt STASI agents. They use her body for their own gratification, while she opts to use her sensual talents in a bid for total freedom!

JOCELYN JOYCE

PRIVATE LIVES
$4.95/309-0
The dirty habits of the illustrious make for a sizzling tale of French erotic life. A widow has a craving for a young busboy; he's sleeping with a rich businessman's wife; her husband is minding his sex business elsewhere!

SABINE
$4.95/3046-6
There is no one who can refuse her once she casts her spell; no lover can do anything less than give up his whole life for her. Great men and empires fall at her feet; but she is haughty, distracted, impervious. It is the eve of WW II, and Sabine must find a new lover equal to her talents and her tastes.

THE JAZZ AGE
$4.95/48-3
An attorney becomes suspicious of his mistress while his wife has an interlude with a lesbian lover. A romp of erotic realism from the heyday of the flapper and the speakeasy—when rules existed to be broken!

SARA H. FRENCH

MASTER OF TIMBERLAND
$6.95/595-6
A tale of sexual slavery at the ultimate paradise resort—where sizzling submissives serve their masters without question. One of our bestselling titles, this trek to Timberland has ignited passions the world over—and stands poised to become one of modern erotica's legendary tales.

MARY LOVE

ANGELA
$6.95/545-X
Angela's game is "look but don't touch," and she drives everyone mad with desire, dancing for their pleasure but never allowing a single caress. Soon her sensual spell is cast, and she's the only one who can break it!

BUY ANY 4 BOOKS & CHOOSE 1 ADDITIONAL BOOK, OF EQUAL OR LESSER VALUE, AS YOUR FREE GIFT

MASQUERADE BOOKS

MASTERING MARY SUE
$5.95/351-1

Mary Sue is a rich nymphomaniac whose husband is determined to declare her mentally incompetent and gain control of her fortune. He brings her to a castle where, to Mary Sue's delight, she is unleashed for a veritable sex-fest!

AMARANTHA KNIGHT
The Darker Passions: CARMILLA
$6.95/578-6

Captivated by the portrait of a beautiful woman, a young man finds himself becoming obsessed with her remarkable story. Little by little, he uncovers the many blasphemies and debaucheries with which the beauteous Laura filled her hours—even as an otherworldly presence began feasting upon her....

The Darker Passions:
THE PICTURE OF DORIAN GRAY
$6.50/342-2

One woman finds her most secret desires laid bare by a portrait far more revealing than she could have imagined. Soon she benefits from a skillful masquerade, indulging her previously hidden and unusual whims.

THE DARKER PASSIONS READER
$6.50/432-1

Here are the most eerily erotic passages from the acclaimed sexual reworkings of *Dracula, Frankenstein, Dr. Jekyll & Mr. Hyde* and *The Fall of the House of Usher*.

The Darker Passions:
DR. JEKYLL AND MR. HYDE
$4.95/227-2

It is a story of incredible transformations. Explore the steamy possibilities of a tale where no one is quite who they seem. Victorian bedrooms explode with hidden demons!

The Darker Passions: DRACULA
$5.95/326-0

"Well-written and imaginative...taking us through the sexual and sadistic scenes with details that keep us reading.... A classic in itself has been added to the shelves." —*Divinity*

The infamous erotic revisioning of Bram Stoker's classic.

THE PAUL LITTLE LIBRARY
TEARS OF THE INQUISITION
$6.95/612-X

Paul Little delivers a staggering account of pleasure. "There was a tickling inside her as her nervous system reminded her she was ready for sex. But before her was...the Inquisitor!" Titillating accusations ring through the chambers of the Inquisitor as men and women confess their every desire....

CHINESE JUSTICE
$6.95/596-4

The notorious Paul Little indulges his penchant for discipline in these wild tales. *Chinese Justice* is already a classic—the story of the excruciating pleasures and delicious punishments inflicted on foreigners under the tyrannical leaders of the Boxer Rebellion.

FIT FOR A KING/BEGINNER'S LUST
$8.95/571-9/Trade paperback

Two complete novels from this master of modern lust. Voluptuous and exquisite, she is a woman *Fit for a King*—but could she withstand the fantastic force of his carnality? *Beginner's Lust* pays off handsomely for a novice in the many ways of sensuality.

SENTENCED TO SERVITUDE
$8.95/565-4/Trade paperback

A haughty young aristocrat learns what becomes of excessive pride when she is abducted and forced to submit to ordeals of sensual torment. Trained to accept her submissive state, the icy young woman soon melts under the heat of her owners....

ROOMMATE'S SECRET
$8.95/557-3/Trade paperback

A woman is forced to make ends meet by the most ancient of methods. From the misery of early impoverishment to the delight of ill-gotten gains, Elda learns to rely on her considerable sensual talents.

TUTORED IN LUST
$6.95/547-6

This tale of the initiation and instruction of a carnal college co-ed and her fellow students unlocks the sex secrets of the classroom.

LOVE SLAVE/
PECULIAR PASSIONS OF MEG
$8.95/529-8/Trade paperback

What does it take to acquire a willing *Love Slave* of one's own? What are the appetites that lurk within *Meg*? The notoriously depraved Paul Little spares no lascivious detail in these two relentless tales!

CELESTE
$6.95/544-1

It's definitely all in the family for this female duo of sexual dynamics. While traveling through Europe, these two try everything and everyone on their horny holiday.

ALL THE WAY
$6.95/509-3

Two hot Little tales in one big volume! *Going All the Way* features an unhappy man who tries to purge himself of the memory of his lover with a series of quirky and uninhibited vixens. *Pushover* tells the story of a serial spanker and his celebrated exploits.

MASQUERADE BOOKS

THE END OF INNOCENCE
$6.95/546-8
The early days of Women's Emancipation are the setting for this story of very independent ladies. These women were willing to go to any lengths to fight for their sexual freedom, and willing to endure any punishment in their desire for total liberation.

THE BEST OF PAUL LITTLE
$6.50/469-0
Known for his fantastic portrayals of punishment and pleasure, Little never fails to push readers over the edge of sensual excitement. His best scenes are here collected for the enjoyment of all erotic connoisseurs.

CAPTIVE MAIDENS
$5.95/440-2
Three young women find themselves powerless against the debauched landowners of 1824 England. They are banished to a sex colony, where they are subjected to unspeakable perversions.

THE PRISONER
$5.95/330-9
Judge Black has built a secret room below a penitentiary, where he sentences his female prisoners to hours of exhibition and torment while his friends watch. Judge Black's brand of rough justice keeps his captives on the brink of utter pleasure!

TEARS OF THE INQUISITION
$4.95/146-2
A staggering account of pleasure and punishment, set during a viciously immoral age. "There was a tickling inside her as her nervous system reminded her she was ready for sex. But before her was...the Inquisitor!"

DOUBLE NOVEL
$6.95/86-6
The Metamorphosis of Lisette Joyaux tells the story of a young woman initiated into an incredible world of lesbian lusts. *The Story of Monique* reveals the twisted sexual rituals that beckon the ripe and willing Monique.

SLAVE ISLAND
$5.95/441-0
A leisure cruise is waylaid by Lord Henry Philbrock, a sadistic genius. The ship's passengers are kidnapped and spirited to his island prison, where the women are trained to accommodate the most bizarre sexual cravings of the rich and perverted. A perennially bestselling title.

ALIZARIN LAKE
CLARA
$6.95/548-4
The mysterious death of a beautiful woman leads her old boyfriend on a harrowing journey of discovery. His search uncovers an unimaginably sensuous woman embarked on a quest for deeper and more unusual sensations, each more shocking than the one before!

SEX ON DOCTOR'S ORDERS
$5.95/402-X
A tale of true devotion to mankind! Naughty Beth, a nubile young nurse, uses her considerable skills to further medical science by offering insatiable assistance in the gathering of important specimens. Soon she's involved everyone in her horny work—and no one leaves without surrendering exactly what Beth wants!

THE EROTIC ADVENTURES OF HARRY TEMPLE
$4.95/127-6
Harry Temple's memoirs chronicle his incredibly amorous adventures—from his initiation at the hands of insatiable sirens, through his stay at a house of hot repute, to his encounters with a chastity-belted nympho, and much more! A modern classic!

LUSCIDIA WALLACE
THE ICE MAIDEN
$6.95/613-8
Edward Canton has everything he wants in life, with one exception: Rebecca Esterbrook. He kidnaps her and whisks her away to his remote island compound, where she learns to shed her inhibitions with both men and women. Fully aroused for the first time in her life, she becomes a slave to his—and her—desires!

JOHN NORMAN
CAPTIVE OF GOR
$6.95/581-6
On Earth, Elinor Brinton was accustomed to having it all—wealth, beauty, and a host of men wrapped around her little finger. But Elinor's spoiled existence is a thing of the past. She is now a pleasure slave of Gor—a world whose society insists on her subservience to any man who calls her his own. And despite her headstrong past, Elinor finds herself succumbing—with pleasure—to her powerful Master....

MASQUERADE BOOKS

TARNSMAN OF GOR
$6.95/486-0
This controversial series returns! Tarl Cabot is transported to Gor. He must quickly accustom himself to the ways of this world, including the caste system which exalts some as Priest-Kings or Warriors, and debases others as slaves. The beginning of the epic which made Norman a household name among fans of both sci-fi and dominance/submission.

OUTLAW OF GOR
$6.95/487-9
Tarl Cabot returns to Gor. Upon arriving, he discovers that his name, his city and the names of those he loves have become unspeakable. Once a respected Tarnsman, Cabot has become an outlaw, and must discover his new purpose on this strange planet, where even simple answers have their price....

PRIEST-KINGS OF GOR
$6.95/488-7
Tarl Cabot searches for his lovely wife Talena. Does she live, or was she destroyed by the all-powerful Priest-Kings? Cabot is determined to find out—though no one who has approached the mountain stronghold of the Priest-Kings has ever returned alive....

NOMADS OF GOR
$6.95/527-1
Cabot finds his way across Gor, pledged to serve the Priest-Kings. Unfortunately for Cabot, his mission leads him to the savage Wagon People—nomads who may very well kill before surrendering any secrets....

ASSASSIN OF GOR
$6.95/538-7
The chronicles of Counter-Earth continue with this examination of Gorean society. Here is the caste system of Gor: from the Assassin Kuurus, on a mission of vengeance, to Pleasure Slaves, trained in the ways of personal ecstasy.

RAIDERS OF GOR
$6.95/558-1
Tarl Cabot descends into the depths of Port Kar—the most degenerate port city of the Counter-Earth. There Cabot learns the ways of Kar, whose residents are renowned for the grip in which they hold their voluptuous slaves....

SYDNEY ST. JAMES
RIVE GAUCHE
$5.95/317-1
The Latin Quarter, Paris, circa 1920. Expatriate bohemians couple wildly—before eventually abandoning their ambitions amidst the temptations waiting to be indulged in every bedroom.

DON WINSLOW
THE BEST OF DON WINSLOW
$6.95/607-3
Internationally best-selling fetish author Don Winslow personally selected his hottest passages for this special collection. Sizzling excerpts from *Claire's Girls*, *Gloria's Indiscretion*, *Katerina in Charge*, *The Insatiable Mistress of Rosedale*, *Secrets of Cheatem Manor*, and *The Many Pleasures of Ironwood* are artfully woven together to make this an extraordinary overview of Winslow's greatest hits.

SLAVE GIRLS OF ROME
$6.95/577-8
Never were women so relentlessly used as were ancient Rome's voluptuous slaves! With no choice but to serve their lustful masters, these captive beauties learn to perform their duties with the passion of Venus herself.

THE FALL OF THE ICE QUEEN
$6.50/520-4
Rahn the Conqueror chose a true beauty as his Consort. But the regal disregard with which she treated Rahn was not to be endured. It was decided that she would submit to his will—and as so many had learned, Rahn's depraved expectations have made his court infamous.

PRIVATE PLEASURES
$6.50/504-2
Frantic voyeurs and licentious exhibitionists are here displayed in all their wanton glory—laid bare by the perverse and probing eye of Don Winslow.

THE INSATIABLE MISTRESS OF ROSEDALE
$6.50/494-1
Edward and Lady Penelope reside in Rosedale manor. While Edward is a connoisseur of sexual perversion, it is Lady Penelope whose mastery of complete sensual pleasure makes their home infamous. Indulging one another's bizarre whims is a way of life for this wicked couple....

SECRETS OF CHEATEM MANOR
$6.50/434-8
Edward returns to oversee his late father's estate, only to find it being run by the majestic Lady Amanda—assisted by her two beautiful daughters, Catherine and Prudence. What the randy young man soon comes to realize is the love of discipline that all three beauties share.

KATERINA IN CHARGE
$5.95/409-7
When invited into a country retreat by a mysterious couple, two randy young ladies can hardly resist! Soon after they arrive, the imperious Katerina makes her desires known—and demands that they be fulfilled...

MASQUERADE BOOKS

THE MANY PLEASURES OF IRONWOOD
$5.95/310-4

Seven lovely young women are employed by The Ironwood Sportsmen's Club, where their natural talents in the sensual arts are put to creative use. Winslow explores the ins and outs of this small and exclusive club—where members live out each of their fantasies with one (or all!) of these seven carefully selected sexual playthings.

CLAIRE'S GIRLS
$5.95/442-9

You knew when she walked by that she was something special. She was one of Claire's girls, a woman carefully dressed and groomed to fill a role, to capture a look, to fit an image crafted by the sophisticated proprietress of an exclusive escort agency. High-class whores blow the roof off!

MARCUS VAN HELLER
KIDNAP
$4.95/90-4

P.I. Harding is called in to investigate a kidnapping case involving the rich and powerful. Along the way he has the pleasure of "interrogating" an exotic dancer and a beautiful English reporter, as he finds himself enmeshed in the sleazy international underworld.

ALEXANDER TROCCHI
YOUNG ADAM
$4.95/63-7

A classic of intrigue and perversion. Two British barge operators discover a girl drowned in the river Clyde. Her lover, a plumber, is arrested for her murder. But he is innocent. Joe, the barge assistant, knows that. As the plumber is tried and sentenced to hang, this knowledge lends poignancy to Joe's romances with the women along the river whom he will love then... well, read on.

N. WHALLEN
THE EDUCATION OF SITA MANSOOR
$6.95/567-0

On the eve of her wedding, Sita Mansoor is left without a bridegroom. Sita travels to America, where she hopes to become educated in the ways of a permissive society. She could never have imagined the wide variety of tutors—both male and female—who would be waiting to take on so beautiful a pupil. The ultimate in Sex Ed!

TAU'TEVU
$6.50/426-7

Statuesque and beautiful Vivian learns to subject herself to the hand of a domineering man. He systematically helps her prove her own strength, and brings to life in her an unimagined sensual fire.

ISADORA ALMAN
ASK ISADORA
$4.95/61-0

Six years' worth of Isadora's syndicated columns on sex and relationships. Alman's been called a "hip Dr. Ruth," and a "sexy Dear Abby," based upon the wit of her advice. Today's world is more perplexing than ever—and Alman is just the expert to help untangle the most personal of knots.

THE CLASSIC COLLECTION
THE ENGLISH GOVERNESS
$5.95/373-2

When Lord Lovell's son was expelled from his prep school for masturbation, his father hired a very proper governess to tutor the boy—giving her strict instructions not to spare the rod to break him of his bad habits. Luckily, Harriet Marwood was addicted to domination.

PROTESTS, PLEASURES, RAPTURES
$5.95/400-3

Invited for an allegedly quiet weekend at a country vicarage, a young woman is stunned to find herself surrounded by shocking acts of sexual sadism. Soon she begins to explore her own capacities for delicious sexual cruelty.

THE YELLOW ROOM
$5.95/378-3

The "yellow room" holds the secrets of lust, lechery, and the lash. There, bare-bottomed, spread-eagled, and open to the world, demure Alice Darvell soon learns to love her lickings.

SCHOOL DAYS IN PARIS
$5.95/325-2

Few Universities provide the profound and pleasurable lessons one learns in after-hours study— particularly if one is young and available, and lucky enough to have Paris as a playground. Here are all the randy pursuits of young adulthood.

MAN WITH A MAID
$4.95/307-4

The adventures of Jack and Alice have delighted readers for eight decades! A classic of its genre, *Man with a Maid* tells a tale of desire, revenge, and submission.

MASQUERADE BOOKS

MASQUERADE READERS
INTIMATE PLEASURES
$4.95/38-6

Indulge your most private penchants with this specially chosen selection of Masquerade's hottest moments. Try a tempting morsel of *The Prodigal Virgin* and *Eveline*, the bizarre public displays of carnality in *The Gilded Lily* or the relentless and shocking carnality of *The Story of Monique*.

CLASSIC EROTIC BIOGRAPHIES
JENNIFER AGAIN
$4.95/220-5

The uncensored life of one of modern erotica's most popular heroines. Once again, the insatiable Jennifer seizes the day and extracts every last drop of sensual pleasure! A thrilling peak at the mores of the uninhibited 1970s.

JENNIFER #3
$5.95/292-2

The adventures of erotica's most daring heroine. Jennifer has a photographer's eye for details—particularly of the male variety! One by one, her subjects submit to her demands for pleasure.

PAULINE
$4.95/129-2

From rural America to the royal court of Austria, Pauline follows her ever-growing sexual desires: "I would never see them again. Why shouldn't I give myself to them that they might become more and more inspired to deeds of greater lust!"

RHINOCEROS

M. CHRISTIAN, ED.
EROS EX MACHINA
$7.95/593-X

As the millennium approaches, technology is not only an inevitable, but a deeply desirable addition to daily life. *Eros Ex Machina: Eroticising the Mechanical* explores the thrill of machines—our literal and literary love of technology. Join over 25 of today's hottest writers as they explore erotic relationships with all kinds of gizmos, gadgets, and devices.

LEOPOLD VON SACHER-MASOCH
VENUS IN FURS
$7.95/589-1

The alliance of Severin and Wanda epitomizes Sacher-Masoch's obsession with a cruel goddess and the urges that drive the man held in her thrall. Exclusive to this edition are letters exchanged between Sacher-Masoch and Emilie Mataja—an aspiring writer he sought as the avatar of his desires.

JOHN NORMAN
IMAGINATIVE SEX
$7.95/561-1

The author of the Gor novels outlines his philosophy on relations between the sexes, and presents fifty-three scenarios designed to reintroduce fantasy to the bedroom.

KATHLEEN K.
SWEET TALKERS
$6.95/516-6

"If you enjoy eavesdropping on explicit conversations about sex... this book is for you."   —*Spectator*

Kathleen K. ran a phone-sex company in the late 80s, and she opens up her diary for a peek at the life of a phone-sex operator. Transcripts of actual conversations are included.
Trade /$12.95/192-6

THOMAS S. ROCHE
DARK MATTER
$6.95/484-4

"*Dark Matter* is sure to please gender outlaws, bodymod junkies, goth vampires, boys who wish they were dykes, and anybody who's not to sure where the fine line should be drawn between pleasure and pain. It's a handful." —Pat Califia

"Here is the erotica of the cumming millennium.... You will be deliciously disturbed, but never disappointed."
—Poppy Z. Brite

NOIROTICA 2: PULP FRICTION
$7.95/584-0

Another volume of criminally seductive stories set in the murky terrain of the erotic and noir genres. Thomas Roche has gathered the darkest jewels from today's edgiest writers to create this provocative collection. A must for all fans of contemporary erotica.

NOIROTICA: An Anthology of Erotic Crime Stories (Ed.)
$6.95/390-2

A collection of darkly sexy tales, taking place at the crossroads of the crime and erotic genres. Here are some of today's finest writers, all of whom explore the arousing terrain where desire runs irrevocably afoul of the law.

DAVID MELTZER
UNDER
$6.95/290-6

The story of a 21st century sex professional living at the bottom of the social heap. After surgeries designed to increase his physical allure, corrupt government forces drive the cyber-gigolo underground, where even more bizarre cultures await....

MASQUERADE BOOKS

ORF
$6.95/110-1

Meltzer's celebrated exploration of Eros and modern mythology returns. Orf is the ultimate hero—the idol of thousands, the fevered dream of many more. Every last drop of feeling is squeezed from a modern-day troubadour and his lady love in this psychedelic bacchanal.

LAURA ANTONIOU, ED.
SOME WOMEN
$7.95/573-5

Introduction by Pat Califia

"Makes the reader think about the wide range of SM experiences, beyond the glamour of fiction and fantasy, or the clever-clever prose of the perverati." —*SKIN TWO*

Over forty essays written by women actively involved in consensual dominance and submission. Professional mistresses, lifestyle leatherdykes, whipmakers, titleholders—women from every conceivable walk of life lay bare their true feelings about issues as explosive as feminism, abuse, pleasure and public image. A bestselling title, Some Women is a valuable resource for anyone interested in sexuality.

NO OTHER TRIBUTE
$7.95/603-0

Tales of women kept in bondage to their lovers by their deepest passions. Love pushes these women beyond acceptable limits, rendering them helpless to deny anything to the men and women they adore. A volume certain to challenge political correctness as few have before.

BY HER SUBDUED
$6.95/281-7

These tales all involve women in control—of their lives and their lovers. So much in control that they can remorselessly break rules to become powerful goddesses of those who sacrifice all to worship at their feet.

AMELIA G, ED.
BACKSTAGE PASSES:
Rock n' Roll Erotica from the
Pages of *Blue Blood* Magazine
$6.95/438-0

Amelia G, editor of the goth-sex journal *Blue Blood*, has brought together some of today's most irreverent writers, each of whom has outdone themselves with an edgy, antic tale of modern lust.

ROMY ROSEN
SPUNK
$6.95/492-5

Casey, a lovely model poised upon the verge of super-celebrity, falls for an insatiable young rock singer—not suspecting that his sexual appetite has led him to experiment with a dangerous new aphrodisiac. Soon, Casey becomes addicted to the drug, and her craving plunges her into a strange underworld, and into an alliance with a shadowy young man with secrets of his own....

MOLLY WEATHERFIELD
CARRIE'S STORY
$6.95/485-2

"I was stunned by how well it was written and how intensely foreign I found its sexual world.... And, since this is a world I don't frequent... I thoroughly enjoyed the National Geo tour." —*bOING bOING*

"Hilarious and harrowing... just when you think things can't get any wilder, they do." —*Black Sheets*

Weatherfield's bestselling examination of dominance and submission. "I had been Jonathan's slave for about a year when he told me he wanted to sell me at an auction...." A rare piece of erotica, both thoughtful and hot!

CYBERSEX CONSORTIUM
CYBERSEX: The Perv's Guide to
Finding Sex on the Internet
$6.95/471-2

You've heard the objections: cyberspace is soaked with sex, mired in immorality. Okay—so where is it!? Tracking down the good stuff—the real good stuff—can waste an awful lot of expensive time, and frequently leave you high and dry. The Cybersex Consortium presents an easy-to-use guide for those intrepid adults who know what they want.

LAURA ANTONIOU
("Sara Adamson")

"Ms. Adamson's friendly, conversational writing style perfectly couches what to some will be shocking material. Ms. Adamson creates a wonderfully diverse world of lesbian, gay, straight, bi and transgendered characters, all mixing delightfully in the melting pot of sadomasochism and planting the genre more firmly in the culture at large. I for one am cheering her on!" —Kate Bornstein

MASQUERADE BOOKS

THE MARKETPLACE
$7.95/602-2
The first title in Antoniou's thrilling Marketplace Trilogy, following the lives and lusts of those who have been deemed worthy to participate in the ultimate BDSM arena.

THE SLAVE
$7.95/601-4
The Slave covers the experience of one talented submissive who longs to join the ranks of those who have proven themselves worthy of entry into the Marketplace. But the price, while delicious, is staggeringly high....

THE TRAINER
$6.95/249-3
The Marketplace Trilogy concludes with the story of the trainers, and the desires and paths that led them to become the ultimate figures of authority.

GERI NETTICK
WITH BETH ELLIOT
MIRRORS: Portrait of a Lesbian Transsexual
$6.95/435-6
Born a male, Geri Nettick knew something just didn't fit. Even after coming to terms with her own gender dysphoria she still fought to be accepted by the lesbian feminist community to which she felt she belonged. A true story.

TRISTAN TAORMINO & DAVID AARON CLARK, EDS.
RITUAL SEX
$6.95/391-0
The contributors to *Ritual Sex* know that body and soul share more common ground than society feels comfortable acknowledging. From memoirs of ecstatic revelation, to quests to reconcile sex and spirit, *Ritual Sex* provides an unprecedented look at private life.

TAMMY JO ECKHART
AMAZONS: Erotic Explorations of Ancient Myths
$7.95/534-4
The Amazon—the fierce woman warrior—appears in the traditions of many cultures, but never before has the erotic potential of this archetype been explored with such imagination. Powerful pleasures await anyone lucky enough to encounter Eckhart's spitfires.

PUNISHMENT FOR THE CRIME
$6.95/427-5
Stories that explore dominance and submission. From an encounter between two of society's most despised individuals, to the explorations of longtime friends, these tales take you where few others have ever dared....

AMARANTHA KNIGHT, ED.
SEDUCTIVE SPECTRES
$6.95/464-X
Tours through the erotic supernatural via the imaginations of today's best writers. Never have ghostly encounters been so alluring, thanks to otherworldly characters well-acquainted with the pleasures of the flesh.

SEX MACABRE
$6.95/392-9
Horror tales designed for dark and sexy nights—sure to make your skin crawl, and heart beat faster.

FLESH FANTASTIC
$6.95/352-X
Humans have long toyed with the idea of "playing God": creating life from nothingness, bringing life to the inanimate. Now Amarantha Knight collects stories exploring not only the act of Creation, but the lust that follows.

GARY BOWEN
DIARY OF A VAMPIRE
$6.95/331-7
"Gifted with a darkly sensual vision and a fresh voice, [Bowen] is a writer to watch out for."   —Cecilia Tan

Rafael, a red-blooded male with an insatiable hunger for the same, is the perfect antidote to the effete malcontents haunting bookstores today. The emergence of a bold and brilliant vision, rooted in past and present.

RENÉ MAIZEROY
FLESHLY ATTRACTIONS
$6.95/299-X
Lucien was the son of the wantonly beautiful actress, Marie-Rose Hardanges. When she decides to let a "friend" introduce her son to the pleasures of love, Marie-Rose could not have foretold the excesses that would lead to her own ruin and that of her cherished son.

GRANT ANTREWS
LEGACIES
$7.95/605-7
Kathi Lawton discovers that she has inherited the troubling secret of her late mother's scandalous sexuality. In an effort to understand what motivated her mother's desires, Kathi embarks on an exploration of SM that leads her into the arms of Horace Moore, a mysterious man who seems to see into her very soul. As she begins falling for her new master, Kathi finds herself wondering just how far she'll go to prove her love.... Another moving exploration from the author of *My Darling Dominatrix*.

MASQUERADE BOOKS

ROGUES GALLERY
$6.95/522-0

A stirring evocation of dominant/submissive love. Two doctors meet and slowly fall in love. Once Beth reveals her hidden desires to Jim, the two explore the forbidden acts that will come to define their distinctly exotic affair.

MY DARLING DOMINATRIX
$7.95/566-2

When a man and a woman fall in love, it's supposed to be simple, uncomplicated, easy—unless that woman happens to be a dominatrix. This highly praised and unpretentious love story captures the richness and depth of this very special kind of love without leering or smirking.

SUBMISSIONS
$6.95/207-8

Antrews portrays the very special elements of the dominant/submissive relationship with restraint—this time with the story of a lonely man, a winning lottery ticket, and a demanding dominatrix.

JEAN STINE
THRILL CITY
$6.95/411-9

Thrill City is the seat of the world's increasing depravity, and this classic novel transports you there with a vivid style you'd be hard pressed to ignore. No writer is better suited to describe the extremes of this modern Babylon.

SEASON OF THE WITCH
$6.95/268-X

"A future in which it is technically possible to transfer the total mind...of a rapist killer into the brain dead but physically living body of his female victim. Remarkable for intense psychological technique. There is eroticism but it is necessary to mark the differences between the sexes and the subtle altering of a man into a woman." —*The Science Fiction Critic*

Jean Stine's undisputed masterpiece, and one of the earliest science-fiction novels to explore the complexities and contradictions of gender.

JOHN WARREN
THE TORQUEMADA KILLER
$6.95/367-8

Detective Eva Hernandez gets her first "big case": a string of murders taking place within New York's SM community. Eva assembles the evidence, revealing a picture of a world misunderstood and under attack—and gradually comes to face her own hidden longings.

THE LOVING DOMINANT
$7.95/600-6

Everything you need to know about an infamous sexual variation, and an unspoken type of love. Warren guides readers through this rarely seen world, and offers clear-eyed advice guaranteed to enlighten the most jaded erotic explorers.

DAVID AARON CLARK
SISTER RADIANCE
$6.95/215-9

A meditation on love, sex, and death. The vicissitudes of lust and romance are examined against a backdrop of urban decay in this testament to the allure of the forbidden.

THE WET FOREVER
$6.95/117-9

The story of Janus and Madchen—a small-time hood and a beautiful sex worker on the run—examines themes of loyalty, sacrifice, redemption and obsession amidst Manhattan's sex parlors and underground S/M clubs.

MICHAEL PERKINS
EVIL COMPANIONS
$6.95/3067-9

Evil Companions has been hailed as "a frightening classic." A young couple explores the nether reaches of the erotic unconscious in a confrontation with the extremes of passion.

THE SECRET RECORD:
Modern Erotic Literature
$6.95/3039-3

Michael Perkins surveys the field with authority and unique insight. Updated and revised to include the latest trends, tastes, and developments in this misunderstood genre.

AN ANTHOLOGY OF CLASSIC ANONYMOUS EROTIC WRITING
$6.95/140-3

Michael Perkins has collected the best passages from the world's erotic writing. "Anonymous" is one of the most infamous bylines in publishing history—and these excerpts show why!

HELEN HENLEY
ENTER WITH TRUMPETS
$6.95/197-7

Helen Henley was told that women just don't write about sex. So Henley did it alone, flying in the face of "tradition" by writing this touching tale of arousal and devotion in one couple's kinky relationship.

MASQUERADE BOOKS

ALICE JOANOU
CANNIBAL FLOWER
$4.95/72-6

"She is waiting in her darkened bedroom, as she has waited throughout history, to seduce the men who are foolish enough to be blinded by her irresistible charms.... She is the goddess of sexuality, and *Cannibal Flower* is her haunting siren song."
—Michael Perkins

BLACK TONGUE
$6.95/258-2

"Joanou has created a series of sumptuous, brooding, dark visions of sexual obsession, and is undoubtedly a name to look out for in the future."
—Redeemer

Exploring lust at its most florid and unsparing, *Black Tongue* is redolent of forbidden passions.

TOURNIQUET
$6.95/3060-1

A heady collection of stories and effusions. A riveting series of meditations on desire.

LIESEL KULIG
LOVE IN WARTIME
$6.95/3044-X

Madeleine knew that the handsome SS officer was dangerous, but she was just a cabaret singer in Nazi-occupied Paris, trying to survive in a perilous time. When Josef fell in love with her, he discovered that a beautiful woman can be as dangerous as any warrior.

SAMUEL R. DELANY
THE MAD MAN
$8.99/408-9/Mass market

"Delany develops an insightful dichotomy between [his protagonist]'s two worlds: the one of cerebral philosophy and dry academia, the other of heedless, 'impersonal' obsessive sexual extremism. When these worlds finally collide...the novel achieves a surprisingly satisfying resolution...."
—Publishers Weekly

Graduate student John Marr researches the life of Timothy Hasler: a philosopher whose career was cut tragically short over a decade earlier. Marr begins to find himself increasingly drawn toward shocking sexual encounters with the homeless men, until it begins to seem that Hasler's death might hold some key to his own life as a gay man in the age of AIDS.

DANIEL VIAN
ILLUSIONS
$6.95/3074-1

Two tales of danger and desire in Berlin on the eve of WWII. From private homes to lurid cafés, passion is exposed in stark contrast to the brutal violence of the time, as desperate people explore their darkest sexual desires.

PERSUASIONS
$4.95/183-7

"The stockings are drawn tight by the suspender belt, tight enough to be stretched to the limit just above the middle part of her thighs, tight enough so that her calves glow through the sheer silk..." A double novel, including the classics *Adagio* and *Gabriela and the General*, this volume traces lust around the globe.

PHILIP JOSÉ FARMER
A FEAST UNKNOWN
$6.95/276-0

"Sprawling, brawling, shocking, suspenseful, hilarious..."
—Theodore Sturgeon

Lord Grandrith—armed with the belief that he is the son of Jack the Ripper—tells the story of his remarkable life. His story progresses to encompass the furthest extremes of human behavior.

FLESH
$6.95/303-1

Stagg explored the galaxies for 800 years. Upon his return, the hero Stagg is made the centerpiece of an incredible public ritual—one that will take him to the heights of ecstasy, and drag him toward the depths of hell.

ANDREI CODRESCU
THE REPENTANCE OF LORRAINE
$6.95/329-5

"One of our most prodigiously talented and magical writers."
—NYT Book Review

An aspiring writer, a professor's wife, a secretary, gold anklets, Maoists, Roman harlots—and more—swirl through this spicy tale of a harried quest for a mythic artifact. Written when the author was a young man.

TUPPY OWENS
SENSATIONS
$6.95/3081-4

Tuppy Owens takes a rare peek behind the scenes of *Sensations*—the first big-budget sex flick. Originally commissioned to appear in book form after the release of the film in 1975, *Sensations* is finally available.

SOPHIE GALLEYMORE BIRD
MANEATER
$6.95/103-9

Through a bizarre act of creation, a man attains the "perfect" lover—by all appearances a beautiful, sensuous woman, but in reality something far darker. Once brought to life she will accept no mate, seeking instead the prey that will sate her hunger.

BADBOY

DAVID MAY
MADRUGADA
$6.95/574-3

Set in San Francisco's gay leather community, *Madrugada* follows the lives of a group of friends—and their many acquaintances—as they tangle with the thorny issues of love and lust. Uncompromising, mysterious, and arousing, David May weaves a complex web of relationships in this unique story cycle.

PETER HEISTER
ISLANDS OF DESIRE
$6.95/480-1

Red-blooded lust on the wine-dark seas of classical Greece. Anacraeon yearns to leave his small, isolated island and find adventure in one of the overseas kingdoms. Accompanied by some randy friends, Anacraeon makes his dream come true—and discovers pleasures he never dreamed of!

KITTY TSUI WRITING AS "ERIC NORTON"
SPARKS FLY
$6.95/551-4

The highest highs—and most wretched depths—of life as Eric Norton, a beautiful wanton living San Francisco's high life. *Sparks Fly* traces Norton's rise, fall, and resurrection, vividly marking the way with the personal affairs that give life meaning.

BARRY ALEXANDER
ALL THE RIGHT PLACES
$6.95/482-8

Stories filled with hot studs in lust and love. From modern masters and slaves to medieval royals and their subjects, Alexander explores the mating rituals men have engaged in for centuries—all in the name of desire...

MICHAEL FORD, ED.
BUTCHBOYS:
Stories For Men Who Need It Bad
$6.50/523-9

A big volume of tales dedicated to the rough-and-tumble type who can make a man weak at the knees. Some of today's best erotic writers explore the many possible variations on the age-old fantasy of the thoroughly dominating man.

WILLIAM J. MANN, ED.
GRAVE PASSIONS:
Gay Tales of the Supernatural
$6.50/405-4

A collection of the most chilling tales of passion currently being penned by today's most provocative gay writers. Unnatural transformations, otherworldly encounters, and deathless desires make for a collection sure to keep readers up late at night.

J. A. GUERRA, ED.
COME QUICKLY:
For Boys on the Go
$6.50/413-5

Here are over sixty of the hottest fantasies around—all designed to get you going in less time than it takes to dial 976. Julian Anthony Guerra, the editor behind the popular *Men at Work* and *Badboy Fantasies*, has put together this volume especially for you—a busy man on a modern schedule, who still appreciates a little old-fashioned action.

JOHN PRESTON
HUSTLING: A Gentleman's Guide to the Fine Art of Homosexual Prostitution
$6.50/517-4

"Fun and highly literary. What more could you expect form such an accomplished activist, author and editor?" —*Drummer*

John Preston solicited the advice and opinions of "working boys" from across the country in his effort to produce the ultimate guide to the hustler's world. *Hustling* covers every practical aspect of the business, from clientele and payment to "specialties," and drawbacks.
Trade $12.95/137-3

MR. BENSON
$4.95/3041-5

Jamie is an aimless young man lucky enough to encounter Mr. Benson. He is soon learns to accept this man as his master. Jamie's incredible adventures never fail to excite—especially when the going gets rough!

TALES FROM THE DARK LORD
$5.95/323-6

Twelve stunning works from the man *Lambda Book Report* called "the Dark Lord of gay erotica." The relentless ritual of lust and surrender is explored in all its manifestations in this heart-stopping triumph of authority and vision.

TALES FROM THE DARK LORD II
$4.95/176-4
THE ARENA
$4.95/3083-0
Preston's take on the ultimate sex club—where men go to abolish all personal limits. Only the author of *Mr. Benson* could have imagined so perfect an institution for the satisfaction of male desire.

THE HEIR•THE KING
$4.95/3048-2
The Heir, written in the lyric voice of the ancient myths, tells the story of a world where slaves and masters create a new sexual society. *The King* tells the story of a soldier who discovers his monarch's most secret desires.

THE MISSION OF ALEX KANE
SWEET DREAMS
$4.95/3062-8
It's the triumphant return of gay action hero Alex Kane! In *Sweet Dreams*, Alex travels to Boston where he takes on a street gang that stalks gay teenagers.

GOLDEN YEARS
$4.95/3069-5
When evil threatens the plans of a group of older gay men, Kane's got the muscle to take it head on. Along the way, he wins the support—and very specialized attentions—of a cowboy plucked right out of the Old West.

DEADLY LIES
$4.95/3076-8
Politics is a dirty business and the dirt becomes deadly when a smear campaign targets gay men. Who better to clean things up than Alex Kane!

STOLEN MOMENTS
$4.95/3098-9
Houston's evolving gay community is victimized by a malicious newspaper editor who is more than willing to boost circulation by printing homophobic slander. He never counted on Alex Kane, fearless defender of gay dreams and desires.

SECRET DANGER
$4.95/111-X
Alex Kane and the faithful Danny are called to a small European country, where a group of gay tourists is being held hostage by brutal terrorists.

LETHAL SILENCE
$4.95/125-X
Chicago becomes the scene of the right-wing's most noxious plan—facilitated by unholy political alliances. Alex and Danny head to the Windy City to battle the mercenaries who would squash gay men underfoot.

MATT TOWNSEND
SOLIDLY BUILT
$6.50/416-X
The tale of the relationship between Jeff, a young photographer, and Mark, the butch electrician hired to wire Jeff's new home. For Jeff, it's love at first sight; Mark, however, has more than a few hang-ups.

JAY SHAFFER
SHOOTERS
$5.95/284-1
No mere catalog of random acts, *Shooters* tells the stories of a variety of stunning men and the ways they connect in sexual and non-sexual ways. Shaffer always gets his man.

ANIMAL HANDLERS
$4.95/264-7
In Shaffer's world, every man finally succumbs to the animal urges deep inside. And if there's any creature that promises a wild time, it's a beast who's been caged for far too long.

FULL SERVICE
$4.95/150-0
No-nonsense guys bear down hard on each other as they work their way toward release in this finely detailed assortment of fantasies.

D. V. SADERO
IN THE ALLEY
$4.95/144-6
Hardworking men bring their special skills and impressive tools to the most satisfying job of all: capturing and breaking the male animal.

SCOTT O'HARA
DO-IT-YOURSELF PISTON POLISHING
$6.50/489-5
Longtime sex-pro Scott O'Hara draws upon his acute powers of seduction to lure you into a world of hard, horny men long overdue for a tune-up.

SUTTER POWELL
EXECUTIVE PRIVILEGES
$6.50/383-X
No matter how serious or sexy a predicament his characters find themselves in, Powell conveys the sheer exuberance of their encounters with a warm humor rarely seen in contemporary gay erotica.

GARY BOWEN
WESTERN TRAILS
$6.50/477-1
Some of gay literature's brightest stars tell the sexy truth about the many ways a rugged stud found to satisfy himself—and his buddy—in the Very Wild West.

MASQUERADE BOOKS

MAN HUNGRY
$5.95/374-0
A riveting collection of stories from one of gay erotica's new stars. Dipping into a variety of genres, Bowen crafts tales of lust unlike anything being published today.

KYLE STONE
THE HIDDEN SLAVE
$6.95/580-8
"This perceptive and finely-crafted work is a joy to discover. Kyle Stone's fiction belongs on the shelf of every serious fan of gay literature."
—Pat Califia

"Once again, Kyle Stone proves that imagination, ingenuity, and sheer intellectual bravado go a long way in making porn hot. This book turns us on and makes us think. Who could ask for anything more?"
—Michael Bronski

HOT BAUDS 2
$6.50/479-8
Stone conducted another heated search through the world's randiest gay bulletin boards, resulting in one of the most scalding follow-ups ever published.

HOT BAUDS
$5.95/285-X
Stone combed cyberspace for the hottest fantasies of the world's horniest hackers. Sexy, shameless, and eminently user-friendly.

FIRE & ICE
$5.95/297-3
A collection of stories from the author of the adventures of PB 500. Stone's characters always promise one thing: enough hot action to burn away your desire for anyone else....

FANTASY BOARD
$4.95/212-4
Explore the future—through the intertwined lives of a collection of randy computer hackers. On the Lambda Gate BBS, every horny male is in search of virtual satisfaction!

THE CITADEL
$4.95/198-5
The sequel to PB 500. Micah faces new challenges after entering the Citadel. Only his master knows what awaits....

THE INITIATION OF PB 500
$4.95/141-1
He is a stranger on their planet, unschooled in their language, and ignorant of their customs. But Micah will soon be trained in every detail of erotic service. When his training is complete, he must prove himself worthy of the master who has chosen him....

RITUALS
$4.95/168-3
Via a computer bulletin board, a young man finds himself drawn into sexual rites that transform him into the willing slave of a mysterious stranger. His former life is thrown off, and he learns to live for his Master's touch....

ROBERT BAHR
SEX SHOW
$4.95/225-6
Luscious dancing boys. Brazen, explicit acts. Take a seat, and get very comfortable, because the curtain's going up on a very special show no discriminating appetite can afford to miss.

JASON FURY
THE ROPE ABOVE, THE BED BELOW
$4.95/269-8
A vicious murderer is preying upon New York's go-go boys. In order to solve this mystery and save lives, each studly suspect must lay bare his soul—and more!

ERIC'S BODY
$4.95/151-9
Follow the irresistible Jason through sexual adventures unlike any you have ever read—touching on the raunchy, the romantic, and a number of highly sensitive areas in between....

1 900 745-HUNG

THE connection for hot handfuls of eager guys! No credit card needed—so call now for access to the hottest party line available. Spill it all to bad boys from across the country! (Must be over 18.) Pick one up now.... $3.98 per min.

LARS EIGHNER
WANK: THE TAPES
$6.95/588-3
Lars Eighner gets back to basics with this look at every guy's favorite pastime. Horny studs bare it all and work up a healthy sweat during these provocative discussions about masturbation.

WHISPERED IN THE DARK
$5.95/286-8
A volume demonstrating Eighner's unique combination of strengths: poetic descriptive power, an unfailing ear for dialogue, and a finely tuned feeling for the nuances of male passion. An extraordinary collection of this influential writer's work.

BUY ANY 4 BOOKS & CHOOSE 1 ADDITIONAL BOOK, OF EQUAL OR LESSER VALUE, AS YOUR FREE GIFT

MASQUERADE BOOKS

AMERICAN PRELUDE
$4.95/170-5
Eighner is one of gay erotica's true masters, producing wonderfully written tales of all-American lust, peopled with red-blooded, oversexed studs.

DAVID LAURENTS, ED.
SOUTHERN COMFORT
$6.50/466-6
Editor David Laurents now unleashes a collection of tales focusing on the American South—stories reflecting the many sexy contributions the region has made to the iconography of the American Male.

WANDERLUST:
Homoerotic Tales of Travel
$5.95/395-3
A volume dedicated to the special pleasures of faraway places—and the horny men who lie in wait for intrepid tourists. Celebrate the freedom of the open road, and the allure of men who stray from the beaten path....

THE BADBOY BOOK
OF EROTIC POETRY
$5.95/382-1
Erotic poetry has long been the problem child of the literary world—highly creative and provocative, but somehow too frank to be "art." *The Badboy Book of Erotic Poetry* restores eros to its place of honor in gay writing.

AARON TRAVIS
BIG SHOTS
$5.95/448-8
Two fierce tales in one electrifying volume. In *Beirut*, Travis tells the story of ultimate military power and erotic subjugation; *Kip*, Travis' hypersexed and sinister take on *film noir*, appears in unexpurgated form for the first time.

EXPOSED
$4.95/126-8
A unique glimpse of the horny gay male in his natural environment! Cops, college jocks, ancient Romans—even Sherlock Holmes and his loyal Watson—cruise these pages, fresh from the pen of one of our hottest authors.

BEAST OF BURDEN
$4.95/105-5
Innocents surrender to the brutal sexual mastery of their superiors, as taboos are shattered and replaced with the unwritten rules of masculine conquest. Intense and extreme.

IN THE BLOOD
$5.95/283-3
Early tales from this master of the genre. Includes "In the Blood"—a heart-pounding descent into sexual vampirism.

THE FLESH FABLES
$4.95/243-4
One of Travis' best collections. Includes "Blue Light," as well as other masterpieces that established him as the erotic writer to watch.

BOB VICKERY
SKIN DEEP
$4.95/265-5
So many varied beauties no one will go away unsatisfied. No tantalizing morsel of manflesh is overlooked—or left unexplored!

JR
FRENCH QUARTER NIGHTS
$5.95/337-6
Sensual snapshots of the many places where men get down and dirty—from the steamy French Quarter to the steam room at the old Everard baths.

TOM BACCHUS
RAHM
$5.95/315-5
Tom Bacchus brings to life an extraordinary assortment of characters, from the Father of Us All to the cowpoke next door, the early gay literati to rude, queercore mosh rats.

BONE
$4.95/177-2
Queer musings from the pen of one of today's hottest young talents. Tom Bacchus maps out the tricking ground of a new generation.

KEY LINCOLN
SUBMISSION HOLDS
$4.95/266-3
From tough to tender, the men between these covers stop at nothing to get what they want. These sweat-soaked tales show just how bad boys can really get.

CALDWELL/EIGHNER
QSFX2
$5.95/278-7
Other-worldly yarns from two master storytellers—Clay Caldwell and Lars Eighner. Both eroticists take a trip to the furthest reaches of the sexual imagination, sending back ten scalding sci-fi stories of male desire.

CLAY CALDWELL
JOCK STUDS
$6.95/472-0
Scalding tales of pumped bodies and raging libidos. Swimmers, runners, football players—whatever your sport might be, there's a man here waiting to work up a little sweat, peel off his uniform, and claim his reward for a game well-played....

MASQUERADE BOOKS

ASK OL' BUDDY
$5.95/346-5

Set in the underground SM world—where men initiate one another into the secrets of the rawest sexual realm of all. And when each stud's initiation is complete, he takes part in the training of another hungry soul....

STUD SHORTS
$5.95/320-1

"If anything, Caldwell's charm is more powerful, his nostalgia more poignant, the horniness he captures more sweetly, achingly acute than ever."
—Aaron Travis

A new collection of this legend's latest sex-fiction. Caldwell tells all about cops, cadets, truckers, farmboys (and many more) in these dirty jewels.

TAILPIPE TRUCKER
$5.95/296-5

Trucker porn! Caldwell tells the truth about Trag and Curly—two men hot for the feeling of sweaty manflesh. Together, they pick up—and turn out—a couple of thrill-seeking punks.

SERVICE, STUD
$5.95/336-8

Another look at the gay future. The setting is the Los Angeles of a distant future. Here the all-male populace is divided between the served and the servants—guaranteeing the erotic satisfaction of all involved.

QUEERS LIKE US
$4.95/262-0

For years the name Clay Caldwell has been synonymous with the hottest, most finely crafted gay tales available. Queers Like Us is one of his best: the story of a randy mailman's trek through a landscape of available studs.

ALL-STUD
$4.95/104-7

This classic, sex-soaked tale takes place under the watchful eye of Number Ten: an omniscient figure who has decreed unabashed promiscuity as the law of his all-male land.

CLAY CALDWELL & AARON TRAVIS
TAG TEAM STUDS
$6.50/465-8

Wrestling will never seem the same, once you've made your way through this assortment of sweaty studs. But you'd better be wary—should one catch you off guard, you just might spend the night pinned to the mat....

LARRY TOWNSEND
LEATHER AD: M
$5.95/380-5

John's curious about what goes on between the leatherclad men he's fantasized about. He takes out a personal ad, and starts a journey of discovery that will leave no part of his life unchanged.

LEATHER AD: S
$5.95/407-0

The tale continues—this time told from a Top's perspective. A simple ad generates many responses, and one man puts these studs through their paces....

1·800·906·HUNK

Hardcore phone action for real men. A scorching assembly of studs is waiting for your call—and eager to give you the headtrip of your life! Totally live, guaranteed one-on-one encounters. (Must be over 18.) No credit card needed. $3.98 per minute.

BEWARE THE GOD WHO SMILES
$5.95/321-X

Two lusty young Americans are transported to ancient Egypt—where they are embroiled in warfare and taken as slaves by barbarians. The two finally discover that the key to escape lies within their own rampant libidos.

2069 TRILOGY
(This one-volume collection only $6.95)244-2

The early science-fiction trilogy in one volume! Here is the tight plotting and shameless all-male sex action that established Townsend as one of erotica's masters.

MIND MASTER
$4.95/209-4

Who better to explore the territory of erotic dominance than an author who helped define the genre—and knows that ultimate mastery always transcends the physical.

THE LONG LEATHER CORD
$4.95/201-9

Chuck's stepfather never lacks money or male visitors with whom he enacts intense sexual rituals. As Chuck comes to terms with his own desires, he begins to unravel the mystery behind his stepfather's secret life.

THE SCORPIUS EQUATION
$4.95/119-5

The story of a man caught between the demands of two galactic empires. Our randy hero must match wits—and more—with the incredible forces that rule his world.

BUY ANY 4 BOOKS & CHOOSE 1 ADDITIONAL BOOK, OF EQUAL OR LESSER VALUE, AS YOUR FREE GIFT

MASQUERADE BOOKS

MAN SWORD
$4.95/188-8
The *trés gai* tale of France's King Henri III, who encounters enough sexual schemers and politicos to alter one's picture of history forever! Witness the unbridled licentiousness of one of Europe's most notorious courts.

THE FAUSTUS CONTRACT
$4.95/167-5
Two cocky young hustlers get more than they bargained for in this story of lust and its discontents.

CHAINS
$4.95/158-6
Picking up street punks has always been risky, but here it sets off a string of events that must be read to be believed. The legendary Townsend at his grittiest.

KISS OF LEATHER
$4.95/161-6
A look at the acts and attitudes of an earlier generation of gay leathermen. Sensual pain and pleasure mix in this classic tale.

RUN, LITTLE LEATHER BOY
$4.95/143-8
The famous tale of sexual awakening. A chronic underachiever, Wayne seems to be going nowhere fast. He finds himself drawn to the masculine intensity of a dark and mysterious sexual underground, where he soon finds many goals worth pursuing....

RUN NO MORE
$4.95/152-7
The sequel to *Run, Little Leather Boy*. This volume follows the further adventures of Townsend's leatherclad narrator as he travels every sexual byway available to the S/M male.

THE SEXUAL ADVENTURES OF SHERLOCK HOLMES
$4.95/3097-0
A scandalously sexy take on the notorious sleuth. Via the unexpurgated diary of Holmes' horny sidekick Watson, "A Study in Scarlet" is transformed to expose the Diogenes Club as an S/M arena, and clues only the redoubtable—and horny—Sherlock Holmes could piece together.

THE GAY ADVENTURES OF CAPTAIN GOOSE
$4.95/169-1
Jerome Gander is sentenced to serve aboard a ship manned by the most hardened, unrepentant criminals. In no time, Gander becomes one of the most notorious rakehells Merrie Olde England had ever seen. On land or sea, Gander hunts down the Empire's hottest studs.

DONALD VINING
CABIN FEVER AND OTHER STORIES
$5.95/338-4
"Demonstrates the wisdom experience combined with insight and optimism can create." —*Bay Area Reporter*

Eighteen blistering stories in celebration of the most intimate of male bonding, reaffirming both love and lust in modern gay life.

DEREK ADAMS
MILES DIAMOND AND THE CASE OF THE CRETAN APOLLO
$6.95/381-3
Hired by a wealthy man to track a cheating lover, Miles finds himself involved in ways he could never have imagined! When the jealous Callahan threatens not only Diamond but his innocent an studly assistant, Miles counters with a little undercover work—involving as many horny informants as he can get his hands on!

PRISONER OF DESIRE
$6.50/439-9
Red-blooded, sweat-soaked excursions through the modern gay libido.

THE MARK OF THE WOLF
$5.95/361-9
The past comes back to haunt one well-off stud, whose desires lead him into the arms of many men—and the midst of a mystery.

MY DOUBLE LIFE
$5.95/314-7
Every man leads a double life, dividing his hours between the mundanities of the day and the pursuits of the night. Derek Adams shines a little light on the wicked things men do when no one's looking.

HEAT WAVE
$4.95/159-4
Derek Adams sexy short stories are guaranteed to jump start any libido—and *Heatwave* contains his very best.

MILES DIAMOND AND THE DEMON OF DEATH
$4.95/251-5
Miles always find himself in the stickiest situations—with any stud he meets! This adventure promises another carnal carnival, as Diamond investigates a host of horny guys.

THE ADVENTURES OF MILES DIAMOND
$4.95/118-7
The debut of this popular gay gumshoe. To Diamond's delight, "The Case of the Missing Twin" is packed with randy studs. Miles sets about uncovering all as he tracks down the delectable Daniel Travis.

MASQUERADE BOOKS

KELVIN BELIELE
IF THE SHOE FITS
$4.95/223-X
An essential volume of tales exploring a world where randy boys can't help but do what comes naturally—as often as possible! Sweaty male bodies grapple in pleasure.

JAMES MEDLEY
THE REVOLUTIONARY & OTHER STORIES
$6.50/417-8
Billy, the son of the station chief of the American Embassy in Guatemala, is kidnapped and held for ransom. Frightened at first, Billy gradually develops an unimaginably close relationship with Juan, the revolutionary assigned to guard him.

HUCK AND BILLY
$4.95/245-0
Young lust knows no bounds—and is often the hottest of one's life! Huck and Billy explore the desires that course through their bodies, determined to plumb the depths of passion.

FLEDERMAUS
FLEDERFICTION: STORIES OF MEN AND TORTURE
$5.95/355-4
Fifteen blistering paeans to men and their suffering. Unafraid of exploring the furthest reaches of pain and pleasure, Fledermaus unleashes his most thrilling tales in this volume.

VICTOR TERRY
MASTERS
$6.50/418-6
Terry's butchest tales. A powerhouse volume of boot-wearing, whip-wielding, bone-crunching bruisers who've got what it takes to make a grown man grovel.

SM/SD
$6.50/406-2
Set around a South Dakota town called Prairie, these tales offer evidence that the real rough stuff can still be found where men take what they want despite all rules.

WHIPs
$4.95/254-X
Cruising for a hot man? You'd better be, because one way or another, these WHIPs—officers of the Wyoming Highway Patrol—are gonna pull you over for a little impromptu interrogation....

MAX EXANDER
DEEDS OF THE NIGHT: Tales of Eros and Passion
$5.95/348-1
MAXimum porn! Exander's a writer who's seen it all—and is more than happy to describe every glorious inch of it in pulsating detail. A whirlwind tour of the hypermasculine libido.

LEATHERSEX
$4.95/210-8
Hard-hitting tales from merciless Max. This time he focuses on the leather clad lust that draws together only the most willing and talented of tops and bottoms—for an all-out orgy of limitless surrender and control....

MANSEX
$4.95/160-8
"Mark was the classic leatherman: a huge, dark stud in chaps, with a big black moustache, hairy chest and enormous muscles. Exactly the kind of men Todd liked—strong, hunky, masculine, ready to take control...."

TOM CAFFREY
TALES FROM THE MEN'S ROOM
$5.95/364-3
Male lust at its most elemental and arousing. The Men's Room is less a place than a state of mind—one that every man finds himself in, day after day....

HITTING HOME
$4.95/222-1
Titillating and compelling, the stories in *Hitting Home* make a strong case for there being only one thing on a man's mind.

"BIG" BILL JACKSON
EIGHTH WONDER
$4.95/200-0
"Big" Bill Jackson's always the randiest guy in town—no matter what town he's in. From the bright lights and back rooms of New York to the open fields and sweaty bods of a small Southern town, "Big" Bill always manages to cause a scene!

TORSTEN BARRING
GUY TRAYNOR
$6.50/414-3
Some call Guy Traynor a theatrical genius; others say he was a madman. All anyone knows for certain is that his productions were the result of blood, sweat and outrageous erotic torture!

MASQUERADE BOOKS

PRISONERS OF TORQUEMADA
$5.95/252-3
Another volume sure to push you over the edge. How cruel is the "therapy" practiced at Casa Torquemada? Rest assured that Barring is just the writer to evoke such steamy sexual malevolence.

SHADOWMAN
$4.95/178-0
From spoiled aristocrats to randy youths sowing wild oats at the local picture show, Barring's imagination works overtime in these steamy vignettes of homolust.

PETER THORNWELL
$4.95/149-7
Follow the exploits of Peter Thornwell and his outrageously horny cohorts as he goes from misspent youth to scandalous stardom, all thanks to an insatiable libido and love for the lash. The first of Torsten Barring's popular SM novels.

THE SWITCH
$4.95/3061-X
Sometimes a man needs a good whipping, and *The Switch* certainly makes a case! Packed with hot studs and unrelenting passions, these stories established Barring as a writer to be watched.

BERT McKENZIE
FRINGE BENEFITS
$5.95/354-6
From the pen of a widely published short story writer comes a volume of highly immodest tales. Not afraid of getting down and dirty, McKenzie produces some of today's most visceral sextales.

CHRISTOPHER MORGAN
STEAM GAUGE
$6.50/473-9
This volume abounds in manly men doing what they do best—to, with, or for any hot stud who crosses their paths.

THE SPORTSMEN
$5.95/385-6
A collection of super-hot stories dedicated to the all-American athlete. These writers know just the type of guys that make up every red-blooded male's starting line-up....

MUSCLE BOUND
$4.95/3028-8
In the NYC bodybuilding scene, Tommy joins forces with sexy Will Rodriguez in a battle of wits and biceps at the hottest gym in town, where the weak are bound and crushed by iron-pumping gods.

SONNY FORD
REUNION IN FLORENCE
$4.95/3070-9
Follow Adrian and Tristan an a sexual odyssey that takes in all ports known to ancient man. From lustful Turks to insatiable Mamluks, these two spread pleasure throughout the classical world!

ROGER HARMAN
FIRST PERSON
$4.95/179-9
Each story takes the form of a confessional—told by men who've got plenty to confess! From the "first time ever" to firsts of different kinds....

J. A. GUERRA, ED.
SLOW BURN
$4.95/3042-3
Torsos get lean and hard, pecs widen, and stomachs ripple in these sexy stories of the power and perils of physical perfection.

DAVE KINNICK
SORRY I ASKED
$4.95/3090-3
Unexpurgated interviews with gay porn's rank and file. Get personal with the men behind (and under) the "stars," and discover the hot truth about the porn business.

SEAN MARTIN
SCRAPBOOK
$4.95/224-8
From the creator of *Doc and Raider* comes this hot collection of life's horniest moments—all involving studs sure to set your pulse racing!

CARO SOLES & STAN TAL, EDS.
BIZARRE DREAMS
$4.95/187-X
An anthology of voices dedicated to exploring the dark side of human fantasy. Here are the most talented practitioners of "dark fantasy," the most forbidden sexual realm of all.

MICHAEL LOWENTHAL, ED.
THE BADBOY EROTIC LIBRARY Volume 1
$4.95/190-X
Excerpts from *A Secret Life, Imre, Sins of the Cities of the Plain, Teleny* and others.

THE BADBOY EROTIC LIBRARY Volume 2
$4.95/211-6
This time, selections are taken from *Mike and Me, Muscle Bound, Men at Work, Badboy Fantasies,* and *Slowburn.*

MASQUERADE BOOKS

ERIC BOYD

MIKE AND ME
$5.95/419-4

Mike joined the gym squad to bulk up on muscle. Little did he know he'd be turning on every sexy muscle jock in Minnesota! Hard bodies collide in a series of horny workouts.

MIKE AND THE MARINES
$6.50/497-6

Mike takes on America's most elite corps of studs! Join in on the never-ending sexual escapades of this singularly lustful platoon!

ANONYMOUS

A SECRET LIFE
$4.95/3017-2

Meet Master Charles: eighteen and quite innocent, until his arrival at the Sir Percival's Academy, where the lessons are supplemented with a crash course in pure sexual heat!

SINS OF THE CITIES OF THE PLAIN
$5.95/322-8

Indulge yourself in the scorching memoirs of young man-about-town Jack Saul! Jack's sinful escapades grow wilder with every chapter!

IMRE
$4.95/3019-9

An extraordinary lost classic of obsession, gay erotic desire, and romance in a small European town on the eve of WWI.

TELENY
$4.95/3020-2

Often attributed to Oscar Wilde. A young man dedicates himself to a succession of forbidden pleasures.

THE SCARLET PANSY
$4.95/189-6

Randall Etrange travels the world in search of true love. Along the way, his journey becomes a sexual odyssey of truly epic proportions.

PAT CALIFIA, ED.

THE SEXPERT
$4.95/3034-2

From penis size to toy care, bar behavior to AIDS awareness, The Sexpert responds to real concerns with uncanny wisdom and a razor wit.

HARD CANDY

ELISE D'HAENE

LICKING OUR WOUNDS
$7.95/605-7

"A fresh, engagingly sarcastic and determinedly bawdy voice. D'Haene is blessed with a savvy, iconoclastic view of the world that is mordant but never mean." —*Publisher's Weekly*

Licking Our Wounds, Elise D'Haene's acclaimed debut novel, is the story of Maria, a young woman coming to terms with the complexities of life in the age of AIDS. Abandoned by her lover and faced with the deaths of her friends, Maria struggles along with the help of Peter, HIV-positive and deeply conflicted about the changes in his own life, and Christie, a lover who is full of her own ideas about truth and the meaning of life.

CHEA VILLANUEVA

BULLETPROOF BUTCHES
$7.95/560-3

"...Gutsy, hungry, and outrageous, but with a tender core... Villanueva is a writer to watch out for: she will teach us something." —Joan Nestle

One of lesbian literature's most uncompromising voices. Never afraid to address the harsh realities of working-class lesbian life, Chea Villanueva charts territory frequently overlooked in the age of "lesbian chic."

KEVIN KILLIAN

ARCTIC SUMMER
$6.95/514-X

An examination of the emptiness lying beneath the rich exterior of America in the 50s. With the story of Liam Reilly—a young gay man of considerable means and numerous secrets—Killian exposes the contradictions of the American Dream.

MICHAEL ROWE

WRITING BELOW THE BELT:
Conversations with Erotic Authors
$7.95/540-9

"An in-depth and enlightening tour of society's love/hate relationship with sex, morality, and censorship." —*James White Review*

Michael Rowe interviewed the best and brightest erotic writers and presents the collected wisdom in *Writing Below the Belt*. Includes interviews with such cult sensations as John Preston, Larry Townsend, Pat Califia, and others.

MASQUERADE BOOKS

PAUL T. ROGERS
SAUL'S BOOK
$7.95/462-3
Winner of the Editors' Book Award

"A first novel of considerable power... Speaks to us all."
— New York Times Book Review

The story of a Times Square hustler, Sinbad the Sailor, and Saul, a brilliant, self-destructive, alcoholic, dominating character who may be the only love Sinbad will ever know. A classic tale of desire, obsession and the terrible wages of love.

STAN LEVENTHAL
BARBIE IN BONDAGE
$6.95/415-1
Widely regarded as one of the most clear-eyed interpreters of big city gay male life, Leventhal here provides a series of explorations of love and desire between men.
SKYDIVING ON CHRISTOPHER STREET
$6.95/287-6
"Positively addictive." — Dennis Cooper

Aside from a hateful job, a hateful apartment, a hateful world and an increasingly hateful lover, life seems, well, all right for the protagonist of Stan Leventhal's latest novel. An insightful tale of contemporary urban gay life.

BRAD GOOCH
THE GOLDEN AGE OF PROMISCUITY
$7.95/550-6
"The next best thing to taking a time-machine trip to grovel in the glorious '70s gutter." — San Francisco Chronicle

"A solid, unblinking, unsentimental look at a vanished era. Gooch tells us everything we ever wanted to know about the dark and decadent gay subculture in Manhattan before AIDS altered the landscape." — Kirkus Reviews

RED JORDAN AROBATEAU
DIRTY PICTURES
$5.95/345-7
Dirty Pictures is the story of a lonely butch tending bar—and the femme she finally calls her own.
LUCY AND MICKEY
$6.95/311-2
"A necessary reminder to all who blissfully—some may say ignorantly—ride the wave of lesbian chic into the mainstream." — Heather Findlay

The story of Mickey—an uncompromising butch—and her long affair with Lucy, the femme she loves.

PATRICK MOORE
IOWA
$6.95/423-2
"Full of terrific characters etched in acid-sharp prose, soaked through with just enough ambivalence to make it thoroughly romantic." — Felice Picano

The raw tale of one gay man's journey into adulthood, and the roads that bring him home again.

WALTER R. HOLLAND
THE MARCH
$6.95/429-1
Beginning on a hot summer night in 1980, The March revolves around a circle of young gay men, and the many others their lives touch. Over time, each character changes in unexpected ways; lives and loves come together and fall apart, as society itself is horribly altered by the onslaught of AIDS.

DONALD VINING
A GAY DIARY
$8.95/451-8
"A Gay Diary is, unquestionably, the richest historical document of gay male life in the United States that I have ever encountered...." — Body Politic

Vining's Diary portrays a vanished age and the lifestyle of a generation frequently forgotten.

LARS EIGHNER
GAY COSMOS
$6.95/236-1
An analysis of gay culture. Praised by the press, Gay Cosmos is an important contribution to the area of Gay and Lesbian Studies.

FELICE PICANO
AMBIDEXTROUS
$6.95/275-2
"Makes us remember what it feels like to be a child..." — The Advocate

Picano tells all about his formative years: home life, school face-offs, the ingenuous sophistications of his first sexual steps.
MEN WHO LOVED ME
$6.95/274-4
"Zesty...spiked with adventure and romance...a distinguished and humorous portrait of a vanished age." — Publishers Weekly

In 1966, Picano abandoned New York, determined to find true love in Europe. He becomes embroiled in a romance with Djanko, and lives la dolce vita to the fullest. Upon returning to the US, he plunges into the city's thriving gay community of the 1970s.

MASQUERADE BOOKS

THE LURE
$6.95/398-8
A Book-of-the-Month-Club Selection
After witnessing a brutal murder, Noel is recruited by the police, to assist as a lure for the killer. Undercover, he moves deep into the freneticism of gay highlife in 1970s Manhattan—where he discovers his own hidden desires.

WILLIAM TALSMAN
THE GAUDY IMAGE
$6.95/263-9
"To read *The Gaudy Image* now...it is to see first-hand the very issues of identity and positionality with which gay men were struggling in the decades before Stonewall. For what Talsman is dealing with...is the very question of how we conceive ourselves gay." —from the introduction by Michael Bronski

ROSEBUD

THE ROSEBUD READER
$5.95/319-8
Rosebud has contributed greatly to the burgeoning genre of lesbian erotica, introducing new writers and adding contemporary classics to the shelves. Here are the finest moments from Rosebud's runaway successes.

DANIELLE ENGLE
UNCENSORED FANTASIES
$6.95/572-7
In a world where so many stifle their emotions, who doesn't find themselves yearning for a little old-fashioned honesty—even if it means bearing one's own secret desires? Danielle Engle's heroines do just that—and a great deal more—in their quest for total sexual pleasure.

LESLIE CAMERON
WHISPER OF FANS
$6.50/542-5
A thrilling chronicle of love between women, written with a sure eye for sensual detail. One woman discovers herself through the sensual devotion of another.

RACHEL PEREZ
ODD WOMEN
$6.50/526-3
These women are sexy, smart, tough—some say odd. But who cares! An assortment of Sapphic sirens proves once and for all that comely ladies come best in pairs.

RED JORDAN AROBATEAU
STREET FIGHTER
$6.95/583-2
Another blast of truth from one of today's most notorious plain-speakers. An unsentimental look at the life of a street butch—Woody, the consummate outsider, living on the fringes of San Francisco.

SATAN'S BEST
$6.95/539-5
An epic tale of life with the Outlaws—the ultimate lesbian biker gang. Angel, a lonely butch, joins the Outlaws, and finds herself loving a new breed of woman and facing a new brand of danger on the open road....

ROUGH TRADE
$6.50/470-4
Famous for her unflinching portrayal of lower-class dyke life and love, Arobateau outdoes herself with these tales of butch/femme affairs and unrelenting passions.

BOYS NIGHT OUT
$6.50/463-1
Incendiary short fiction from this lesbian literary sensation. As always, Arobateau takes a good hard look at the lives of everyday women, noting well the struggles and triumphs each experiences.

RANDY TUROFF
LUST NEVER SLEEPS
$6.50/475-5
Highly erotic, powerfully real fiction. Turoff depicts a circle of modern women connected through the bonds of love, friendship, ambition, and lust with accuracy and compassion.

ALISON TYLER
**THE SILVER KEY:
MADAME VICTORIA'S FINISHING SCHOOL**
$6.95/614-6
In the rarefied atmosphere of a Victorian finishing school, a circle of randy young ladies share a diary. Molly records an explicit description of her initiation into the ways of physical love; Colette reports on a ghostly encounter. Eden tells of how it feels to wield a switch; and Katherine transcribes the journey of her love affair with the wickedly wanton Eden. Each of these thrilling tales is recounted in loving detail, making *The Silver Key* a treasure trove of scalding prose....

MASQUERADE BOOKS

COME QUICKLY:
For Girls on the Go
$6.95/428-3
Here are over sixty of the hottest fantasies around. A volume designed a modern girl on a modern schedule, who still appreciates a little old-fashioned action.

VENUS ONLINE
$6.50/521-2
Lovely Alexa spends her days in a boring bank job, saving her energies for the night. That's when she goes online... Soon Alexa—aka Venus—finds her real and online lives colliding deliciously.

DARK ROOM:
An Online Adventure
$6.50/455-0
Dani, a successful photographer, can't bring herself to face the death of her lover, Kate. Determined to keep the memory of her lover alive, Dani goes online under Kate's screen alias—and begins to uncover the truth behind Kate's shocking death....

BLUE SKY SIDEWAYS
& OTHER STORIES
$6.50/394-4
A variety of women, and their many breathtaking experiences with lovers, friends—and even the occasional sexy stranger.

DIAL "L" FOR LOVELESS
$5.95/386-4
Katrina Loveless—a sexy private eye talented enough to give Sam Spade a run for his money. In her first case, Katrina investigates a murder implicating a host of lovely, lusty ladies.

THE VIRGIN
$5.95/379-1
Seeking the fulfillment of her deepest sexual desires, Veronica answers a personal ad in the "Women Seeking Women" category—and discovers a whole sensual world she had only dreamed existed!

K. T. BUTLER
TOOLS OF THE TRADE
$5.95/420-8
A sparkling mix of lesbian erotica and humor. An encounter with ice cream, cappuccino and chocolate cake; an affair with a complete stranger; a pair of faulty handcuffs; and more.

LOVECHILD
GAG
$5.95/369-4
One of the bravest young writers you'll ever encounter. These poems take on hypocrisy with uncommon energy, and announce Lovechild as a writer of unforgettable rage.

ELIZABETH OLIVER
THE SM MURDER:
Murder at Roman Hill
$5.95/353-8
Intrepid lesbian P.I.s Leslie Patrick and Robin Penny take on a really hot case: the murder of the notorious Felicia Roman. The circumstances of the crime lead them through the leatherdyke underground, where motives—and desires—run deep.

SUSAN ANDERS
CITY OF WOMEN
$5.95/375-9
Stories dedicated to women and the passions that draw them together. Designed strictly for the sensual pleasure of women, these tales are set to ignite flames of passion in any reader.

PINK CHAMPAGNE
$5.95/282-5
Tasty, torrid tales of butch/femme couplings. Tough as nails or soft as silk, these women seek out their antitheses, intent on working out the details of their own personal theory of difference.

LAURA ANTONIOU, ED.
LEATHERWOMEN
$6.95/598-0
"...a great new collection of fiction by and about SM dykes."
—SKIN TWO

A groundbreaking anthology. These fantasies, from the pens of new or emerging authors, break every rule imposed on women's fantasies. The hottest stories from some of today's newest writers make this an unforgettable exploration of the female libido. A bestselling title.

LEATHERWOMEN II
$4.95/229-9
Another groundbreaking volume of writing from women on the edge, sure to ignite libidinal flames in any reader. Leave taboos behind, because these Leatherwomen know no limits....

AARONA GRIFFIN
LEDA AND THE HOUSE OF SPIRITS
$6.95/585-9
Two steamy novellas in one volume. Ten years into her relationship with Chrys, *Leda* decides to take a one-night vacation—at a local lesbian sex club. She soon finds herself reveling in sensual abandon. In the second story, lovely Lydia thinks she has her grand new home all to herself—until strange dreams begin to suggest that this *House of Spirits* harbors other souls, determined to do some serious partying.

MASQUERADE BOOKS

MASQUERADE BOOKS

A VICTORIAN ROMANCE
$5.95/365-1
A young woman realizes her dream—a trip abroad! Soon, Elaine comes to discover her own sexual talents, as a Parisian named Madelaine takes her Sapphic education in hand.

A CIRCLE OF FRIENDS
$6.50/524-7
A group of women pair off to explore all the possibilities of lesbian passion, until finally it seems that there is nothing—and no one— they have not dabbled in.

ANNABELLE BARKER
MOROCCO
$6.50/541-7
A young woman stands to inherit a fortune— if she can only withstand the ministrations of her guardian until her twentieth birthday. Lila makes a bid for freedom, only to find that liberty has its own delicious price....

A.L. REINE
DISTANT LOVE & OTHER STORIES
$4.95/3056-3
In the title story, Leah Michaels and her lover, Ranelle, have had four years of blissful, smoldering passion together. When Ranelle is out of town, Leah records an audio "Valentine:" a cassette filled with erotic reminiscences....

A RICHARD KASAK BOOK

LARRY TOWNSEND
THE LEATHERMAN'S HANDBOOK
$12.95/559-X
With introductions by John Preston, Jack Fritscher and Victor Terry

"The real thing, the book that started thousands of bikes roaring to the leather bars..."
—John Preston

A special twenty-fifth anniversary edition of this guide to the gay leather underground, with additional material addressing the realities of sex in the 90s. A volume of historical value, the *Handbook* remains relevant to today's reader.

ASK LARRY
$12.95/289-2
For many years, Townsend wrote the "Leather Notebook" column for *Drummer* magazine. Now read Townsend's collected wisdom, as well as the author's contemporary commentary—a careful consideration of the way life has changed in the AIDS era.

PAT CALIFIA
DIESEL FUEL: Passionate Poetry
$12.95/535-2
"Dead-on direct, these poems burn, pierce, penetrate, soak, and sting.... Califia leaves no sexual stone unturned, clearing new ground for us all."
—Gerry Gomez Pearlberg

Pat Califia reveals herself to be a poet of power and frankness, in this first collection of verse. A volume of extraordinary scope, and one of this year's must-read explorations of underground culture.

SENSUOUS MAGIC
$12.95/610-X
"*Sensuous Magic* is clear, succinct and engaging even for the reader for whom S/M isn't the sexual behavior of choice.... When she is writing about the dynamics of sex and the technical aspects of it, Califia is the Dr. Ruth of the alternative sexuality set...."
—Lambda Book Report

"Captures the power of what it means to enter forbidden terrain, and to do so safely with someone else, and to explore the healing potential, spiritual aspects and the depth of S/M."
—Bay Area Reporter

"Don't take a dangerous trip into the unknown—buy this book and know where you're going!" —SKIN TWO

SIMON LEVAY
ALBRICK'S GOLD
$20.95/518-2/Hardcover
"Well-plotted and imaginative... [Levay's] premise and execution are original and engaging." —Publishers Weekly

From the man behind the controversial "gay brain" studies comes a tale of medical experimentation run amok. Is Dr. Guy Albrick performing unethical experiments in an attempt at "correcting" homosexuality? Doctor Roger Cavendish is determined to find out, before Albrick's guinea pigs are let loose among an unsuspecting gay community... An edge-of-the-seat thriller based on today's cutting-edge science.

SHAR REDNOUR, ED.
VIRGIN TERRITORY 2
$12.95/506-9
Focusing on the many "firsts" of a woman's erotic life, VT2 provides one of the sole outlets for serious discussion of the myriad possibilities available to and chosen by many lesbians.

VIRGIN TERRITORY
$12.95/457-7
An anthology of writing by women about their first-time erotic experiences with other women. A groundbreaking examination of contemporary lesbian desire.

MASQUERADE BOOKS

MICHAEL BRONSKI, ED.
TAKING LIBERTIES: Gay Men's Essays on Politics, Culture and Sex
$12.95/456-9

Lambda Literary Award Winner

"Offers undeniable proof of a heady, sophisticated, diverse new culture of gay intellectual debate. I cannot recommend it too highly."
—Christopher Bram

An essential look at the state of the gay male community. Some of the gay community's foremost essayists—from radical left to neo-conservative— weigh in on such slippery topics as outing, identity, pornography, pedophilia, and much more.

FLASHPOINT: Gay Male Sexual Writing
$12.95/424-0

Over twenty of the genre's best writers are included in this thrilling and enlightening look at contemporary gay porn. Accompanied by Bronski's insightful analysis, each story illustrates the many approaches to sexuality used by today's gay writers.

HEATHER FINDLAY, ED.
A MOVEMENT OF EROS: 25 Years of Lesbian Erotica
$12.95/421-6

A roster of stellar talents, each represented by their best work. Tracing the course of the genre from its pre-Stonewall roots to its current renaissance, Findlay examines each piece, placing it within the context of lesbian community and politics.

MICHAEL FORD, ED.
ONCE UPON A TIME: Erotic Fairy Tales for Women
$12.95/449-6

How relevant to contemporary lesbians are traditional fairy tales? Some of the biggest names in lesbian literature retell their favorites, adding their own sexy—and surprising—twists.

HAPPILY EVER AFTER: Erotic Fairy Tales for Men
$12.95/450-X

An eye-opening appreciation of these age-ol tales. Adapting some of childhood's beloved stories to the adult gay reader, the contributors to *Happily Ever After* dig up the erotic subtext of these hitherto "innocent" diversions.

CHARLES HENRI FORD & PARKER TYLER
THE YOUNG AND EVIL
$12.95/431-3

"*The Young and Evil* creates [its] generation as *This Side of Paradise* by Fitzgerald created his generation."—Gertrude Stein

Originally published in 1933, *The Young and Evil* was a sensation due to its portrayal of young gay artists living in Greenwich Village. From drag balls to bohemian flats, these characters followed love wherever it led them.

BARRY HOFFMAN, ED.
THE BEST OF GAUNTLET
$12.95/202-7

Gauntlet has always published the widest possible range of opinions. The most provocative articles have been gathered by editor-in-chief Barry Hoffman, to make *The Best of Gauntlet* a riveting exploration of American society's limits.

AMARANTHA KNIGHT, ED.
LOVE BITES
$12.95/234-5

A volume of tales dedicated to legend's sexiest demon—the Vampire. Not only the finest collection of erotic horror available—but a virtual who's who of promising new talent.

MICHAEL ROWE
WRITING BELOW THE BELT: Conversations with Erotic Authors
$19.95/363-5

"An in-depth and enlightening tour of society's love/hate relationship with sex, morality, and censorship."
—James White Review

Rowe speaks frankly with cult favorites such as Pat Califia, crossover success stories like John Preston, and up-and-comers Michael Lowenthal and Will Leber.

MICHAEL LASSELL
THE HARD WAY
$12.95/231-0

"Lassell is a master of the necessary word. In an age of tepid and whining verse, his bawdy and bittersweet songs are like a plunge in cold champagne."
—Paul Monette

The first collection of renowned gay writer Michael Lassell's poetry, fiction and essays. As much a chronicle of post-Stonewall gay life as a compendium of a remarkable writer's work.

MASQUERADE BOOKS

WILLIAM CARNEY
THE REAL THING
$10.95/280-9

"Carney gives us a good look at the mores and lifestyle of the first generation of gay leathermen.   —Pat Califia

With a new introduction by Michael Bronski. *The Real Thing* returns from exile more than twenty-five years after its initial release, detailing the attitudes and practices of an earlier generation of leathermen. An important piece of gay publishing history.

RANDY TUROFF, ED.
LESBIAN WORDS: State of the Art
$10.95/340-6

"This is a terrific book that should be on every thinking lesbian's bookshelf."   —Nisa Donnelly

The best of lesbian nonfiction looking at not only the current fashionability the media has brought to the lesbian "image," but considerations of the lesbian past via historical inquiry and personal recollections.

ASSOTTO SAINT
SPELLS OF A VOODOO DOLL
$12.95/393-7
Lambda Literary Award Nominee.
"Angelic and brazen."   —Jewelle Gomez

A spellbinding collection of the poetry, lyrics, essays and performance texts by one of the most important voices in the renaissance of black gay writing.

EURYDICE
F/32
$10.95/350-3

"It's wonderful to see a woman...celebrating her body and her sexuality by creating a fabulous and funny tale."
     —Kathy Acker

A funny, disturbing quest for unity, *f/32* tells the story of Ela and her vagina—the latter of whom embarks on one of the most hilarious road trips in recent fiction. An award-winning novel.

ROBERT PATRICK
TEMPLE SLAVE
$12.95/191-8

"One of the best ways to learn what it was like to be fabulous, gay, theatrical and loved in a time at once more and less dangerous to gay life than our own."   —*Genre*

The story of Greenwich Village and the beginnings of gay theater, fictionalized by this world-famous playwright.

FELICE PICANO
DRYLAND'S END
$12.95/279-5

Dryland's End takes place in a fabulous techno-empire ruled by intelligent, powerful women. While the Matriarchy has ruled for over two thousand years and altered human society, it is now unraveling. Military rivalries, religious fanaticism and economic competition threaten to destroy the mighty empire.

SAMUEL R. DELANY
THE MOTION OF LIGHT IN WATER
$12.95/133-0

"A very moving, intensely fascinating literary biography from an extraordinary writer....The artist as a young man and a memorable picture of an age."   —William Gibson

Samuel R. Delany's autobiography covers the early years of one of science fiction's most important voices. A self-portrait of one of today's most challenging writers.
THE MAD MAN
$23.95/193-4/Hardcover

"What Delany has done here is take the ideas of the Marquis de Sade one step further, by filtering extreme and obsessive sexual behavior through the sieve of post-modern experience...."   —*Lambda Book Report*

"Delany develops an insightful dichotomy between [his protagonist]'s two worlds: the one of cerebral philosophy and dry academia, the other of heedless, 'impersonal' obsessive sexual extremism. When these worlds finally collide ... the novel achieves a surprisingly satisfying resolution...."
     —*Publishers Weekly*

For his thesis, graduate student John Marr researches the life and work of the brilliant Timothy Hasler: a philosopher whose career was cut tragically short over a decade earlier. Marr notices parallels between his life and that of his subject—and begins to believe that Hasler's death might hold some key to his own life as a gay man in the age of AIDS.

LUCY TAYLOR
UNNATURAL ACTS
$12.95/181-0

"A topnotch collection..."   —*Science Fiction Chronicle*

A disturbing vision of erotic horror. Unrelenting angels and hungry gods play with souls and bodies in Taylor's murky cosmos: where heaven and hell are merely differences of perspective; where redemption and damnation lie behind the same shocking acts.

MASQUERADE BOOKS

MARCO VASSI
THE EROTIC COMEDIES
$12.95/136-5

"The comparison to [Henry] Miller is high praise indeed.... But reading Vassi's work, the analogy holds—for he shares with Miller an unabashed joy in sensuality, and a questing after experience that is the root of all great literature, erotic or otherwise...." —David L. Ulin, *The Los Angeles Reader*

Scathing and humorous, these stories reflect Vassi's belief in the power and primacy of Eros in American life.

THE STONED APOCALYPSE
$12.95/132-2

Vassi's autobiography, financed by the other erotic writing that made him a cult sensation.

A DRIVING PASSION
$12.95/134-9

Famous for the lectures he gave regarding sexuality, *A Driving Passion* collects these lectures, and distills the philosophy that made him a sensation.

THE SALINE SOLUTION
$12.95/180-2

The story of one couple's affair and the events that lead them to reassess their lives.

CHEA VILLANUEVA
JESSIE'S SONG
$9.95/235-3

"It conjures up the strobe-light confusion and excitement of urban dyke life.... Read about these dykes and you'll love them." —Rebecca Ripley

Touching, arousing portraits of working class butch/femme relations. An underground hit.

STAN TAL, ED.
BIZARRE SEX
AND OTHER CRIMES OF PASSION
$12.95/213-2

Over twenty stories of erotic shock, guaranteed to titillate and terrify. This incredible volume includes such masters of erotic horror as Lucy Taylor and Nancy Kilpatrick.

ORDERING IS EASY

MC/VISA orders can be placed by calling our toll-free number
PHONE 800-375-2356/FAX 212-986-7355
HOURS M-F 9am—12am EDT Sat & Sun 12pm—8pm EDT
E-MAIL masqbks@aol.com
or mail this coupon to:
MASQUERADE DIRECT
DEPT. BMMQ98 801 2ND AVE., NY, NY 10017

BUY ANY FOUR BOOKS AND CHOOSE ONE ADDITIONAL BOOK,
OF EQUAL OR LESSER VALUE AS YOUR FREE GIFT

QTY.	TITLE	NO.	PRICE
			FREE

DEPT. BMMQ98 (please have this code
available when placing your order)

We never sell, give or trade any
customer's name.

SUBTOTAL	
POSTAGE AND HANDLING	
TOTAL	

In the U.S., please add $1.50 for the first book and 75¢ for each additional book; in Canada, add $2.00 for the first book
and $1.25 for each additional book. Foreign countries: add $4.00 for the first book and $2.00 for each additional book. No
C.O.D. orders. Please make all checks payable to Masquerade/Direct. Payable in U.S. currency only. NY state residents add
8.25% sales tax. Please allow 4–6 weeks for delivery. Payable in U.S. currency only.

NAME_____

ADDRESS_____

CITY_____ STATE _____ ZIP_____

TEL( ) _____

E-MAIL _____

PAYMENT: ☐ CHECK   ☐ MONEY ORDER   ☐ VISA   ☐ MC

CARD NO. _____ EXP. DATE _____